Sunrise

Fires

Heather LaBarge

Exalted Peacock

ISBN: 978-0-9888203-0-2

eISBN: 978-0-9888203-1-9

Library of Congress Control Number: 2012951697

Chapter One

"*H*ey you," the deep bass in Ryan's voice, cut with its gravely rumble, always made me melt.

"Hi, love." I smoothed a spot for him on the cool cotton blanket beside me. "Sleep well?"

"Right until the very end there...that little part where I woke up alone." He leaned into me, his lips brushing mine as he settled on the blanket next to me. The sun was still low on the horizon, its light barely beginning to cast the yellow hues of morning across the California sky.

This place, particularly at sunrise, felt divine and magical to me. I dug my feet deeper into the cold damp sand and continued to gaze out across the ocean swells. I breathed in deeply. The smell of seaweed and salted air revived me and filled my lungs with air fresher than any I could get in my home in the desert of Las Vegas. Sometimes I was still shocked at how different it felt to breathe in air that wasn't laced with fine desert dust.

My hand absently massaged the cotton blanket under me as I said, "I love the beach — you know that. I had to see the sunrise."

"I'd have watched it with you." He draped his arm around me, and I leaned into him settling against his shoulder.

"Tomorrow morning then. We still have one more day out here. I promise I'll wake you tomorrow."

He smiled. "So have you decided?"

"Ugh, don't bring that up. Let's just enjoy the morning here." A gull swooped down to say good morning — I returned the greeting. "Hello, Mr. Gull," I told him, and then to Ryan, "How could anyone not love it here?" I smiled at him. "Thanks for bringing me."

"How could anyone not love *you*?"

I smiled even broader and my cheeks hurt. "Stop that," I said, feigning surprise.

"Stop what? Loving you? Okay. The beach then. The beach and my dirt bike. Maybe I'll ride off into the sunset with my motorcycle."

"Hah! Your dirt bike and all the guys you ride with — they'd never let you go." I poked his ribs, chiding him.

He brought his other arm around in front of me and tackled me to the blanket. "Is that so? And what will they think when I decide that it's me and you to the end?"

"Pppsshhhaww — they'll love it — of course! I'm a great cook."

"That's not the only thing you're great at." And he kissed me, his lips warm and sensuous on mine, plying, pressing, wanting for more. And I gave him more. My tongue forged into his mouth, seeking his as my hands roamed the frame on top of me. He had a wrestler's body, muscular and stocky. I loved the feel of his muscles in my hands, strong and sinewy. I traced his outline until I reached his ass and pulled him more fully onto my body. As he settled between my legs, he pulled away from our kiss. I reached for his cheek, cupping his jawline. "I love you, Ryan Riverton. You know that, right?"

"Yeah. I know. I can feel it." He smiled as he leaned to the side and his hands moved over my body. "I can feel it here," his hand settled on my sternum, "in your heart. And here..." He squeezed my right breast.

I exhaled sharply and slapped his hand. "Ryan!"

"...and here!" He cupped and squeezed my pubic bone.

I cringed and laughed as we rolled together on the blanket, him kissing me and me fighting him. "Right there, huh? Is that your favorite place to feel my love?"

"Come back to the tent, and let's see if it is."

We lay there kissing and playing for a few more minutes before I did exactly as he asked. But isn't that what I always did?

***

A shrill trademark cell phone ringtone woke us from a beautiful beachside slumber. "Yours or mine?" Ryan asked as we both scrambled from our shared sleeping bag bed, ignoring the fact that we were naked as each of us searched for our phones.

"Definitely yours," I replied, "mostly because I don't want it to be mine."

"That's because they're expecting an answer, and you don't have one." I hated it when Ryan was right.

Three high-pitched frantic rings later, I found my phone amongst the pile of my clothes that we'd hastily peeled off and discarded just a few hours earlier. "Hah! Not mine," I said triumphantly as he fished his out of the back pocket of the jeans he'd been wearing.

"Hello?" he said, slightly winded from the scramble. I poked him in the ribs, as he tried to be serious on the phone. "Yeah, Johnnie, yeah, it's me." His earnest tone was such a contrast from our playful morning on the beach and the sexual romp we'd just had. "What's up?" Teasing him and keeping playful embers burning in him was fun. I ran my fingers along his bare skin and delighted as his body responded, goose bumps rose, and he tensed and released his cock, making it jump. I loved seeing his body respond. Smiling, I took his still soft cock into my hand and began to stroke it, teasing him specifically because he was on the phone, but also hoping to continue the playful theme of the day. "What!?" He jerked away from me and waved me off with his arm. Turning back to our sleeping bags, I laid back pouting and feigning hurt feelings, folding my arms across my chest. "What hospital?!" He frantically pulled on his boxer shorts and reached for his shirt.

I threw on a pair of comfortable old jean shorts and a soft cotton T-shirt before rolling up the sleeping bags and beginning to pack up the contents of the tent. Whatever this phone call was about, it wasn't going to be good. It was ten minutes before he clicked off his cell, and then he set to helping me pack up the rest of the tent in silent fury.

"Do you want to tell me?" I ventured.

The golden rims that lined his brown irises were nearly glowing as his eyes met mine, and when he spoke, the words that shot out of his mouth were tight compact statements of fact, "It's Chris. He might be paralyzed."

Chapter Two

$\mathcal{W}$e'd been camped on the soft sand dunes of

the beach; it was one of our favorite pastimes. Being here always brought a sense of joy, playfulness, and relaxation to both of us individually and as a couple. We made some of our best memories on beaches like this one. But now, as we stepped outside the empty nylon tent, the sunshine that normally brought a smile to my face somehow seemed out of place. The cackle of the gulls and the splash of the waves all seemed far too fun for the stark somber mood change at our campsite. Ryan's concern was etched into his face, making him look angry. His brow furrowed, casting a shadow over his normally bright eyes, and his jaw flexed and released over and over again. He moved methodically as we packed the remainder of camp and pulled the tent down in near silence. Ryan gave some direction here or there, guidance on what he needed next, but there was no real conversation.

"We can talk later," he had said. "It's a long ride to Vegas. Let's get this shit packed up." And now, hours later, heading north up the interstate, we were still in a tense haze so thick that I felt uncomfortable. His old American pickup seemed cavernous. He'd bought it specifically for camping so that he could always bring his dirt bike and still have room for everything else, and at the moment, I thought that 'everything else' might've included an elephant sitting on my chest. Ryan was distant, his eyes glassed over. I felt miles away from him, sitting all the way over on the passenger side, eyeing him as he stewed in the driver's seat. I tried to bridge the distance, reaching across the gap between us and placing my hand on his thigh. "Baby, no matter what it is I am sure it will be okay."

The warmth of his hand settling on top of mine was instantly reassuring, but his words slapped. "You don't know that. Johnnie said he couldn't feel his feet when they put him in the helicopter." He didn't look at me as he spoke.

I unbuckled my seat belt and slid across the aging canvas bench. "I am here with you. It will be fine. No matter what it is." I settled my head onto his shoulder.

He put his hand on my thigh. "Buckle up. How about we don't have two motor vehicle accidents in one day?"

I straightened up and buckled, tensed and irritated that I was unable to help soften this tension hanging over us. He glanced in my direction and his face softened. He reached for me, putting his arm behind my head and drawing it down to my shoulders, pulling me into him. "I'm sorry, baby. I'm just worried about him. Chris is the least experienced rider among us. I think he's only twenty-two. And he works construction — it's not like he has a desk job." He told me about what Johnnie had said: the guys had been riding and Chris tried to do a move well beyond his skill level. He ended up hurting himself bad enough to need to be medically evacuated on a helicopter.

The group of guys that Ryan rode with had been friends, some of them since high school, and they'd taken up this hobby together, gradually meeting and making friends with more people whom they occasionally rode with as well. They had a sense of camaraderie and friendship that was more like family than men who enjoyed the same hobby. An event like this was likely to be distressing to all of them. And Ryan, in particular, took responsibility for things. It was his nature and something that endeared me to him. At times like this, though, it was even more stressful for him than perhaps for the others.

With the flat of my palm against his chest, I pressed into him and breathed deeply. I matched my breathing to his and stayed settled into his body. "I love that you are so concerned about him, hun. It is one of the things I love the most about you — how protective you are when you care." We exhaled deeply together, and I think I saw his lip quiver a little.

***

I had met Chris only once; we'd been out at the usual dirt track where Ryan rode. I watched from the sidelines and fed the guys when it was done, usually something I'd brought that was recently home cooked. On this day, we had had lasagna, and Chris was so flattering that I couldn't help but remember him. He was young looking and slim, with baby blond hair and sky blue eyes. I'm not even sure he grew facial hair, and if he did, it would have been an easy shave.

There was a core group of six or seven men who were Ryan's closest companions in life and in the riding world, and among them, Chris fell into the little brother role. The men took care of him, not only coaching him as he learned the ropes of dirt biking, but also coaching him in life. Chris was predictably exuberant and excited at times, making him reckless and foolhardy. He had had girl troubles, hadn't planned accordingly to pay his bills, had taken irresponsible risks at the blackjack tables, or had made other foolish mistakes, and each time, Ryan and the guys rallied around him to educate and support him in ways that only trusted peers can.

When I'd met him, he nearly effervesced with enthusiasm, his cheeks pink with excitement as he took his helmet off. He barely introduced himself before raving about some of the jumps and runs he'd done.

"Didja see me? That ridge right there," he pointed toward the track as if I would differentiate one ridge from the next, "I got some air there — real air. I bet I was ten feet up." His eyes scanned the group expectantly. His energy was infectious as he continued to rave about one hill or another and how he'd moved around the track. And he didn't stop raving once he was eating — he was just as excited about my lasagna as he had been about the ride.

I could see why the guys had adopted him. Hell, even I had a soft spot for him.

***

Despite the fact that traffic was in our favor, the drive from LA back to Las Vegas was interminable. It was an hour and a half before we reached Fontana — a really good time, considering what typical California traffic from the beaches was like, but not fast enough when racing to get to the hospital after a catastrophic event. As we passed the last few Fontana/Riverside exits, I thought of the times I'd driven down to California to meet Ryan when he lived here — our first uncomfortable date for coffee and a movie, his old bachelor pad with comfortable furniture but not a speck of décor, the first time he took me with him dirt biking, the smell of the gas, the engines, the kicked up dirt and dust, and the smell of Ryan, musky and happy, sipping a Bud light at the end of the day. The thoughts carried me well into Death Valley as the sun beat down on the windshield.

And now, sitting here beside him, my head on his shoulder and his arm loosely around me, it felt like eons ago when we had been such strangers. He absently stroked my arm as he drove or fumbled with a strand of my hair. His tension was so evident, but his warmth and love seemed the persistent undercurrent to everything, always. I wondered how I could ever go even one day of the rest of my life without him. I looked up at his profile, stoic and determined. I kissed his cheek and then wiped my fingers over my kiss...rubbing it in or wiping it off, I was not sure. He glanced over at me and smiled, "I love you, babe; I'm not trying to be distant, but this drive is killing me, and I just want to get there and be sure he'll be okay. He's like a kid brother to me..."

"I know, hun. I know." I kissed his cheek again and settled into his side with one arm behind him at the small of his back, and the other draped across his chest. I traced small designs in his T-shirt with my fingers, and then erased them with my palm.

***

We finally arrived at the hospital hours later, and Ryan nearly ran inside. By the time I met him in the emergency room, he was nearly frantic. "They won't let me back." The grayish-blue hues of the fluorescent lights made him look ill, pale, and weak.

"Okay, hun," I placed my hand on his shoulder and rubbed in small circles, "the guys probably weren't allowed back either. Have you looked around the waiting area and snack bar for them? They can at least tell you what happened." This place smelled of antiseptic; the wire seating stood screwed to the floor, ready to hold up the ill and their loved ones; and medics and doctors bustled about in the background with medical charts in hand, calling names of patients and discussing cases in hushed tones.

Ryan scanned the faces of people in scrubs and of the random passersby, his eyes narrowed to slits as he searched the area. And in an instant, his eyes flew open wide and his mouth rounded in recognition. I turned to see Johnnie approaching.

He had seen Ryan, and made his way across the room toward us. He was tall, at least four inches taller than Ryan, thinner, and more businesslike. His sharp jawline, always shaved baby smooth, stood out even more now as worry settled into it. His camel brown hair parted to the side made it hard to believe he'd been wearing a helmet not so long ago, though I suspected he kept a comb at the ready to ensure he always looked his best. He was something of a ladies' man, always sought after but seldom taking women seriously. His friends and his professional future were his primary motivators, and today, one of them was in trouble.

As soon as they were within comfortable earshot, Johnnie began, "It doesn't look good, man. He said he couldn't feel his legs, and we definitely couldn't get him up after he landed." Even this debonair chiseled man looked grey and ill in this environment under these circumstances. We all exchanged hugs and sat down on the nearest of the wire bench seats.

Ryan was animated as he pressed for more. "What the fuck happened, man?"

"We were up at Apex, and he tried to do that nearly vertical push up the side of the ridge — that one on the high-speed turn, the one intended for —"

"I know the one."

Johnnie continued as it Ryan hadn't interrupted him. "I thought he was going to make it. He got up there pretty high, at least twenty-five feet. But then something happened...not enough throttle, I'm guessing. He fell back, and his bike kinda bounced on top of him."

"Damn."

"I originally thought he knocked the wind out of himself and definitely must've broken some ribs. But he was talking right away. The bike had fallen to the side, and Mark pulled it away. This kid was really excited about nearly making it up there. That was what he was talking about!" Johnnie sounded like a proud parent and both men laughed and smiled at Chris's exuberance. Johnnie's faced darkened as he remembered the events. "But then he tried to get up, and he couldn't move, man." He looked at his hands, calloused from riding so often. Absently, he stroked the palm of one hand with the thumb of the other. "Ryan, man, he said...he said...well," he looked up and met Ryan's eyes, "he said his legs were dead."

"Dead legs?"

"That's what he said, and we were all wondering what that meant, too. I mean, you can guess, and everyone all looked at each other really serious out there on the track, but I don't think we wanted to believe it."

"Fuck, man. Fuck. Have you seen the doctor yet?"

"No, we haven't seen anybody or heard anything. We probably arrived at least an hour after him because of the drive out of there. He got the high-speed trip on that helicopter."

Silence hung between them. My chest tightened with the realization that Chris might be paralyzed at twenty-two. I thought of Ryan's natural big brother role and how he would take it, knowing he hadn't been there. I stared at Ryan, captivated by the pattern on his shirt; it was black with tan design on it. I couldn't see the design, my eyes wouldn't focus, but it felt good to watch it move as Ryan inhaled and exhaled in a natural rhythm. It calmed me to allow myself to focus on nothing in particular. I thought of Chris's light enthusiastic personality and how it might be impacted by such bad news. I thought of what I would do and how our lives would change if Ryan had been the one in the accident.

As the silence dragged on, it felt heavy, stretching the tension between the three of us until Johnny's voice finally snapped it. "He really couldn't move his legs, man," he was almost whispering, his eyes bloodshot and glassy. "I checked to see if he broke one or something, but I didn't see anything." He didn't finish the statement, there was no need.

Silence fell between us again and stretched on for long minutes.

"What do you think is taking so long?" Ryan's frustration and impatience blasted through the silence.

"I don't know, man," Johnnie tried to sound soothing, but his nervous energy tightened his voice to a near squeal, making it anything but soothing.

"Well, fuck, Johnnie. Where's everybody else? Where the hell is Mark? And who else was there? I mean, who was on this ride with you?"

Johnnie bristled, his shoulders tight as he sat more upright and eyed Ryan through squinted eyes, his lips a thin tight line. His jaw flexed before he spoke, "Pat had to get home. His wife had to go to work so he had to watch the kids." His tone was matter-of-fact and controlled. "Mark is outside smoking a cigarette and calling to see if he can get off work tonight. Paul is down the hall in the bathroom." As he completed the laundry list, he leaned forward, resting his elbows on his knees and clasping his hands. His eyes were still narrowed and defensive as he stared Ryan down. He looked like a mountain lion, ready to pounce. I half expected to see a tail twitching behind him in warning.

Ryan's response was softer, almost inaudible. "Damn — bunch of people on that ride. Shoulda been a good day."

Johnnie softened as well. "It was, Ryan, you should've been there."

"Maybe if I had been, I could've talked the kid out of trying that hill."

"Don't start that shit, Ryan. We all tried. He wanted it. There was nothing we were gonna say that would stop him."

"Yeah..." But Ryan's voice trailed off as if he didn't believe that.

Chapter Three

$\mathcal{W}$e spent the next week in and out of Mercy Hospital, visiting Chris and supporting his family. It took three days before he was awake again from surgery. It turned out that they had taken him to the back, done some x-rays and tests, and immediately taken him in for surgery hoping to prevent permanent paralysis. They said something about swelling against the spine. Between work and Mercy Hospital, Ryan was consistently on the run. It was a twenty-five minute drive to the hospital from our house, and since Ryan stayed until visiting hours were over, I was never going to see Ryan if I didn't go with him to see Chris. Thankfully Ryan and I both worked similar hours so I had time in the evenings to accompany him to the hospital, trying to maintain a sense of normalcy to our relationship while also supporting Chris through his recovery.

In the truck, I had changed to sitting in the center seat as my norm and settling against Ryan as I would if we were at home watching TV on the couch, comfortable, leaning against his side, breathing him in, and chatting about our day. I liked the feel of him next to me, the deep rumble of his voice resonating off my body and eardrums at the same time, lifting me to a happy place while also grounding me with the heavy deep weight of the bass in it. As he drove, I nestled into his side and let my hand trace his chest and belly. His body was muscular, stocky and beefy. I liked the feel of him beneath my hands, strong and full, it felt like he could take me, make me do as he pleased if he wanted to. And knowing that he loved me enough to be tender and loving instead made me feel special.

In the past week, it seemed he must've lost at least five pounds for lack of eating and perhaps dehydration. On one particular trip to the hospital, I pleaded with him for the thousandth time to eat and drink something, suggesting that he stop so we could grab dinner at a drive through on our way to the hospital.

"I'm not hungry," he answered.

"You've been 'not hungry' since Chris's accident. Babe, you've gotta eat."

He sucked his teeth, sighed heavily, and pulled into a fast food place. We ordered a couple of burgers and fries, and as we pulled out, I asked, "Have you talked to your mom about what happened?" This past week had been stressful on Ryan, and it seemed there was nothing I could do to alleviate his feelings of guilt and his drive to take responsibility now, no matter what the cost in terms of his own health and stress. His mother was the person he most trusted, the person who had the most sway and influence in his life, even now that he was nearing thirty and plenty capable of taking care of himself. I hoped that he had called her and that she might've helped get him to see that this was really stressing him out and that perhaps we could skip a day or two so that he might rest. Maybe she could convince him to eat or perhaps she'd invite us over for dinner - an invitation he only refused when he had a rock-solid reason.

"Yeah, on the phone yesterday."

"What'd she say?"

"She said the same thing everyone says," he crammed another bite into his mouth, "'it'll all work out' or 'quit stressing over it,'" he air quoted the words as they sarcastically dripped off his tongue. "Or some other dismissive crap...I don't remember exactly."

His resentful tone was rare for him, in particular, when talking about her. Knowing better than to continue that conversation, I pressed another direction. "Someone was hungrier than he thought."

"Yeah, I guess." He shrugged, swallowing another bite of his burger, almost without chewing it. "I could actually go for another burger." He sounded surprised by the idea.

I smiled, feeling vindicated for having insisted that we stop to grab something. I was tempted to remind him of his heavy sigh and eye roll. Instead, I said, "Okay, baby, take mine. I'll leave you at the hospital and go grab something around there for myself."

He didn't balk. Instead, he reached right into the bag and grabbed the second burger. "If I didn't know better, I'd say that sounded like wife-talk."

I punched him in the arm. "Funny man, eh?" We hadn't talked about marriage in more than a year. It was a sore subject. Ryan asked me to marry him, and I refused. I had been married twice before, and I knew how marriage changed things. There was no way I was going to ruin this thing with Ryan by exchanging rings and vows and spending tens of thousands of dollars to do it. No, when things are perfect, my policy was why screw it up by changing anything?

We'd been at the beach when he'd asked me the last time, and it nearly ended us.

He had me pinned on the blanket, kissing me. My shirt was unbuttoned nearly to my bellybutton and his pants were already undone. He stopped us midstream. "Marry me."

"What?"

"I said 'marry me.' It's been four years and still we poke at this thing," he thrust his hips at me and his rod stabbed at my already swollen pussy, "I want you to be my wife."

"First, it has only been two years. Those first two, before we met, those don't count. And second, you know, I won't marry again. We've been over this." He sat up abruptly.

"We already live like we are married, and I want everyone to know."

"They know, Ryan. They know because of how we love each other, how we act around one another, because we cannot hide it." I sat up and put my hand on the center of his back. "Because it's real. No piece of paper or ring is going to change that."

He reached around his knees and clasped his hands together. "Do you love me? Really love me in the way you say you do, not some fairy tale bullshit, but really love me?"

"I just told you I did, and I know that you know it already in the way I treat you."

"Then why not? Why not make me that happiest man in the world and become my wife?"

Tears welled in my eyes, and I tried desperately not to let them spill. "Why do you torture us like this?" I smiled weakly and tried to lean into him, to break his hands apart and hold him. I could only manage to rest my cheek on his shoulder and wrap my arms around the tight ball that he had become.

"C'mon, let's just break camp." He got up abruptly and stepped toward the tent despite my hands grabbing at him.

"Baby," I pleaded, "don't be like this."

"Like what?" He reeled around. "Like the man who loves you? Like a devoted lover and boyfriend? Like your best fucking friend? Like fucking what? Tell me."

"Don't ruin this moment by giving me that same ultimatum again." I was standing now, and I crossed to him. "I *am* married to you. I'm married to you already in all the ways that count. You *are* all those things you said. And that sums you up as my life mate. I want to be with you and live just like this forever or for until you don't want it anymore." His jaw clenched.

"'Until I don't want it anymore'? What is that supposed to mean? I'm so fucking tired of trying to prove that I love you."

"I know that you love me, Ryan. I know you do. And I love you, too. Please, let's just go into the tent. Let's continue the amazing good morning we started."

"Fuck? That's what you want? You want to fuck this away? Do you think you can fuck me into forgetting that you've rejected me so many times?"

We degraded into one of the biggest fights we'd ever had, and he actually moved out for a period of time. And I'd written him off. Despite how perfect we'd been, I chalked him up to 'like all other guys,' and I'd let him go. Initially, I was saddened by his absence and felt stupid for daring to believe that we might've been different. When weeks went by and he didn't call, I was sure that he wasn't missing me like I was missing him, sure that I'd not meant as much to him as he had to me. And I flipped the switch from missing to resentment. Resentment was a wonderful salve. I decided that I didn't want him anymore, that he was the one to blame, that he was childish and silly for trying to force my hand and coerce me into marrying him. Good riddance, I didn't need someone like that in my life anyway.

When he finally did call, I was cold and aloof. My position on marriage hadn't changed so I was confused when he reached out. I was sure that he thought we would become friends with benefits and it offended me. Did he seriously think I would be available at his beck and call? On again, off again? Maybe he'd dated others and now thought he could come back to his trusty standby. I definitely couldn't let him think I was his on-call lover. Had he really even missed me? Or was he just lonely in general?

I loved him and had missed him dearly in our separation, but I couldn't bear to let him know that. It was difficult trying to appear unaffected, cautious, and independent while also letting him know that I was open to a conversation about reconciliation. It was an awkward, difficult, and painful road back, despite how much our separation had hurt me and how much I'd hoped we might one day get back together.

When we finally reunited, we agreed that we each feel whole and happy around each other unlike with anyone else. We hadn't talked about marriage since, but sometimes Ryan dropped little comments like this one, reminding me that he resented that door was locked.

***

When we got to the hospital, the overflow from the ER was apparent. Some kind of flu must've hit. Every wire bench was occupied, and people lined the walls, huddled together in little pods of illness and injury. Instead of the antiseptic smell that normally permeated the place, it smelled of musk, grass, leaves, sweat, and bad breath. It felt surreal and postapocalyptic the way people murmured in hushed tones and eyed us as we passed, as if we had something they might want, and they were considering taking it from us. We hurried through the madness, and I was glad to be clear of it, shaking off the unsettling feeling with a chill as I punched the up arrow in the elevator lobby.

We made our way to Chris's ward and signed in at the nurses' station. It was much brighter up here and the nurses knew us by now.

"Welcome, back, Ryan, Jen," the head nurse greeted us as we headed down the hall to Chris's room. This place was an altogether more pleasant experience than anything the emergency room and trauma center downstairs had to offer. The fluorescent lights here didn't seem so grayish blue; instead, they cast a more yellowish peach color to the ward, brightening it. And the smell of flowers dotted the hallway as we passed in front of rooms where they'd been recently delivered 'get well' bouquets of sunflowers, carnations, roses, and others, intended to keep the spirits high as the body recuperated. No matter what the impact it had on the patients, it was working on me, and by the time we knocked on Chris's door, I was feeling rather cheery.

"Come in!" His boyish voice matched my mood.

Ryan heaved the solid wood door open, and we stepped inside. The room was intended for two patients, though Chris presently had it to himself. He'd taken up residence on the far side nearest the window. The lights were off, and the room was shadowed and cool inside. Whatever light we had came from the large windows across the room; evening was approaching, but the desert summer meant that sunset was still at least an hour away. The first bed looked dark and dreary. The curtain drawn, separating the two 'rooms' from one another, blocked most of the light from reaching it. The bed was made and pillow fluffed at the head of it. A clear Plexiglas clipboard was attached at the foot, hanging in wait for the next victim's medical chart. There was a side table as well, with little tags in the upper right-hand corner of each likely naming what medical supplies were in each of the drawers. The entire scene was sterile and uninviting, unless you wanted to lie down and allow the Reaper direct easy access.

In just a few steps, the room's energy changed completely. The bed, the clipboard, the side table—all the furniture was the same, and yet the place seemed entirely different. The light from the window brightened up the back half of the room, and Chris's bubbling personality made it shine.

"Hey! My favorite couple!" Chris greeted us, smiling broadly. His bed was mechanically adjusted to the seated position, and Chris was clearly ready for company.

"Yep. How are you holding up, old man?" Ryan's tone was warm and loving as he leaned over and hugged Chris.

"Are you kidding? I wiggled my big toe today!" He raised and lowered his eyebrows repeatedly. "Huh huh? How cool is that?"

Ryan snorted. "You can do some pretty good things with a big toe, man. Don't knock it. Know what I'm saying?" And he raised and lowered his eyebrows in a similar fashion.

"Ewww. Nobody said anything else was paralyzed! Just the legs, man. I still can handle anything you're getting at. And do it well!"

"Well, then get up and get to handling. There's a city full of girls waiting on you."

"I will. I will. They say six months to a year, but I'm walking out of this hospital even if I am just hopping on that one big toe."

We all laughed.

I stepped over and gave Chris a hug and kiss on his cheek. "I'm gonna go grab something to eat, hun. I am so glad you are feeling better...well, that you're feeling your big toe, at least." And we laughed again. "You want something? Or is hospital food suiting you?"

"Hell yeah, I want something! An animal style burger and a shake. This food in here is really terrible. But damn, you just got here. Stay a while. Go in a bit."

"Can't. Starving. Someone ate my burger on the way over here." I jerked a thumb in Ryan's direction.

"Hey! You offered me that burger! You damn near insisted!"

I winked at Chris and then kissed Ryan on the cheek. "I know, babe. And I am glad you ate it." I ran my hand down his spine, squeezing him at the small of his back, as I kissed his neck and whispered in his ear, "I love you, hun. I'm just being silly with Chris." And then I straightened up and turned back to Chris, tugging my shirt down to straighten it and holding my palm up in front of me, feigning a writing utensil in the other hand, "Okay." I dotted the 'pen' to my tongue quickly to get it started, "One animal style burger," I spoke slowly as I took the order, "and one shake." I looked up from my hand, "Flavor?"

"What?"

"What flavor shake?"

"Uhhh...What do they got?" He paused and thought for a second and then continued, "Bah, chocolate. Every place has chocolate."

"Okay." I waved my hand, scribbling furiously on my makeshift notepad. "You want fries with that?"

"Sure. I'll take fries."

Ryan stood with his hands on his hips, looking back and forth between us with disapproving eyes and pursed lips. His heavy sigh and sideways glances were half the fun of this process.

"Ketchup?"

"Yep."

"Salt?"

"Extra."

"Any beverage besides the shake?"

"Miller light."

I looked up from my palm. "Excuse me, sir, but we do not recommend beer for people in the hospital. And, anyway, this establishment doesn't serve beer."

"Is that so? Well, I wanna see the manager!"

We both looked at Ryan. "No way! Keep me outta that little corny charade!"

"Well, you're no fun." And I jabbed him in the ribs. Turning my attention to Chris, I said, "Can I trust this fuddy duddy in your care while I'm gone?"

"Sure can. I might just lighten him up a bit."

I turned and headed for the door. "But he doesn't need to lose any weight." I chuckled, listening to Chris's laughter and Ryan's groan.

Chapter Four

$\mathcal{I}$t was a month before Chris left the hospital, and

he wasn't walking on his own, though he used his crutches really well. I made lasagna that night and tried to think of Chris while I did, pouring some extra thoughts and love into it. We all gathered up at our house; I preferred it that way since I was cooking. Nobody complained since we were the only ones who lived in a house. Even Pat, who was married with two children, lived in an apartment.

We lived in a quiet gated community. The streets were lined with old oaks and green well-manicured lawns maintained by whomever the home owners' association hired. It reminded me of my New England roots back East, making the exorbitant home owner's association fees well worth it. Each home was painted in similar neutral tones of beige, tan, brown, peach, and terra cotta—signature desert colors that survived well in the blazing summer sun. Ours was in the middle of the block, a cookie-cutter copy of the house three doors down to our left and two down to the right—tract housing at its finest. Still, I loved the place. Ryan and I had chosen it together, and that alone made it special. He had found a rental agency that helped us find precisely what we wanted, and we'd selected a few to go see every few days until we found something we could agree on. This had been only the fourth or fifth house we looked at. Once we saw it, we knew there was no point in continuing to look. It was a two-story, two-bedroom place. The downstairs was open and welcoming while the upstairs was more cozy and private.

The place reeked of garlic and basil by the time people started arriving. Barefooted, I crossed the tiled floor to answer the door. The tiles were one of the many things I loved about this home, particularly in the summer time when carpet might've held the heat and made the place feel stifling. My toes gripped the natural surface of the ceramic tiles. They were cool and firm beneath my feet. I opened the door and wasn't surprised to find Mark standing there. He was the quietest and seemingly most melancholy of the bunch, but he maintained an air of cordiality and respect. Seeing him arrive on time wasn't a shock. Neither was it a shock to see him with a woman I'd never seen before. Bringing a new woman to an event was his signature. In fact, I wondered if anyone ever got a second date.

"Hey, hun." I reached up to hug him as he leaned down to me. He was much taller than me, likely six foot three or four, and rail thin. He was brooding and dark, wearing clothes that matched his demeanor. Today, he wore black skinny jeans held up by a belt fashioned from a car's seat belt and a black button-down shirt, with the sleeves partially rolled up. He had one eyebrow piercing and snake bite piercings on his bottom lip, any of which he was prone to fiddle with when he was nervous or brooding. His jet-black hair swept across his forehead toward his left ear, never quite succeeding in staying out of his eyes. His face was sharp and angular— marked by gaunt cheeks, a pointed nose, and sharp-jutted chin—and dotted by deep charcoal eyes. In all, he was a shadow until you got to know him. He was shy and reserved, never speaking until spoken to, and resigned to remain a background figure.

I smiled at him coming away from our hug. "You're the first one here." He shrugged and handed me a bottle of wine. "Well, thank you," I said, and then looking at the bottle, I was surprised that he'd chosen my favorite red wine. "Did Ryan tell you to get this? I think it's the only red I drink. It's perfect for tonight."

"Nope, thought of that all on my own," he sounded resentful, or maybe I was just reading into his usual sad reserved tone.

"Well, damned good thinking then. I'm pretty picky as far as wine goes, and it's rare to find a decent sweet red." I turned to the date, "And who do we have here?" She was waif thin and probably not taller than five foot two. Her floral print sundress hung from her shoulders as if it were three sizes too big. And other than her fluffed, curled, and sprayed Texas-sized hairdo, there was nothing big about her. I offered her my hand; she placed hers in mine, but it was cold, limp, and weak, a wet fish of a handshake for sure. Mark said her name, but it didn't register. She had already been named 'wet fish.' It was a name she would only have for this night, and only in my head. In the end, their names were irrelevant. "A pleasure to meet you, hun. Make yourselves at home. The rest of everyone should be arriving any minute now."

They slunk off to the living room as I padded back to the kitchen. I still had a Caesar salad to make and garlic bread to crisp under the broiler. The smell of garlic and cheese hit me as I reentered the kitchen and, immediately, I remembered the sound of Chris's enthusiasm the first time he tasted my lasagna—hell, the first time anyone tasted my lasagna. Even Ryan was bound to love this meal and give me plenty of appreciation for it afterwards.

I set the wine on the island in the center of the kitchen; it joined two loaves of Italian bread, halved and slathered with garlic butter. I looked at the bottle.

Mark was a curious character. Even after more than a year, he was an enigma in many ways. Truth was it had taken months before I was able to get Mark to converse with me beyond stilted hellos and awkward forced polite conversation about the weather or the track. I had finally achieved a special standing with him, though I wasn't sure why. Maybe it was because I persisted in pestering him until he let me get to know him better. Maybe it was because I was Ryan's girl, and after being there for so long, the other guys had already fully accepted me, so he finally gave in. No matter what the reason, it was nice to be in this special place. And nice that he brought the wine.

I turned my attention to the sink where the Romaine lettuce waited in a colander. As I began rinsing it, I looked out the window as the sun was just barely beginning to set. I loved this kitchen; it was spacious and well-lit, with plenty of pantry space and an extra large refrigerator. The sinks were against the far wall directly in front of two large windows that looked out toward the mountains. Sunrises were gorgeous. Sunbeams cut through the windows, making the kitchen seem alive in the morning. It made cooking breakfast a joyous way to start the day. And sunsets were just as beautiful, with orange and red hues that played out on the mountains, until dusk silenced them. It made the evening meal preparation feel intimate and special.

Tonight was no exception to the rule. The sunset was an amazing vista of blood orange fading to salmon, with white wisps of clouds contrasting the mountains' silhouettes. I sighed as I shook the water from the lettuce and set it on a bed of paper towels to drain. I was really looking forward to the company and seeing Ryan interact with his friends.

I had just finished the garlic bread when my phone rang. Assuming it must be Ryan with news of being delayed with Chris and the guys, I answered immediately. After all, my Caesar salad was at stake.

"Hey, gorgeous!" I said cheerfully.

"Excuse me?" Whoops that wasn't Ryan's voice. I pulled the phone away from my cheek and saw that it was actually Mr. Dullberth, the human resources chief at the office.

"Ummm, I'm sorry, Mr. Dullberth, I thought you were someone else."

"Indeed," he replied matter-of-factly.

Dullberth was a stodgy businessman who was ill suited to be anything other than a human resources person or perhaps a quality assurance guy. He was detail-oriented, took everything just a little too seriously, and expected both life and people to be predictable—a sure sign of the kind of person he himself was. In fact, I found that his name suited him. He was as dull as anyone I'd ever met. He drove a solid safety-rated four-door sedan with amazing gas mileage; he brought his lunch each day, always a sandwich, a fruit, and a bag of baked chips; he wore the same style of slacks and shirt each day, varied only in shades of grey or black; and he spoke in monotones and seldom raised his voice. His promotion to corporate HR should have been reason for celebration, and yet on the day I met him, he was moving into his office completely nonplussed. In all, Dullberth was a man the company needed, and that I tolerated. "What was it you needed, sir?"

"We've not heard from you in regards to our offer yet, and I wanted to remind you that the deadline is approaching."

"I know, sir. I'm aware."

"And you do realize that we have already hired someone for your position here in Las Vegas?"

"I understood that to be a contingent offer, pending my departure, should I choose to accept the other position."

"Unfortunately, that has recently changed."

"Excuse me, what?" I was aghast.

"Madam, you have not yet committed to either position, and the company had to protect their interests."

"What exactly are you saying, Mr. Dullberth?"

"I thought I was clear. The young man hired on contingency for your position here in Las Vegas has now been hired and is on payroll."

"What?! How could you possibly do that? There is no way!" I took a deep breath, realizing that I was raising my voice, and that Dullberth would see me as unreasonable and emotional. More slowly and clearly, I began again, "Mr. Dullberth, I've been with the company for five years! Productivity is up in my sectors and sales have never been higher."

"Which is precisely why you were given the offer abroad."

"That's not fair."

"Ms. Simmons, we have waited for nearly two months on your answer. It is clear the offices in Germany want to hire you, and yet you make them wait. And you expect us to absorb your loss should you take the position on short notice? Surely, you can't be serious."

"I just mean that you should have made this phone call before telling the other guy he was hired. So, now you are telling me that I'm going to Germany or else I'm fired. Is that about right?"

"We will let you go, yes...either way. One for your further success. The other would be..." he cleared his throat, "less fortunate."

"The deadline is..." I looked at the calendar hanging on the kitchen wall, "Thirteen days, right?"

"That is precisely right...*if* you waited until the last day." He emphasized the word 'if' as if it had been a threat.

"Thank you, Mr. Dullberth. I'll let you know."

"So, then, you still have not—" I hung up before he could finish. Tears stung my eyes.

They streamed down my cheeks while I finished the salad. I sniffled and sobbed uncontrollably, staring at but not seeing the mountains. Suddenly, I didn't want to have dinner here at the house.

I wanted to be alone with Ryan.

I wanted to cry and to rage, and these people were an intrusion to that or at least a delay of it. If he were here right now, he would say he told me so, and that he's been reminding me to call them. He would give me disapproving parent eyes. And then he would hold me while I cried and tell me that it will be all right. And he'd say, "Who cares if I was right," and then he'd muttered under his breath, "Except me, of course." And we'd laugh while I bawled. I needed him to lie with me and talk to me. I wanted to hear his voice thrumming against my eardrums, saying anything at all. I just needed the reassurance of it.

"Hey, my gorgeous woman." I hadn't heard him come in, and now here I was, a mess, and about to ruin dinner with my drama. I sniffled once really hard and dabbed my eyes on my T-shirt, grateful that I had my back to the door. Deep breaths and long slow exhales helped clear the tears and settle the distress. And then his lips were on the back of my neck and his arms around my waist, his hands pulling my hips into him. "Did you miss me?"

I smiled and stretched my neck to give him more area to kiss. "Yes, love," I sounded surprisingly calm, "I missed you terribly." I took another deep settling breath. "And how does it smell in here? Are you ready to eat?"

He massaged my hips. "Dinner smells almost as good as you do." He let a hand wander to my mound. "God, I've missed you. I miss you every time I go away." His words hung in my ears. Germany. 'I miss you every time I go away.' It had only been a few hours since he had last seen me. What would he do if I went to Germany? "I can't wait for dinner, baby. It smells amazing," he squeezed my crotch, "and dessert later." The warmth and strength of his grip sent ripples of a tremble through my pelvis and stomach.

The doorbell rang before I had to respond to him, and it was a good thing, because a short trip to the bathroom revealed a raccoon-eyed, cry-baby-faced mess. I tidied myself up for dinner and had a good strong talk with myself about Mr. Dullberth's revelation not ruining our dinner for Chris.

Chapter Five

*C*onversation had swept the time by quickly and kept thoughts of Dullberth and Germany at bay. The lasagna was wonderful, cheesy, and full of garlic, basil, and other Italian spices; it was met with rave reviews, as were the salad and garlic bread. Mark's wine complimented everything really well. The night was topped off with cannoli that Johnnie brought from a nearby bakery. The moon was full and bright by the time dinner waned, and we stood at the door, sending everyone on their way.

"I'm so glad you're home, man. You'll be back on that bike by the summer." Ryan hugged Chris.

"Thanks for everything," he replied. Turning to me, he said, "Thanks for the dinner; it was awesome."

"Oh...that old thing?" And we both chuckled. "You're headed home with Mark and...Mark's girl?" I chuckled to myself remembering my nickname for her.

"Yeah, they're gonna drop me at my parents' house on their way to…well…on their way."

Again, we smiled, and I leaned out the door. "Thanks again, Mark, for the wine. And bye, honey, it was nice meeting you." They mumbled something inaudible as Chris joined them.

I leaned into Ryan as he closed the door. "I'm exhausted."

"That's one word for it. You want to tell me what's up?"

"Huh?" I stood up again and faced him. "Come again?"

"Baby, you've been off all night - ever since I got back from the hospital with Chris. You got something you wanna tell me?" My eyes immediately burned and my nose tingled. God, I didn't want to cry again. "What the hell is it, baby?" His arms were around me now, warm and supportive.

My lower lip quivered. I knew I had to tell him. But once I did, we would never be the same again. Tonight may be the last night we would consider ourselves a couple. Anything could happen, and I hated Dullberth for it. What if Ryan decided it was time for us to be over, before it hurt more, before the day I had to leave for Germany? I couldn't handle that. And I couldn't refuse Germany because I wouldn't be able to find another job like this in the Las Vegas area, at least, not quickly. I knew that Dullberth had forced my hand, and that I would indeed be going to Germany, but I wished there was a way I could keep this a secret from Ryan. I wished that we could stay the way we were just a few hours ago, and that he would never have to know about Germany.

I walked toward the couch. As he followed, I choked it out. "Dullberth called..." It was all I could manage before breaking into body wracking sobs. I plopped down on the couch in real rag doll fashion, legs straight out into the living room and head flung back against the back cushion. The tears flowed into my hair, drenching it at my temples. I didn't care. This was probably the end anyway.

Initially, Ryan gaped at me. I was too overwhelmed with my own thoughts of his abandonment that I didn't care that he was staring. In the end, he was likely to recognize this as our end anyway. He knew who Dullberth was and what Dullberth would want, so he surely would recognize that I had to leave for Germany, and that we were done.

I continued to sob uncontrollably. The couch material had begun to dampen; darkening the beautiful beige microfibers to something more of a chocolate brown. But, at the moment, I didn't care. Ryan was standing over me, surveying the situation, trying to make sense of the dramatic scene that was unfolding, or else checking out the deluge of tears now staining our somewhat expensive sectional. A couple of times I tried to speak, wanted to say something that made sense of the entire thing, but all that came out were choked sputters and snot-filled coughs.

Gradually, the consequences of the Dullberth call settled in, or maybe the initial shock of witnessing me lose it wore off. Regardless, he settled on the couch next to me and lay his head on my chest. He drove his arm under my body and wrapped the other over my belly. We lay there quietly, absorbing the truth of it for quite some time. It seemed like an eternity before my sobbing finally subsided.

"You okay?" He raised his head and looked into my ridiculously puffy eyes.

"No." I smiled weakly. "But I think I'm cried out."

He chuckled. "Really? Cried out? Not one more tear left?"

I smiled despite myself and drew him closer to me. "I fucking love you. I love you so goddamned much." My lower lip quivered even as I spoke. "What other guy can make a woman smile even in a moment like this? Nobody. That's who!"

"So," he began treading slowly and carefully, "Dullberth calling doesn't feel like the end of the world to me, baby. You are so good at what you do, and your name is already known. Another company, another country, they'll come knocking. Just wait." He paused, looking into my eyes before continuing with a smile. "And until then, I get you all to myself." He squeezed me more tightly. "Plus I get to say 'I told you so,' which is a bonus as far as I'm concerned. I told you to call them back weeks ago. They probably waited as long as they could for you to give them a ring. If it was gonna make you this upset, why didn't you take the job?"

I blanched. He thought Dullberth called to say someone else got the job in Germany. He had no idea what was really happening. He had just held me, so I could cry it out. He wasn't sad at all. He didn't realize that I had to leave him, leave us, leave our beautiful wonderful life behind. And he definitely didn't realize that it was going to happen soon. Tears sprang anew.

"Hey, hey, hey. You said you were fresh outta those. Liar!" he chided me as he reached up and wiped my tears. "So, I'm gonna go back to my initial question, you wanna tell me what's up?"

"That's not what he called to say." I paused, choking back more uncontrolled sobs. "Ryan," I took a deep breath and sat up, unsettling him from my chest, "Ryan, baby, they..." I started to cry again. "They hired somebody for my position here in Vegas." I sniffled. "The job in Germany is still available, but regardless, my job here..." I trailed off, hoping he wouldn't make me say it. My lips trembled. I had the nervous shakes.

"Regardless, what, baby? If you don't go to Germany, then whomever they hired will be un-hired." He air quoted hired and un-hired for emphasis.

"No, honey. They said they couldn't keep him contingency-hired for so long, and since I have made them wait this long, they hired him for real. Basically, they decided for me."

"Are you serious?! So, either you go to Germany or...you're fired?" I nodded as tears overtook me again. "That's such bullshit. They can't do that!

"They wouldn't say they fired me."

"How can they not? They hired someone for your position while you still work there! How is that not firing?!"

"'Offered a promotion and refused it'...that's what they'll say."

"Well...fine, baby, fuck it. I told you that you should go to Germany anyway. So go. I support you, baby. Go to Germany. It's a promotion after all. And it's only a year. Twelve months isn't that long – consider it an extended well-paid vacation."

"It doesn't include a job for boyfriends...." I fished for his feelings about us, and how they'd change if I went to Germany.

"I never said I would go with you, hun. I like it here. My family is here, my bike, my friends, my job, my life. I never even thought about going with you. You never even put that on the table."

"If I did, would you? Would you at least think about it?!"

"That's heavy, baby. That's really heavy."

"Why do you think I'm crying? I feel like I have to choose between the man who makes me the happiest I've ever been or else my career! I don't want to leave you. That's what it boils down to. The promotion is great, but I don't want to leave you."

He kissed me. Tenderly at first, and then again and again. His lips drew the sadness out of me, or at least made me temporarily forget it. So intense were his kisses. My hands flew to his face, pulling him in. We fell back into the depth of the couch and the kiss broke. I was desperate to feel him here again, making me forget. I whimpered. He crawled to me, pulling my shirt collar down a little and kissing the chest he revealed, and then my collarbone and my neck. He worked his way back to me slowly, tenderly. My hands pulled at him, but he would not be rushed. And when he finally reached my face, he paused and looked at me, his gaze so intense that I almost looked away. "I love you. I love you deeply, Ms. Simmons."

"C'm'ere ya big lug." And I stretched my neck toward him, pushing my tongue into his mouth as soon as our lips met. He placed a hand on my chest and pushed me into the couch, his weight pinning me exquisitely. His lips abandoned mine again, and he worked his way over to my neck. I turned my head and exhaled, my belly trembling as he reached my ear. His tongue snaked into my ear and then behind it. He bit and nibbled my neck and began working his way down to my chest again. His hands were already working the button of my jeans. I arched my back, and he slid a hand under me and up to my bra strap. In one swift movement, it was open, and his hand was covering my breast. He flicked the hardening nipple with his thumb, and I jolted. I reached down and yanked at my shirt, finally wriggling free of it and my bra. He licked one breast from ribs to nipple and then the other. I squirmed and squealed. "Please, baby."

He looked at me, and the corners of his mouth drew upward. He sucked one breast while massaging the other, twisting the nipple between his thumb and forefinger. My hand flew to the back of his head, pulling him more deeply into my breast as I moaned with pleasure. He moved slowly downward, stroking each rib with his tongue and nibbling at my sides while he slid my jeans off my hips and my panties with them. Squeezing my own breasts, I tried to push my pelvis in his direction. He held my hips still and stopped kissing my body long enough to give me a warning look. He was kneeling on the floor in front of me, and the heat of his presence so close to my already aching pussy was torture. Slowly, he removed my jeans from my left leg. Tenderly, he kissed his way back up my inner thigh and nearly to the apex of my legs before moving to my right leg and removing my jeans from it. By the time he made it back to my pelvis, my quim was vibrating with anticipation. One hand on the tender skin of each inner thigh, he inhaled deeply and exhaled a steamy breath onto my swollen glistening lips. I tensed and pushed my pubic bone toward him. My heart was pounding, breathing shallow. With a flat tongue he licked me, starting from deep in my pussy and moving to my clit, flicking it as he passed. My breath caught in my throat, escaping merely as a sharp yelp.

He rose and kissed me, settling between my legs as both of us savored my taste, sharing in its exquisite sweet pungent flavor and the anticipation of where we were going. I wrapped my legs around him and pulled him more deeply into me. Even through his jeans, I could feel his cock hard and full. I reached between us, unbuttoning his jeans and sliding my hand inside, fingering the tip of his cock and reveling in the slick feel of the pre-cum oozing from it. I sighed, he groaned, and we broke away from our kiss.

I moved to his neck and nuzzled it, trying to simultaneously slide his pants down over his hips. "I love you."

"Shhh..." He placed a finger over my lips and moved back down to his knees, the head of his cock barely peeking out from his boxers. He covered my clit with the warmth of his mouth, sucking and releasing in time to the fingers he slid inside me. In and out slid his fingers; in and out of his mouth my clit pulsed. He drove me closer and closer to orgasm. My hips bucked and rolled in time with his tongue and fingers. He moaned, his voice thrumming my pubic bone and sending me ever closer to the edge. My moaning and whimpering increased, louder and faster, breath coming in rasps. "Yes, oh, yes. Please, baby...ahhh."

Filling me with fingers and working the pace to frenzy, his thumb joined his tongue at my clit, and I gave into him. I gave him my vulnerability, my love, my fears, my lust. My cum spilled all over his fingers and into his hand. My body tensed, froze, and then twitched as I screamed out his name. He was relentless in drawing every bit of that orgasm out of me, and, as I slowed, my legs trembling, stomach quivering, he came up and laid beside me on the couch, head on my chest.

"I love you," I whispered again.

"Shhh," he replied.

I lay there for long moments, catching my breath and feeling him beside me. His course dark hair was on my chest, his five o'clock shadow a rough reminder that he was there. His breath was warm and moist, blowing across my chest while it rose and fell more slowly as I regained composure. At last, I looked at him and smiled, reaching for his pants and fully unzipping them. I reached inside and grabbed his shaft, finding him still rock hard and throbbing, very near release himself. He grabbed my wrist. "Relax. There's plenty of time for that."

I placed my finger on his lips. "Shhhh," and I smiled lovingly at him as I lowered myself down to his waist and took the head of his cock into my mouth. The salty slick taste of his pre-cum was enough to wet my pussy all over again. God he tasted good. I wanted more of him. I yanked at his jeans, and he finally acquiesced and lifted his pelvis for me. I slid his pants to his knees and gaped at his rock hard cock jutting out at me. "Fuck, you're gorgeous," I said more to his dick than to him. He laughed, almost shyly.

My mouth watered as he oozed another glistening drop of cum for me. I licked it away and slid my tongue around the swell where the shaft meets the head, flicking and teasing all the way around. I worked slowly down his shaft, letting the continuing stream of pre-cum drip freely over my fingers that gripped him. The base of his rod was so hard and my tongue played at the transition from rod to his tightening ball sack. Then I carefully gave each ball individual attention, sucking and drawing them into my mouth one at a time, applying enough pressure to pull a groan from him. And now that he was lubricated and primed, I rose back to his head, purple glistening and dripping profusely. I slid him quickly into my mouth, taking in as much of his cock as I could, striping my tongue with pre-cum all the way back to my throat. As he slammed into the back of my throat, I swallowed hard, squeezing the head of his cock with my throat muscles. Working quickly, I slid him into and out of my throat over and over again, each time increasing in intensity and speed. My hand worked his shaft in time with my mouth. I wanted to taste his cum. I reached up with my other hand and coaxed his balls to give me what I wanted. Balls, tongue, throat, stroke, balls, tongue, throat, stroke. He tensed and his balls drew up as I felt the first spurt of cum surge through his dick. I pushed him all the way to the back of my mouth, stretching my soft pallet but not letting him all the way into my throat. I wanted to taste him, to feel his cum spurt forcefully into my mouth.

He placed a hand gently at the back of my head and groaned loudly as one word defined his feelings: "Fuck!" And then he filled my mouth with shot after shot of warm seed. I swallowed and swallowed, and sucked and swallowed, until I had sucked him soft again.

I crawled up to him and kissed his neck as I lay on top of him, one leg between his and the other on his left side. It felt good to cover him with my body, sharing warmth and connectedness. He moved my hair from around my face and looked at me before kissing me tenderly on my forehead; grabbing the blanket that was draped over the back of the couch, he covered us.

"I love you," I whispered.

"I love you, too, baby."

Chapter Six

*I*n the days that followed Chris's welcome home dinner, Germany came up multiple times, but Ryan never agreed to go, and I never had the balls to ask him directly if he would. Instead, we poked at the subject and kept sliding it off to the right more and more. Mr. Dullberth called twice more, but I didn't answer. *Fuck him,* I thought. *Just fuck him for wanting an answer.*

I went to work, but being a regional manager meant that, more often, I could visit my stores rather than spend much time in my office at corporate. I didn't want to be there; I resented what was happening and didn't want to deal with it. I had one week to make a decision. Regardless, I needed to clean out my desk, so I made short trips to the office at odd hours to accomplish the task piecemeal.

"Nice to see you in the office for a change." It was Jackie, my best coworker friend. Jackie and I had both started at Huntington's on the sales floor. When we worked together, we were often paired to design and set up sales displays. Over time, we became close, going for drinks after work or hiking and camping together. At that time in our lives, Jackie and I talked nearly daily and helped each other with everyday struggles, including, at times, the frustrating parts of working the sales floor at Huntington's. As I rose through the sales ranks, Jackie continued to go to college, and the frequency of our contact gradually faded. Still, my affection for her had not waned, and when we saw each other, our friendship was always rekindled.

"Hey, babe, how've you been?" I hugged her warmly; she smelled of rose water and berries. She was slight, barely ninety pounds and less than five feet tall. She was one of the spunkiest, sportiest, most independent women I'd ever met, and she was a spitfire to anyone who doubted her. Her thin blond hair had just a hint of strawberry hues to it that accented her mint green eyes beautifully.

"I've missed you." Jackie wasn't one to speak of emotional topics, so the admission that she missed me was a stretch for her and a heartwarming surprise. I raised an eyebrow and smiled appreciatively as I met her eyes. She looked away and poked at the loose papers on my desk. "I heard what they did to you."

My lips tightened to a thin line. "Yeah. Well. Whatever." I shrugged, suddenly wanting to run straight into Dullberth's office and kick him in the dick.

"Really, Jen? Just 'whatever'? That's the summary of your feelings on the matter?"

"I mean, seriously... what the fuck am I supposed to say?" And then lowering my voice I said, "Dullberth is a dick, and he's trying to force my hand. It's manipulative, and you know how I feel about being played. But..." I paused, letting the feelings wash over me, "that fucker bested me, and I have no choice: unemployment or Germany. And both are shitty."

She squinted at me and then scoffed. "Are they equally shitty? I mean unemployment is just as bad as a prestigious promotion to start up Huntington's first ever European chain?" I looked down at those papers on my desk, my jaw set, trying not to be mad at her for pointing out how silly my feelings were. The air hung thick between us. "Look, Jen, this plays well for you. Just go to Germany. It's a year. What bad can possibly happen in a year? Ryan supports you, right? Wants you to go?"

"Jackie, don't... I can't... I mean," I sighed. "I love him, and, in a year, maybe he would decide to love somebody else. Is professional success really worth that? Is Huntington's worth losing the love of my life?"

"Damn. Low self-image talking there or what?"

I knew she was right...that my fears were based in my own insecurities and nothing Ryan had ever shown me. "Fuck you for saying it."

"I call 'em as I see 'em. You've been with Ryan for three years now, and he has given nothing but love and support. I'm jealous of your relationship as I'm sure most couples are."

"Ha! You're single. You're jealous because you don't have a man."

"And fuck you for saying *that*," she mocked, emphasizing the word 'that.' Both of us laughed. "I'm serious, Jen. He loves you. A husband's love. A lifetime love. He'll be here when you get back."

Before I could stop it, I blurted, "What if I want him to go with me?"

"What?!"

"I mean, Jackie," I hesitated feeling suddenly vulnerable, "what if I want him to go with me? We don't have to be apart. I don't have to miss him. We can just stay like we are."

"You!? The woman who won't marry him? The woman who won't commit? The woman who says, 'let's just let things happen naturally' wants to package him up and ship him off to Germany with you? Well, now, isn't this a twist?!"

"Stop it," my lips were tight. I wished I hadn't said it. I wanted to inhale those words all back again.

"I'm serious. You want to pack him up and take him with you because you're afraid to lose him. You don't want to share the experience with him, you want to drag him out there so you can keep an eye on him."

My eyes ran hot and bloodshot at her words. My lower lip trembled, "Jackie…"

"C'mere, girl." She drew me into a hug. "Have you talked to Ryan about it?"

"I can't. He tries but I keep delaying. I know it isn't fair to ask him, but I don't want to tell him I am going to Germany for sure. It feels so final. I am sure he knows. I mean, I'm not the kind to be without a job and the ability to be independent. And I'm too proud to ask him to support both of us while I sit home and do nothing. He has to know that Germany looms just ahead. But somehow, it feels like, if I tell him I'm going, then I am saying good-bye to him, to us. I want to ask him to go with me, but that seems so unfair now that he's just gotten the promotion… and his family is here and all of his friends and Chris…"

"Jesus, you've been fighting with this since Dullberth originally offered you the position, haven't you?"

I looked at my desk and smirked, suddenly interested in those papers we'd both been eyeing. "Maybe..."

"Okay, that's it. Dinner and drinks. Tonight. No excuses. You need a girls' night out."

"The decision is seven days away..."

"Ha. So funny how you see it. The offer was made a month and three weeks ago, so I see it as...the decision is seven weeks overdue!" She laughed, scoffing my procrastination.

"I don't know if I can."

"If you can make the decision? Seems Dullberth has done that for you, and good thing because I don't know if you could either. But as far as going out tonight, I'm sure you can. Text Ryan and tell him you are with the coolest chick in Vegas. He'll get it and definitely let you go."

"He'll say that *I'm* the coolest chick in Vegas and ask who else is going." I stuck my tongue out.

"I bet he will," she mused. "I just bet he will. Why are all the good ones taken?"

"If I go to Germany... maybe he won't be..."

"Shut up that idiot talk," she turned and headed out of my office. "Be ready to go at seven, I'm driving."

***

"I like Jackie. How come you don't go out with her more?"

"I dunno, Ryan," I pecked him on the lips, "because I can't tear myself away from you, I suppose." I turned back to the bathroom mirror and dotted some cover-up on the dark circles under my eyes.

"Germany will likely change that."

"Now? Right now, baby? You have to start that conversation when Jackie will be here any minute?"

He sat on the counter, watching me swirl my mascara wand in its cylinder. "Start? Funny you should use that word since I've been trying to have this conversation with you for more than a month now."

I drew the mascara brush away from my eye and looked directly at him. "I love you, baby. I really do. And the decision about Germany feels really scary to me."

"So you've said a thousand times. But why? Why can't you allow yourself to be successful? Why are you so stuck in your present that you can't see your future?"

"You know, this might be easier if you were possessive and begged me to stay." I said it in an accusatory tone, and part of me meant it. I resented him for not making this easier for me.

His eyes narrowed, and he looked at me for a long time. I continued putting on my makeup and acting as if what I'd said hadn't been incendiary at all. "Is that really what you want?" he finally said, his face incredulous. "Is that who you expect me to be?"

I didn't have time for this conversation right now, and even if I did, I wasn't ready for it. I changed my demeanor, switching to a playfully flirtatious voice as I replied, "I don't expect you to be anything, love." I pressed my lipsticked lips into a piece of tissue and stepped over to him. "Except the beautiful man that you are." I stood between his parted legs, pressing my pelvis against the counter and leaning into him. "And, of course, the phenomenal lover part is nice, too." I winked at him and kissed his cheek, leaving a big red lipstick impression. As I leaned back, I admired my work, smiling.

He grabbed my ass. "You look good tonight. Am I going to lose you to some irresistible stranger in the bar?" He raised a hand and delicately moved my bangs away from my eyes with one finger.

"Not a chance."

"Maybe he'll try really hard. I know if I saw you across the bar, I would."

I smiled. "You already tried as hard as you needed to get me, and now, you're stuck with me." I nestled into his chest.

"Well, good, because you're stuck with me, too."

My heart thumped in my ears at the thought. "Even if I go to Germany?"

"What?!" He pulled back and tried to look me in the eyes.

I looked down at his crotch, "Nothing." I hadn't meant to say that out loud.

"Oh, my God, that's it. This whole time..." He smacked his forehead. "Holy fuck!"

"This whole time, what?!"

"Jen, you've got to be kidding me. You keep deflecting Germany and refusing to talk about it because you think we're done. Is that it? You think somehow Germany ends us?"

My stomach was lead, and I prayed for Jackie's arrival. I looked at my hands as my fingers tangled and untangled themselves. "I think a year is a long time, and I don't know what comes after Germany either. So maybe more than a year...and next thing you know..." I shrugged. "It's the way of things. And I wouldn't blame you."

"Wow. Holy shit. I don't even know where to begin with you sometimes. I wonder if I know you at all."

Honk, Honk. "That's Jackie," I said. And her timing could not have been better. I felt my shoulders relax as the horn interrupted us.

"I know," Ryan replied, rolling his eyes. He brushed my lips with an exasperated kiss and lightly smacked my ass. "Go. Have a good time. We'll talk when you come home."

***

Jackie took me to an amazing Teppanyaki place I had never tried. Japanese cooking was always one of my favorites, and Jackie had chosen well. The place was well appointed, decorated in an Asian theme complete with an aquarium at the entrance and a sushi bar near the front. It smelled of ginger, soy, and incense spices, making me suddenly hungry for anything Asian. As they guided us toward our table, we passed a Buddha statue with coins stacked all over him and crossed an indoor bridge that extended over a coy pond. Our table seated eight, and we ended up being guests number five and six to arrive—perfect seating. It was dark enough inside that you could maintain a sense of private dining, and everyone could be sufficiently wowed by the flames of the Teppanyaki finale. The lighting was still bright enough that we could see each other and make light conversation. We spoke cordially with the other guests at the table, finding out that two of the couples were on first dates and the third couple was a pair of friends from Montana who ate at steak places far more often than at a place like this one.

The tang of the ginger salad dressing was barely disappearing from my palate as the chef slid some shrimp and chicken onto my plate to join the already steaming soy-sauced fried rice. Jackie and I made small talk and caught up on all that had happened since we'd last spent any real time with one another.

She'd taken up dirt biking with her most recent boyfriend who was—as all her boyfriends were—on again, off again. She also had enrolled in scuba classes and planned her next adventure to Hawaii to scuba in the coral reefs. I told her of the guys and of Chris's accident. And I caught her up on my children, Kelsea and Zion. My kids were fledgling adults, and I loved how far they'd come in finding themselves. My daughter, now married, lived in my old house and worked toward her master's degree. Her husband was a tall, dark, and handsome professional running his own podiatry practice in town. And my son, determined to be a comedian since he was in elementary school, was already touring as an opener for other comedians. I was a proud momma and loved catching up with Jackie. It was an amazing meal, possibly paired with a bit too much plum wine.

We left the Teppanyaki place, and I knew that Jackie was going to find a place where we could talk about Germany and Ryan. I had successfully avoided the conversation thus far and intended to continue to dodge for as long as possible. She took us to a nearby bistro with a live acoustic band and an attached microbrew. The place smelled of hops and ale. The distressed wood floors made the whole place feel as if you stepped inside of an old world wooden European beer cask.

We settled into a u-shaped booth lined with padded vinyl benches and a circular solid wood tabletop reminiscent of the end of a keg, only larger. The tabletop was heavily lacquered that the food menu permanently glazed into it. The brewmaster's selections were written in chalk on boards that were strategically placed all around the bistro; I selected the Alaskan

Amber. Neither of us had room for any more food. This place was for the brew, the band, and, regardless of what I wanted, the conversation that Jackie had been building up all night.

As we awaited our beers, we listened to the band. Their acoustic sound was calm and smooth, a step beyond the smooth background music of a coffee shop, but definitely a step back from so many other breweries in town that allowed over-the-top electric guitar riffs to overwhelm the atmosphere. I loved the ambiance. Jackie had outdone herself this evening.

A few minutes later, I sipped my ale. The brewmaster had done well, finding a balance between the basic amber and customized blends of sweet honey and spices like clove. The brew was refreshing and heady. My eyes widened as I swallowed that first sip. "Wow! That's good! How'd you hear about this place?"

"One of the benefits of being single—dates." We both laughed.

"Was this place the scene of a good date? Or did you run screaming from the place, and I'm supposed to be the one that erases that memory?"

"Let's just say, I'm still single." She took a deep breath and exhaled in a cleansing way—the kind of breath that said we were about to get serious. I had hoped she wouldn't dive right in so soon, but I guess she'd waited all through Teppanyaki. I tensed. "Soooo...."

"He already knows." I tried to cut her off at the pass. If she was going to demand that I talk to Ryan, maybe I could convince that I was well on my way, and we could talk about something else.

"What?"

"Before we came out tonight, we sort of broke the topic open. He knows I am afraid of losing him."

"And...."

I shrugged.

"How'd it go?"

"It went like it always goes with him," I said with a sigh. "Really well." No matter what the topic was, Ryan had a knack for handling it ideally. It was actually somewhat exasperating that he never seemed to break through and become imperfect like the rest of us. "He actually acted surprised, like he had no idea that I would feel this way. And then he said that he sometimes thinks he doesn't even know me." I shrugged again. "We're supposed to talk again tonight, but maybe I'll be too drunk." I took a good long swig of my Amber.

"As strong as you are, you really slay me sometimes. You were the fastest sales associate to regional manager. You had the highest grossing sales in that region that they've ever seen. And the store managers in your region love you! Those things together are like an act of God. Plus you single-parented two kids right out of the house and off to successful lives of their own. And here you sit on the brink of further success, and you seem like some namby-pamby weak little girl over losing a guy who is head over heels for you. What is *up* with you?"

I shrugged.

"Nope, that's not gonna work for me tonight, girlfriend. Maybe you need to chug a few more beers before you can find a better answer than that, whatever it takes, cuz that," she pointed in my direction, moving her finger in a circle to be sure that I was clear that she meant all of me, "that is not gonna work for me."

The band took a break, and the place suddenly felt more intimate and private. I excused myself to the bathroom, feigning a call of Mother Nature. I fixed my lipstick and texted Ryan to tell him I was having a great time. Then I hemmed and hawed, trying to use up more time. Eventually, I knew I needed to go back out there and face Jackie, and, unlike Ryan, she wasn't patient when it came to holding me accountable and expecting me to explain my behavior. I took one last look in the mirror before reporting back for what I was sure would be an inquisition.

I had barely sat back down when Jackie began, "Let's talk like girls. We used to hang out a lot more when we were both entering sales. And you talked to me back then. I realize that I am not a fast-track fancy regional sales manager like you, but I'm still the same Jackie."

"Jackie, stop. It isn't about you. It's definitely me. In all facets of my public life, I'm successful. But after two failed marriages and a string of terrible boyfriends, I'm privately a failure, and I know that..." I trailed off.

We sat in silence. I sipped my beer, and Jackie sat there looking stunned. As I looked at her, mouth gaped open; I couldn't tell if she was angry or surprised. But given our history, I assumed the latter. "A real shocker, huh?" I said. "Here you were envying me and little did you know..."

"That's not it, Jen. Yeah, sure, I envy you, but for what you have with Ryan as much as any professional success you've had. I don't understand you. I really don't get why you keep looking for ways to personally fail. You aren't like that at work."

"That's because I don't fail at work."

"Maybe you don't fail at work because you look for ways to succeed, instead of looking for ways that you might fail. Avoiding failure is not the same as succeeding."

"I dunno, Jackie." She had a point, and I'd not really ever looked at it that way. I wanted success in all areas of my life, but on one side, I sought success and on the other, I hoped not to fail. Just having this reality served up to me made me feel silly for working this way and for the answer being so seemingly obvious to Jackie and likely others. "I don't have the answers. I feel good at work," I floundered to explain myself, "and competent. I can connect when I'm there. and with friends and family, too, I have no problems. I trust you and Talia, and I know we will be fine even if I don't see you for months. And the kids? They are my heart and soul, always my first priority, and I don't feel doubts or fears about my relationship with them." I looked at my hands, and then up to her, shrugging and pursing my lips.

She shrugged back. "So where's the 'privately a failure' part? All of those things sound like the woman I know."

I swigged my beer and exhaled heavily, rolling my eyes. Jackie was asking the questions, but it was me who needed the answers. There was only one place where I felt inadequate, one place where failure always seemed imminent. "Men," I said, as if the one word alone could explain. She shrugged and slapped her hands on the table. "I mean, that's what I know," I said defensively. "That was the whole answer. It is the one place in my life where I consistently fail, and it seems that the best I can hope to do is to 'avoid failure,' as you so eloquently put it. And Ryan is special. He is the first guy I've been with where I've not thought about it that way or at least the first guy since whenever I can remember. And goddamn it. I don't wanna risk losing that."

"Who says, you're gonna lose it? Who said your relationship with Ryan hangs in the balance?" Jackie seemed genuinely confused.

My mind hurt. I knew Germany would jeopardize the one perfect relationship I'd ever had in my life. It had taken years to build this beautiful perfect thing with Ryan, and Germany threatened to take that away. Men get bored. Men leave. Men don't generally need excuses like Germany. Yeah, Ryan was different than most, but a one-year separation is no walk in the park. I knew that if Ryan and I made it through, it would be a miracle. And I didn't need to defend that reality to Jackie or anyone else. I eyed her. "Isn't this a girls' night out? This conversation is too deep to qualify to be here."

"This conversation is exactly why I brought you out here. I wanted to loosen you up a little and talk some sense into you." I grimaced and rolled my eyes, dropping my hands from the table to the tops of my thighs. "Look, I'm just saying, talk to him. He loves you. He loves you enough to let you go to Germany and continue your success. Maybe you should love him enough to be honest with him. Your fears are likely unfounded but, at least telling him will allow him to tell you that himself, and maybe to alleviate some of them." I rolled my eyes and exhaled loudly in her direction. "Fine. Fine. I've said my peace. But you'd be a jackass if you just let him slip through your fingers, and stupid if you try to tie him down. You guys work fine just as you are, so be at peace with it."

"I'm presently at peace with this beer. And it looks like the band is back, thank God. Maybe they can shut you up." I smiled and stuck my tongue out as she pushed my elbow off the table.

Chapter Seven

*S*ettling into bed a few hours later, I felt relieved to find Ryan there. I didn't expect him to have left, but somehow, every day that I found him still here, I felt a sense of muscular release and an emotional sigh.

Our sheets were soft and satiny, a high thread count and years of wear had made them feel buttery smooth. I delighted in the sensation as I slid across from my side of the bed and snuggled into the warmth of his side. He stretched and slid an arm out. I accepted the invitation and laid my head on his chest. His arm curled around my back and slowly stroked my hip. "Hey, babe. Didja have fun?"

"Sure. I had a good time. Jackie's really good people."

"Good...I'm glad." He reached up and stroked my cheek, his hand coming to rest again on his chest as his breathing deepened and he drifted back to sleep.

I felt at peace here in his presence. Even in the stillness of the early morning hours, lying next to Ryan was my most harmonious place. I didn't want to go to Germany without him. I didn't want to let go of this. I didn't care that it wasn't fair that he would have to give up his friends and family and quit his job. I wanted to be enough for him. I knew it was asinine and unfair, but I didn't care. The crying child inside me wanted to bring him, her harmony, her peace with us. The crying child inside of me was a demanding and somewhat selfish little so-and-so. Today would have to be the day that Ryan and I would talk, and I'd make my decision. I would tell him how I feel and we'd figure it out, or we wouldn't. Otherwise, at some point, I'd lose both this Vegas job and the Germany one, and that would be an even worse conversation.

I wrapped my arm around his broad chest and massaged his side as I drifted off.

***

The shrill ring of someone's cell phone was a rude awakening a few hours later. "Mine or yours?" Ryan's voice did little to soften the sound.

Barely functioning, I mumbled, "I dunno, but somebody needs to change their ring tone." I didn't even move toward my phone.

"Not mine," he announced.

The ringing stopped.

"They'll call back," I said. "If it's important, they'll call back or leave a message." I peeked one eye open to see him walking away. Squeezing my eyes shut again, I called after him, "Where're you going? Come back to bed. I don't have enough energy to chase you..." The room was far too bright this morning, a feature that I usually loved about this house. The master bedroom faced southeast allowing just enough light from sunrise to shine diffused through the sheers in a way that made everything look airbrushed. Normally, it made the room feel heavenly and made everyone in it look like an angel. But today, I wished for heavy drapes with vinyl linings so that I could block out the bright beauty in favor of a dungeon's lighting.

After a few moments, Ryan came back into the room. "Can't a man go to the bathroom? Geez." He settled back under the covers, leaning, seated against the headboard. I squirmed over to his lap.

"I missed you," I whined like a two-year-old.

"I was only a few steps away." He scratched and rubbed my back, firmly applying pressure in all the places my sore body needed.

"I'm hung-over, and that distance seemed like...like...as far as...Germany...?"

His hand paused briefly and then resumed its massage. "Hmmph. Germany, eh? So then, finally, we can talk about it?"

I rolled onto my back, keeping my eyes closed from the brightness. "Meh. Maybe..." I peeked at him again. He had slid down onto his side and was propped on one elbow looking at me. I stretched, and one naked breast sprang loose of the warmth of the covers, immediately angry at the cold air and tensing into a tight little peak.

He covered it with a warm hand and massaged it. "Someone doesn't like the cold."

I chuckled, ending my stretch prematurely. "Well, it's a good thing you have mittens for hands then, isn't it?"

He kissed me tenderly. As we pulled away, I dared to open one eye in a squint. *Yep, angelic.* I closed my eye again and thought of everything that one glimpse had shown me. He looked amazing in the morning. His five o'clock shadow had filled in even more and given him a distinguished scruff that I wanted to scratch. His eyes were smoky and warm, still too sleepy to be bright, and his naked shoulders and chest begged to be touched and kissed. He spoke again, "So, then... Germany?" I was still distracted by my own thoughts of how he looked, and with his hand still massaging my breast, I was even more distracted.

I took a deep breath. It was time for this conversation. I couldn't procrastinate any longer. I rolled toward him and scooted into the shadow of his body, feeling the warmth of my own breath bouncing off his chest and back onto my face and neck. I curled my head so that the top of it was against his chest, creating a space for my warm air to circulate between us, and creating a safe place to put my words. I couldn't bear to look at him.

"Germany," I began.

Pulling the pillow under the side of his head, he wrapped his arms around me and completed my cocoon of safety. "Germany."

"I love you, Ryan."

"I know."

"And I don't want to lose you."

"I'm gettin' that."

"And I want success, I suppose."

"Mmhmm."

"But I don't want to lose you." He stroked my hair and rubbed my shoulder. "If I go to Germany..." my voice started to crack. I stopped to breathe and tried to control my tears.

"I love you, Jen. You won't lose me."

"I'm afraid."

"Afraid of what? I really don't understand."

I pushed away from his chest and looked at him, his arms still bracing me. "I want you to go to Germany with me."

"Jen..." He looked baffled and stumbled over his words. "I...I...I can't. You know that. I mean...my family is here...and my job." He squinted at me, almost scowling. "What—?!"

"Do you want me to go because you're ready for us to end?"

"What!?" He released me and sat up.

"Ryan, I just...I'm so fucking afraid. And I can't even find the words, and I feel like you think I'm stupid, and I just wish things could stay how they have been for these past three years. And Germany changes everything. And by everything, I mean these three years are all I get with you. It means I chose Germany, and that means I didn't choose you. And if I didn't choose you, then..." I had picked up such speed as I went that I was out of breath. I stopped, gasping and spluttering, tears spilling out. Much more quietly, I began again, "I am afraid that if I don't choose you, you'll find someone else who will."

He sat there in stunned silence, looking at me, watching me cry and try to regain composure. His eyes were a mixture of confusion and something else I didn't recognize. Maybe he pitied me? He took a deep breath.

"Germany seems to mean an awful lot more to you than I ever anticipated. It's no wonder you've been nearly two months brewing this conversation." He sounded like a chastising parent, and I resented his tone.

"It does mean a lot. It will likely mean everything."

"Did you consider asking me how I feel about it?" I lay back flat on the bed, staring at the ceiling, jaw set, arms folded across my chest. "Well...did you?" he pressed.

"Too afraid," I whispered, feeling emotionally raw and vulnerable.

"What?"

I looked at him and scowled, "I said I was too afraid, all right. Fucking scared. Fearless at work and an imp at home. Okay?! There, I said it. Are you happy now?"

Ryan giggled. "Yep. Happy as a clam." He slid back down onto the bed next to me, propping himself on his elbow again. He cupped my chin and drew my gaze toward him. "Listen here, my scared little imp." He kissed me. "I love you. And Germany is nothing but a place. And in that place, you'll find more success. I want you to shine. You're brilliant at work. And clearly, they need someone like you there to take the German sporting goods market by storm. I'm proud to be with someone so successful. And when you're gone, I'll be bragging about you the whole time."

"And what about us?" I looked down at his chest.

"What about us?"

"Why won't you come with me?"

"You know the answer to that. Is it really fair of you to expect me to traipse over the globe after you? I have a job here and a life. My family and friends are here. Just as I want you to have success and happiness in your life, I want to find that in my own life as well. And that life is here. And in a year, when you get back, I will still be here, still loving you, still proud of you, still wanting to be with you."

"But I'll miss you," my eyes searched his for reassurance.

"And I'll miss you, babe." He drew me into his chest and held me close. I entangled my legs in his and tried to lose my body inside his. "I'll miss you a lot," he said. We lay in silence for long minutes. I wept silently.

**

The call that had come that morning had been Dullberth again. I finally called him back and accepted the job in Germany. I spent the next month in a flurry of training my replacement and getting ready to go; making sure I had my passport, and that the offices in Germany had everything set. Did I have an apartment? Was there a company vehicle? What did I need aside from my bags and my passport?

And I made sure to spend time with those who mattered to me.

I started with my best friend, Talia.

I took a weekend trip to California to see her, and as my plane touched down in central California, the months that had passed since I'd last seen her suddenly felt like years. As I walked through the airport, making my way to baggage claim, my heart hastened along with my steps.

She was standing by my baggage conveyor, five foot six and with an attitude that made her seven feet tall. We'd met more than a decade ago in a class on developing successful business training strategies. The class was taught poorly and dragged on miserably. It was nearly unbearable, so much so that we built six months of a relationship during the three weeks we spent in Detroit attending it. We had similar work ethics and similar views on personal accountability. And we both loved Italian food. We did our assignments in tandem, and then searched Detroit for its redeeming qualities. Talia was one of the first women I loved and accepted in spite of our vast differences. First, her salsa music was so abhorrent to me that I graciously offered to drive whenever we went out on the town. Secretly, I was hoping that being the driver meant that I had more than a fifty percent say about what was played on the radio. Talia saw things in their objective reality, whereas I always added an emotional 'human factor' when I analyzed the same problem sets. She charged me with being blinded by emotion while I jovially called her heartless. She was stoic, strong, and unapologetic while I was strong, independent, but hoping to find friendly footing with everyone I met. Our differences were many and yet... we worked. We loved and respected one another wholly and even sometimes joked that if it weren't for the lack of sexual interest, we'd be married.

And there she stood now in the baggage claim, unaware that I was approaching. As soon as I saw her, I felt calm. I wanted a cup of coffee and a drive around the block. I approached at a normal pace, enjoying watching her without her realizing I was there. Her long thick black hair was tied back in a single pony running down her back, her lips colored a natural rose hue, and her coral rouge bringing out her Puerto Rican olive skin. Her complexion was perfect, her skin always silky, and she smelled of the tropics.

"Boo!" I said, sneaking up behind her.

She turned around with eyes like razors, and then softened immediately. "You know I might've cut you if there wasn't something familiar in that voice," she warned.

I shrugged and then hugged her. "You know I got ninja moves. Never would've been a scratch on me."

"You must've forgotten who you're talking to." She sucked her lips and feigned irritation.

"Gonna be a long weekend with you, I see. You do know I have only a couple of days, right?"

She hugged me. "No. It's not that. It's just been a long morning." Her tone lightened. "How was your flight?"

We talked about the cheap airlines I had used for this flight—how cramped the cabin was, how unorganized the gate processing had been, and so forth. Eventually, my bag came, and we headed out into the beautiful California summer air.

We spent the weekend talking, shopping, and planning her trip up to Vegas the following month. We'd been friends for so long at this point that each time we saw each other needn't be filled with special occasions—presence was enough. She was the one I trusted implicitly, the one who knew me, the only person to whom no door was locked. It was no surprise then when she started the conversation about the impact that Germany might have on my feelings about Ryan.

"So, hun, how are you feeling about Ryan and you?"

"Talia, I love him so much, and things are so amazing between us."

"And Germany? Did you ever get that sorted out—your feelings about him staying while you leave?" I looked at my hands. I couldn't pretend with Talia. I couldn't act like it was going to be okay, that I had faith, and that the sky was filled with stars and rainbows. I knew she would want the truth, and I really needed to vent it out anyway.

I took a deep breath. "We talked it out, and I supposedly feel better about it. And we'll call and IM and Skype and e-mail, and things will be great, and..." I paused for effect, and then began singing in the softest whisper, "Pink fluffy unicorns dancing on rainbows...?"

She laughed and joined me in singing the meme, and then she put an arm around me. "Oh, honey, is it really feeling that bad?"

"A lump in my throat, Talia. A pill I can't swallow. I really don't think we'll last a year. I bet we won't last 'til Christmas."

"You might," she began weakly. "I mean, Jen, this guy loves you pretty seriously. So, unless you force the issue, I doubt it's going to simply end because he got bored waiting. He doesn't strike me as that kind of guy."

"He isn't. But long distance doesn't work."

She pursed her lips and made a sound like she was trying to cough up a hairball. "Really? That simple, huh? 'Long distance doesn't work?' That's what you're going with?"

"It's true."

She rubbed my back. "I hate to be the bearer of logic here. I realize that you wanna live in some other world where logic doesn't exist, but one of my jobs is to keep your perspective aligned to some variation of realistic. Sure, yep, you guys might break up, but probably not because long distance doesn't work. Let's just get that part outta the way. How long were you guys together before you ever met?"

"We weren't."

"Weren't you talking for like two years or something?"

"Talking isn't *together*." I air quoted 'together' and said it snidely.

"I think I'm in this conversation alone." She looked around. "Where'd Jen go? Can you bring her back? Because this little three-year-old thing isn't working for me."

"Not funny."

"Neither is this weak-ass woman sitting here, trying to split hairs over when this relationship began. You guys have been talking for five years now and physically living in the same house for three."

"We've been together for three and living in the same house for two and a half, unless you count the time he moved out because I won't marry him. In which case, we can subtract—"

"Shhhh." I stopped talking and gave Talia a dirty look. "You're making my head hurt. Stop it."

"Well, it's the truth."

"Girl, here're the facts as I see them. One, this guy is a good catch, quit trying to act like he's some run of the mill guy. Two," she grabbed her fingers, counting off her points for visual effect, "Germany is a really good opportunity, and you will do amazing there and find more professional success than you know what to do with, and three, you'll come home to find this guy still wanting to marry you when you get back here...unless you get stupid and push him with some insecure silliness like I'm being forced to endure."

I sat there feeling like a chastised child. "Talia, I'm just scared. I'm afraid that if I'm not here to be with him, to hold him, to make love to him, to cook for him, or to do all the things that I do when we're together, he'll start thinking about why I'm not there, about the fact that I chose Germany. And then maybe some woman will appear and make herself available. And anyways, I'll be in Germany. I'm just so afraid to lose him over this. I know my fears don't make mental sense, but since when are people's brains and hearts on a first name basis? I mean, really, my *heart* says we won't make it to Christmas."

"I know how you feel, and I can picture the faces of the men who made it so. Ryan's face isn't there. And, hun, I really hope that you won't personally, prematurely, add Ryan to the list of guys who broke your heart. I just don't get that from him. Maybe I'm wrong, but I don't think so. He feels like a lifetime thing. From where I sit, you two will be together long after Jesse and I break up."

My eyes widened. "What?! Is something going on with Jesse?"

She picked at the edge of her cuticle. "I'm looking for apartments."

"Oh, my God, hun! With all my life changes and such, we haven't even talked about you. I am so sorry. When he wasn't here, I just assumed he was out of town on business, as usual. Tell me what happened."

"Turns out 'business' also goes by the name Becky..." she began. And so, conversation ebbed and flowed for the rest of the weekend as was typical for us, and Sunday night came far too soon. As I boarded the flight, she reminded me that this was 'to be continued' when she got to Vegas in one short month.

***

In the weeks that followed my trip to California, Ryan and I spent time together doing all the things we loved and hadn't recently made time for. We spent time lounging on the couch, watching movies, or reading books. We cooked together, took walks along the strip, and visited some of our favorite places in town. And we made love; we had sex often and everywhere. It was an extended good-bye of sorts, and I appreciated every minute.

Ryan also spent time with the guys, riding and hanging out. I went to watch as many times as I could, sitting on the sidelines with Chris and talking about his accident, the guys, his recovery, our lives. He really was a great kid. I still brought food, though more often, it was fast food as I was short on time for cooking.

The track was less than a half hour from the house, out on the edge of town. There were thin aluminum bleachers near the parking lot. They faced the track, but the truth was that you really couldn't see much of what was going on out there until the riders came back around again. The place smelled of two-stroke oil/gas mix that burned in the smaller dirt bikes, and of dirt and dust kicked up by the riders. It was a place to inhale your desert environment and let it settle in your nose.

And yet I loved it here. I loved to watch the guys ride. And as I watched Ryan in these last few weeks, I wished that I had done it more often these past three years. Ryan was a natural on his bike and seemed in his most joyous and complete self when he was riding. Seeing him like that made me love him all the more.

Chapter Eight

*S*uddenly, I only had a week to go before my departure. I no longer had to go to work; the new guy had successfully taken the reins. He was 'good enough' but not quite living up to my sales records just yet. A secretly prideful side of me felt satisfaction in that. And Germany was ready for me as well. I had packed my entire dresser and most of my closet, though I did leave behind my sexy lingerie and a lavender sachet in Ryan's underwear drawer. We'd need those when I came home.

We went to see Kelsea and drop my car off with her, checking on the house that she now rented from me. Typically, we were a close mother and daughter pair, but now that she was married and trying to get her career off the ground, we talked much less than we used to and saw each other infrequently. I think she had gotten a recent case of the 'catch-ups' because her younger brother had already been hired as an opener for a fellow stand-up comic on tour around the United States.

"I won't stay, hun. I left Ryan out in his car waiting," I said as I stood in the foyer.

She kissed my cheek. "How rude, Mom. He can come in, you know."

"I know, doll, but if he comes in, the next thing you know, we've eaten up your entire evening. I just came by to drop off the Honda."

Her eyes brightened as I waved the key. "Remember the deal: start her at least once a week; drive her at least once per month." She reached for the key, but I drew back, "Right?"

"Yeah, Mom. Jesus Christ, I'm not sixteen anymore." Even though Kelsea was shorter than me, she was a powerhouse of a young woman, shrewd and intelligent, determined and pragmatic; I had no reason to worry.

"I know, hun. You've just been so preoccupied lately and..." I trailed off, having run out of excuses. I scanned around the foyer, formal living room, and as much of the rest of the house as I could see from the main entrance. "Place looks great, baby. Thanks for taking such good care of it. How's the pool look?"

"Looks great. Looks really great. And the solar heater made it swim-ready in late April."

"That's cool. I'm so glad you guys can enjoy it. Please keep the service while I'm gone, too. The house will run fine if you just leave everything how I had it. If stuff is already running perfectly—"

"Don't change a thing." She completed my sentence and rolled her eyes. "I know, Mom, I know. Your fear of change is hilarious, considering that you decided to go to Germany." She looked at me with inquisitive golden hazel eyes, but there was no time nor need to reopen the mental trunk holding all my fears and concerns about Germany. She would understand and likely already suspected, but I really couldn't revisit it again. She waited long enough to allow me to reply before shrugging and continuing awkwardly. "Well...okay, keep that one locked up for now, but eventually, I suspect we'll be talking about it." She twirled the key ring around her finger. "I'll take her for a spin at least once a week, and I'll keep the pool service and pay all the bills." She paused, looking at me mischievously. "I'll also buy groceries and feed myself. I might go to work, and I might do laundry sometimes, too, though I am considering both of those optional at the moment."

"Okay. Okay. I can take a hint." I hugged her and kissed her forehead.

She sighed. "You smell good, like always."

I didn't want to let her go. "Thank you, baby. When your brother comes back from tour, you give him his piece of this hug, okay?"

She was stroking my back. She sniffed. "I will." Her voice cracked slightly.

"It's only a year, hun. I'll be back before you know it."

She broke from the hug. "I know." Her face was red from crying, and my own eyes stung, too. "Your man is waiting. Better not make him wait too long..." she said in mock warning.

"Speaking of men, tell Blaine that I said he better take care of you while I'm gone."

She beamed at the thought of her husband. "I will."

"Okay, beautiful, I love you." I kissed her again and gave her another hug. "Take care of the car, and be sure to give your brother that piece of my hug."

As we pulled away from the house, I finally allowed the tears to flow.

***

After breakfast the next morning, Ryan helped me with cleaning the kitchen. "How do you feel, babe?"

"I dunno. Nervous I guess." I rinsed another plate and put it in the dish drainer as Ryan's hand chased up my back to my neck. He massaged gently.

"I s'pose that's to be expected, right?"

"I guess. Still don't like it."

He pushed my hair aside and kissed the back of my neck, sliding his hands down to my hips and pulling me close. "I know you aren't comfortable at the moment, but how do you feel about the future?"

"Mostly good, I guess." I bent my head forward and offered him my neck. I loved when he nuzzled me there; I'd stand at the sink all day if that was my reward. He nibbled and nuzzled, and I leaned into him. "What will I do without these moments?"

"We'll have them—video calling and such."

"It's not the same as your hand firmly at my hip and your luscious lips at my neck. No video can capture that."

"That's when we buy plane tickets."

I turned around. "Where did you come from?" I cupped his face and kissed him lovingly. "Where the hell do men like you come from?"

"Men? Men?! Bah," he scoffed. "There is only one me." I threw my head back and laughed, putting my hands up. He bit my neck. "What's so funny?"

I looked at him again. "Ahhh. Fuck, hun. Nothing. Nothing at all is funny." I rested my upper arms on his shoulders, wrapping one around them and coiling the other atop his head. "It's so true. You are unique and special. And I love you." I melted into our kiss, savoring the taste of him in my mouth as his hands stroked down my back and cupped my ass. He lifted me and set me onto the counter, stepping between my now open legs. My mini-skirt rose up to my panty line, exposing my dusty rose thong. His right hand came away from my ass and traced the outside of my thigh, finding the hem of my skirt and following it around the top of my thigh and between my legs. I wrapped my heels behind his knees and opened my legs even farther. He teased the seam of my thong, following it from high on my thigh to the juncture of leg and pelvis. He tickled the tendon that was stretched taut. I inhaled and tilted my hips for him. He rubbed a thumb over the silky material, pushing it against my body and causing it to absorb the juices that were already flowing. We moaned simultaneously as his thumb reached my clit. "I want you…" I breathed.

"I see that." He slid my panties aside and teased my slit, coating his finger without pushing it inside me. I pulled his shirt over his head and stroked his chest. Hopping off the counter, I kissed and licked his nipples as I undid his pants. Sliding my thumbs into the sides of them, I pushed them down. I had barely gotten them below his ass when he pulled me back to standing and stepped into me, pinning me between him and the counter. His cock was a rod between us, pressing against my pelvis. He stripped my shirt off, yanked my skirt up to my waist, and hooked my panties with his thumb, sending them sliding down my legs. As he lifted me, I wrapped my legs around him, opening my pussy and adjusting our alignment. He eased into me so slowly. I twisted and tilted my hips, settling lower and lower onto his shaft. With me pinned against the counter, he drove into me, sucking my breasts as his ribbed cock scraped against my engorged clit.

One centimeter at a time, he pressed into me, and then, just as slowly, he withdrew. He was intentionally teasing me, moving too slowly. I wanted him to drive into me with more speed and force than he was giving. I tried to hasten him, grinding faster, but he moved his hips in opposition. I unlocked my legs from behind his and stood up, his cock sliding out of me.

"On the floor," I rasped, tugging his arm as I knelt down. "Come here." He got on his knees in front of me, kissing me, squeezing my breast with one hand and my ass with the other. I leaned toward him until he sat down. I pulled his legs out in front of him and straddled them. In the morning light, his muscular body was a racetrack of its own, and my mouth and hands wanted to experience every inch.

His cock was still wet and glistening from having been inside me; my mouth watered. In one swift movement, I took his cock all the way into my throat, and then slowly withdrew it, sucking all my juices from him before moving up his chest, kissing, licking, and crawling my way to his neck. I nuzzled him and brought my knees up alongside his ribs and settled my plump wet pussy onto his belly, feeling his cock against my lips. "Mmmmm..."

He grabbed my hips and held me still as he tilted his hips to push inside me. I raised just enough to align him and leaned forward to be sure he'd be able to stab into me with one movement. Together I seated myself, and he thrust, ramming into me. His hands moved to my sides, thumbs at my hips and fingers gripping my ass. I sat upright and bounced up and down on him, feeling his cock deep inside my body, faster and harder with each bounce as I came closer and closer to exploding. He moved a hand to my breast and his other to my clit.

"Yes...oh...yes..." I loved fucking this man. My free breast was bouncing wildly while he pinched the nipple of the other. His thumb stroked my clit at a pace matching my rhythm, and each flick became its own mini orgasm. "Cum with me, baby. Cum inside my throbbing pussy. Fuckkk!"

I screamed. He held me up above him and continued to relentlessly thrust in and out of my convulsing pussy. Again and again, he slammed into me, slapping against my fiery hot clit. I squeezed and sucked his cock with each intense wave of my orgasm, and finally, he groaned and slammed into me as deeply as he could, and then slowing the pace as he filled me with his cum.

I collapsed onto his chest, knees sore, pussy still throbbing, as he began to go soft inside me. I drew my arms into my chest to capture some of our body heat and to feel safe again as I came back to reality. Lying there on his chest, gasping for air, I settled into him and rocked ever so slightly side to side, settling my hips onto his more fully. He dragged his hands softly up and down my back, too softly to feel my ribs, just the slightest touch of his fingertips delicately bringing me back. "Damn, babe. You needed that, eh?"

I pinched him near his armpit. "I'm not the only one. Tell me you didn't want that as badly as I did."

"You can need me that badly any time you'd like."

I pushed up from his chest. "It's a tad chilly in here." My nipples hardened at the exposure.

"I see that, baby." He reached up appreciatively and covered each breast with a meaty hand. "I love your breasts. You have the most amazing tits I've ever seen."

I sat more fully upright on top of him, a hand fisted on each of my hips, pulling my shoulders back and filling my lungs with air. "How about now, huh? Work of art?! I should be a Greek statue, right? Maybe you should sculpt me."

"I couldn't keep my hands off you long enough to ever finish."

I slid my thumbs between his hands and my breasts as if peeling away suction cups. "Well, my dear, they must come off me for the moment while I go find some warm clothes. I'm freezing, and these little mitts are only saving the tits." Still holding his hands, I leaned forward and kissed him. Then using his hands for leverage, I pressed against them to get up. "If you wait there, I'll get a warm washcloth for you and some fresh boxers."

"Well, hurry up, then, because it's really cold without my blanket of Jen to keep me warm."

I walked to the bedroom, turning on the sink as I found each of us some clothes. I washed myself and threw on some panties and a robe before rinsing the washcloth and squeezing it out for him. As I came back to the kitchen, he had drawn his knees up and was lying on his back with his arms wrapped around his torso. "Awww, baby. I'm so sorry. I was as fast as I could be. Here..." I settled down beside him and opened my hands, revealing the steaming rag. Slowly and carefully, I washed him of our sex—his belly, his cock, even between his legs has all gotten coated with our juices. "Damn, where'd all this come from?"

"I know, I know. Now, gimme those boxers; it's too damned cold."

I held the boxers above my head. "What? *These* boxers?"

He scrambled to his knees, wrapped one arm around my waist, and grabbed the boxers with the other. "Yeppers. Precisely those ones."

I stayed on the floor as he stood. When he was fully standing, and before he could pull on his boxers, I knelt and took his soft dick into my mouth one last time, squeezing it with my lips and using my tongue to press it into the roof of my mouth. Slowly, I pulled away and let it slide out into my hand. "Damn, I love your dick!" He laughed in an embarrassed way and pulled on his boxers as I stood up. "I mean that, hun. I'll miss that when I'm gone."

"Is that all? Just the dick? If I could package it up for you, would you take it with you?"

"Now, there's a thought. I could keep it in a box on a shelf in my flat. I'd write on the side of it 'open in case of emergency.' Would it be bad if I had an emergency every day?"

"You do when you're here, so why not in Germany, too?"

I smiled and thought about what he said. "We do have sex almost every day, don't we? I don't really keep track."

"It's one of the things I love about you, baby. You're sexy in everything you do—the way you talk, the way you move, the way you cook. All of it is so sensual that you keep me hard for you. You think I don't see the guys looking at you sometimes?"

"What guys?"

"When we ride. The guys I ride with. Mark especially. I know he's jealous. I think he wants you so bad he can hardly stand it."

I sucked the back of my teeth as my mouth opened, scoffing, "Oh, my God, hun. I think you're wrong."

Nobody has ever done anything that would imply...they're your friends, babe. They've never done or said anything inappropriate."

"Hold your horses. I'm not accusing anybody of anything. Just commenting that I got the best woman out there, and they know it. I can see it in their faces." He paused, looking at me appreciatively. "I love you, babe. And Germany won't change that.

"Now, come on, let's figure out what you're making for the ride tomorrow."

As we shopped that evening and cooked the next day, I took Ryan in. I watched him and took mental images to bring with me to Germany. We made macaroni and cheese and a bratwurst to take to the track. As we cooked, we laughed and joked and played with food, with each other. It was pure joy, and I wanted to capture it to carry with me on my trip. I wished I could videotape us in a way that included the feeling of his hands on me, his voice filling my ears, the smell of the food cooking, the taste of his mouth and body, the smell of our sex, the warmth of his embrace, the sound of his laugh, the smell as I opened the oven door and the heat that blasted me in the face while he aligned himself behind me, pretending there was no other way to get a look into the oven. These moments would be unavailable for a time, and it still petrified me to think of it.

Chapter Nine

I wept watching him ride at the track that day. He was a sight to see. Even with a helmet on, I could feel his smile beaming through the visor. The sun was shining, but it was a relatively mild day for Vegas—barely 90 degrees. The bleachers were ablaze from the sun. Whoever thought aluminum was a good choice must never have spent a summer in Vegas. The bikes added to the desert heat and mystique, filling the air with fumes that made the scene look like a mirage, blurry and gassy. I wore sunglasses and sun block and came armed with a blanket to put on the bleacher bench; I felt like an old pro at this.

And today, Chris was next to me on the bleachers. It had been awhile since I'd seen him here, and even when I didn't come, Ryan said his appearances had become rare. He was still using crutches even though it had been more than two months since he came home. His hair was longer and a little more unkempt, and he'd grown what little facial hair was possible. He slouched, his elbows on his knees, head resting on his fisted hands. I playfully punched his arm, "What's up, tiger?"

He recoiled from my touch, cutting his eyes in my direction. "What's that supposed to mean?"

My eyes narrowed. "Nothing, hun..." I moved to place my hand on his back, but he waved me away. "It's just that I haven't seen you in a while, and I was wondering how you've been." My hand found its way back to my lap.

"You know, this," he jerked his hand pointing at the bleachers and track, "isn't the only place to find me. Strangely enough, guess where I can usually be found." He paused as if I was actually supposed to answer. I eyed him, surprised at the apparent venom in my surrogate sibling's attitude. When he didn't continue, I shrugged. "Home! That's where. Folks who can't ride don't generally hang out at a dirt bike track."

I stared open-faced at the man who used to be my fun-loving, light-hearted friend. Was this some form of grief phase? Maybe he was upset about his recuperation, and he was taking it out on friends and loved ones. "Chris, honey, I don't...."

"Save it. It's fine. I don't need excuses. I get enough of those from the guys. *'Too busy, can't make it. Maybe next week, catch ya later.'*" He mocked. "It's all bullshit. If I didn't come to the track, they'd never see me. You don't owe me anything, but I get more attention and conversation from you than my riding bros."

"What?! That's not true, hun. Ryan loves hanging out with you. He talks about you all the—"

"You know the last time he saw me? The last time he saw me and we *weren't* at the track? When he helped me move back to my parents' house. How depressing is that? And he couldn't even stick around afterwards for a beer." And then he muttered, "I guess getting home to you was more important."

I remembered the day well. Ryan had worked overtime for three days so that he could take the entire day off to help Chris move. It had only been little more than a week since he had helped Chris move out of his parents' house, and now, he was heading back again. It was frustrating for me, though Ryan didn't complain, and he didn't question the sudden change of heart either. He dutifully went to help Chris despite the personal sacrifice it took. He'd come home exhausted and tense that night. Chris had insisted on trying to help despite the crutches making it nearly impossible. And more than once, Chris and his father had exchanged hushed terse words. Over the course of the day, each of the other guys from the riding group had come to help, though none of them could spare the entire day. By the time the last of the boxes and furniture was moved, Ryan told me that he nearly ran from the place to avoid the awkward tension.

"Chris," I tried to remain calm and fight the urge to defend Ryan, "the guys love you like a brother, and Ryan probably more than the rest of them."

"They pity me," he said through gritted teeth.

"No, they don't!"

"Yes, they do! The young one who barely got started riding and now gets to drool jealously from the sidelines." He looked down at his hands. "I may never be able to ride again. Fuck, I might never walk again...not like a normal person." He turned his head away from me and then said more softly, "If they cared, I wouldn't have to beg them to spend time with me. It wouldn't matter that I can't ride." He wrung his hands together, clenching and releasing his jaw. "Do you think I *like* sitting on the sidelines like this? An invalid?" His voice began to rise, and he turned back to me, eyes bloodshot and glassy. "You think I like drooling over what I *used to* do? Waiting in the wings to break bread with guys who otherwise don't have time for me? I mean, I love these guys, but I kinda hate them, too. They are partly the reason I'm like this."

"Wow. Hun... do you really believe that?" I looked at him intently.

"They fucking knew I couldn't handle it."

"And they tried to tell you—"

"Maybe they should've tried harder."

"And maybe you should've listened harder." The words came out as a reflex, and I knew they were the wrong ones as soon as they rang in my ears.

He fumbled with his crutches and got up. "I have no fucking clue what I'm even doing here," his voice cracked; "groveling like some..." he bit his lip, though not before I saw it quiver.

I jumped off the bleachers and grabbed him by the shoulders, shaking him as I spoke, "Stop it, Chris. Jesus Christ, man, stop talking like that!" I pulled him into a hug. "Sweetheart, it simply isn't true," I said to his neck and ear. Breaking away, I looked into his eyes as tears threatened to spill onto his cheeks. "You're like a little brother to me, y'know. And as your big sister, I won't let you keep heading down that road. This kind of thinking...it's not helping." I smiled at him softly. "I tell you what, riddle me this, Batman: what's going right? At this moment, tell me something that's going right for you."

He sniffed and he swiped his face with the back of his hand. "Nothing. That's what's going right. A big fat fucking nothing." In that moment, he looked like a child, helpless and friendless, abandoned in the corner of a schoolyard.

I pursed my lips and cocked my head skeptically. "Nothing?! Absolutely not one single thing?" I sighed heavily. "Tell me about physical therapy. I see you graduated to a new crutch," I stroked the forearm cuff of the new, shorter crutch and raised an eyebrow at him.

"Hate 'em." He fumbled with the grips. "The first ones messed up my armpits, and these aren't much better on my forearms." He rubbed one of his arms as if making the point, though I saw no signs of chaffing. "And physical therapy," he continued, resettling back onto his crutch, "is painful and tiresome, and it's not getting me anywhere. I mean, I haven't gotten much better since I left the hospital, still can't even stand on my own." He looked down at his feet and spoke almost inaudibly. "Y'know, one of the biggest reasons I moved back home?" He looked around as if making sure no one had snuck up on us. "I fell once getting out of the shower. I mean, I had been doing so well. I barely moved back into my apartment when it happened. Mom and Pop insisted that I move back home again. And now, my mother won't let me shower until my father or brother is around to help me get in and out. I feel like a fucking four-year-old."

"Work? What about work?" I was grasping at straws. "What do you do, now that construction is...?" Damn I shouldn't have said that. "Now that you..." I paused again. "What are you doing for work now?"

"Another nothing. How about that? A whole bunch of nothing. You are looking at a four-year-old nothing. And I'm not sure how the fuck to get back to where I was." His lip quivered and tears fell. This time he didn't try to hide them.

I thought of Dullberth and the sales staff. Dullberth kinda screwed me over, probably for my own good or that of the company. But still, maybe he'd feel like he should make good on that.

"What about sales? How do you feel about sales?"

"Like telemarketing? No thanks."

"No, hun. Do you not know what I do?"

"Guys don't talk about that kinda stuff. I have no clue. Best guess is you're a chef."

I smiled broadly. "Well, thanks for saying that, but no. I'm not. I'm the regional manager for Huntington's Sports. We sell all kinds of outdoor equipment—the heavy outdoor stuff. Not running shoes and stuff, but tents and camping gear, quads and dirt bikes, helmets and knives, stuff like that. In fact, that's where I met Ryan, back when I was on the sales floor."

"Really? I never pictured you for a sales person. To me, sales feels like used car shit."

"Retail is different. And this is stuff you know about. You'd be great at it. You have charisma and charm...well...when you aren't so busy being whomever this guy is." I waved in his general direction.

"Fuck. I'm sorry. It just sucks. This whole fucking thing sucks. I mean a few months ago, I was a 'rising star' at Ace construction, site supervisor in training. I was making good money, had my own place..." he trailed off, looking down and toeing the dirt. "I was going places. My life was right on track. And one fucking day ruined everything. Now, Ace won't even let me stay on and do the paperwork until I get better." He stabbed at the dirt with his right crutch before continuing again but more softly. "I was fucking stupid to even try that ridge. I know now that I was. And I hate it."

I had an idea. I'd take Chris to Huntington's. If it went well, maybe I could secure him a sales position until something better came through for him. If it didn't, at least, it would be a distraction, and maybe I could shake him of this funk. "How about you come with me to our flagship store tomorrow? Ryan has to work anyway, and I'm off until I leave."

"I heard about Germany. What about you and Ryan?"

"I love him, hun. And I'm gonna miss him terribly, but we'll talk and video chat and stuff. We'll get through it I'm sure."

"He won't be the same without you. I don't think any of this will be. We sort of expect you to come with him. At least then, we know there'll be food," he laughed and then said more softly, "and a really cool chick."

"Well, now, that's a compliment coming from a badass like you! Now, what do you say about that trip to the store tomorrow?"

"Ahhh, fine. I'll do it, but only as a favor to you. I'm no used car salesman."

I tousled his hair. "You're no four-year-old either."

***

That night, as we drove to his parents' house, Ryan asked about Chris. "What was up with you two today?"

I smiled, remembering our exchange. "He's worse than you know, babe."

"It didn't look bad by the time we came off the track."

"He's really upset at how slowly he is recovering. And he feels alone—"

"But we're always there for him!" Ryan interrupted. "I mean, we arrange our schedules around checking up on him. What more does he want?"

I wiggled my head a little, shaking loose from my surprise at Ryan's strong emotions. "Whoa, baby. Nobody is blaming you for anything. Nobody said you and the guys aren't some damned amazing friends. He's just upset. If you couldn't walk, wouldn't you be pissed? He's not pissed at anyone in particular; he's pissed at the situation." Ryan looked unconvinced. "Look, baby, he feels like a kid. He's living at home again. He has no job. And he had been in training to be a site supervisor, did you know that?"

He shook his head at me and pursed his lips. "We don't talk about shit like that. We talk about riding and chicks and sports and stuff."

"Hun, he went from feeling like he was building a life for himself on his own to living at home again, jobless and feeling helpless. I mean, honey, he needs his father or brother to help him in and out of the shower because he fell once. None of those things are yours to own."

"I feel like shit that I wasn't there that day. I could've stopped him. That was a dumb move, and I could've prevented this whole thing." Ryan's frustration and defensiveness became suddenly clear. More than a brother to him, Chris had become a responsibility. Ryan wanted him to get better, wanted to see him do well, and felt helpless to do more than he already had.

"But you weren't there, and you can't be sure that you could've stopped him. To hear the guys tell it, he had a full head of steam about getting up that ridge that day. I think he was bound to try regardless."

I took a deep breath before blurting, "I'm going to take him to the flagship tomorrow."

"What? Why?"

"He needs to get back to work. He needs something to keep him busy."

"And what's the flagship got to do with it? He knows construction, not sales."

"He knows outdoor equipment. He camps, he goes four-wheeling, and he rides dirt bikes. He can be a good salesman, at least until he gets his legs back."

Ryan parked in front of his parents' house, and as he shut the car off, he looked at me, his lips pressed together, his eyes examining me. "Where did you come from?"

"What?"

"Where do women like you come from?"

"Women?!" I gasped in mock horror. "There is but one of me in all the land, sir. And you've lucked up and caught me," I said in singsong.

He kissed me tenderly. "Well, then, aren't I the lucky one?"

It was nice to visit with Ryan's parents one last time. They'd been married nearly forty years and their love for one another was still obvious. It was an inspiration to see them together, and it made me hopeful about Germany.

Ryan's mother had made a homemade cheesecake, and as she went to get it from the kitchen, Mr. Riverton lit up. "You just wait," he said, "you are in for a treat. My Caroline makes the best cheesecake west of the Mississippi." And with that, he was gone, scurrying to the kitchen behind his wife.

A few minutes later, Mrs. Riverton reemerged carrying napkins and looking a bit embarrassed. "Jim will be right out with the cheesecake," she explained.

Ryan chuckled. "He wouldn't let you carry that tray, Mom, would he?"

"I could've, though," she announced proudly as if someone in the room doubted her.

Ryan shook his head smiling, "I know you could've." He hugged her lovingly. "After forty years, you have to know he does it because he loves you and not because you can't."

Her face softened and she smiled knowingly. "It's just on thirty-seven years. Don't make me sound older than I am," she chided.

Watching Ryan and his mother interact was heartwarming. He was her youngest. And no matter how independent and capable he was, he was still a momma's boy. Seeing their bond made me feel nostalgic about my own son, wondering how we would interact when I reached Mrs. Riverton's age.

The cheesecake was indeed amazing, and so was the freshly ground Amaretto-laced coffee. We settled easily into conversation, talking of Germany, of how Ryan and I expected to make it through the separation, and what kind of touristy things we would do when he came for Oktoberfest.

"It would be great if you guys came, too," I suggested. "Have you ever traveled abroad?"

"That trip will be for you two," Mrs. Riverton pointed at Ryan and I. "There's nothing we could do but get in the way of that. If we want to go to Germany, we don't need excuses." Her voice was warm and loving. Between her cooking and her demeanor, I could see why Ryan was still single. The example his mother gave him had set his bar high. A woman would be lucky to win his heart.

And I did feel lucky.

At the door, while his mother and I hugged, she whispered in my ear, "He loves you, Jen, like I've never seen him. He lights up around you. Remember that when you're missing him in Germany." She pulled away and looked into my eyes. "Okay, my unofficial daughter-in-law, take care of yourself." She smiled as if we had a secret and then she winked. "And you remember what I said...."

As we drove back home, joy and feelings of privilege washed over me. Was I everything he wanted? Was I really all that he could imagine in a wife? Should I have accepted his proposal? He had given me multiple opportunities, and each time I had stubbornly said no. Today, feeling so overwhelmed at how blessed I was to have him, it somehow seemed petty that I had not accepted the privilege of being his wife.

***

The next day, I picked up Chris at ten, and we headed to the store. I took him in through the back entrance so he could see the warehouse first. It was slow going as he moved with his crutches, but that gave him time to soak it all in.

"This isn't a store; it's heaven." I laughed. "I love white water rafting...and those kayaks over there are really top quality. And...how many different kinds of tents do we carry?" He couldn't stop chattering. It almost seemed like he was taking mental inventory.

"It sounds like someone has considered taking a job here."

"I meant you. How many different kinds of tents do *you* carry?"

"Mmmhmm..."

Chris oohed and aahed through the warehouse, pointing out all the equipment he'd either owned or rented in the past and mentioning pros and cons of some of the brands we carried. About halfway through the warehouse, I noticed that we'd picked up a tail. It was Bill, the store manager. He was watching and listening intently to the conversation, and Chris was making this hire a pretty easy sell.

By the time we got to the floor, Bill was waiting for us.

"Hi, Bill. It's so nice to see you." We shook hands.

"And you, too, Ms. Simmons. How have you been, ma'am?"

"I'm fine, Bill. Just fine. A little nervous about the trip to Germany, but otherwise really happy. How's the store doing?"

"Sales are steady. Not the spring spikes we saw when you were here, but I'm happy with our overall performance so far this year."

"Sales should be spiking this time of year. We're in mid-May. At this point, people should have been ramping up for their summer activities. Hmmm. I'll take a look around your sales floor and displays and see what I can do to help. In the meantime...." I turned to Chris. "Bill, this is Chris, Chris Jacobs. And Chris, this is Mr. Rasmussen; he runs the flagship."

Chris shook Bill's hand enthusiastically. "I love the place. It's amazing. And I haven't even seen the store yet."

"You were happy then ...with the warehouse?" His Danish accent and linguistic pace were obvious but charming. Bill Rasmussen was a dutiful man. He stood about six foot three, with ebony hair parted precisely to the side, and perfect porcelain skin. His teeth were white as if he got them cleaned and whitened regularly, and he always wore suit slacks and a dry-cleaned, heavily starched button-down.

"Are you kidding? That place is the Taj Mahal of any outdoorsman!"

"Well, perhaps I shall show you around the sales floor?"

"I'd love it." This time I took the trail position, letting the men walk ahead of me while I texted Ryan.

"It's going amazingly well, baby. I think he'll fit right in." Ryan was busy at work, but I wanted him to be able to relax about Chris and about this morning.

I wandered around the store and saw that displays were functional but lackluster in some areas. The sales staff needed to work on being more creative about staging in the key moneymaking areas of camping and outdoor vehicles. I grabbed some sales staff and gave them my suggestions, and then met back up with Chris and Bill.

"How's it going, boys?"

"This young man is really something special, Ms Simmons. He knows things about the equipment that most sales staff cannot talk about even after being here for a year or more. People always have an area of expertise, but this one is...well, he is something."

"I told you, Bill." I winked at Chris. "Turns out that Chris might be available for hire."

"This has already been handled, ma'am. I could not help but offer him a sales staff position, and thankfully, he has accepted."

I slapped Chris on the back, almost knocking him off his crutches. "Congratulations! How about we get out of Mr. Rasmussen's hair and go celebrate?"

Chris beamed from ear to ear. "That sounds great."

"Okay, hun, give me a minute to talk to Mr. Rasmussen, and we'll head out."

"Mmm'kay." Chris wandered off toward the hunting knives as I turned back to Bill.

"Okay, Bill. Your store is really functional, so no surprise that you are maintaining the quarterly sales quota, but..."

"There is a problem?"

"Some of your displays need work. I think if you fix them, you can increase your revenue." We walked through the store, and I explained to Bill what I had instructed his staff to do and why.

"Thank you. Thank you very much, Ms Simmons. We miss you as regional. We do. All the store managers, we are talking about this."

It felt good to hear, though it was bittersweet as I was down to the last few days before my departure. "You're in good hands, Bill. James will do fine as regional. Just give him time."

"Perhaps..." Bill shrugged.

And with that Chris and I headed out to lunch to celebrate and talk about his new beginning.

By the time I dropped Chris off at his parents' home, he was overflowing with appreciation and excitement. "I start next week! I can't believe it. He didn't even care that I can't walk right. He hired me right there on the spot."

"I knew you'd fit in." I beamed like a proud mother. "It'll be good for the store and good for you."

"Thanks, Jen. Thanks so much."

"Make me proud, Chris. I know you will."

***

I called Dullberth before dinner and told him I brought a talented new kid through the flagship.

"It's not a tourist stop, Ms. Simmons."

"Nope. I know that."

"So what's your angle? You're no longer regional manager."

"I know that, too. But this kid knows a lot about the outdoors. He can be a really good asset to the store."

"So then, you're calling for a favor?"

"No. I'm calling to inform you that you'll be hearing from Rasmussen. And that this kid will likely be a fast burner."

"And if I say no?"

"Rasmussen hired him already. I was just giving you a heads up. This kid has real potential. You may find he'll be fit for upper management faster than I was."

"A bit optimistic, considering your record."

"Clear a career path for this kid, Mr. Dullberth. His name's Chris. Chris Jacobs."

As I hung up, it felt good to know that it was likely the last conversation Dullberth and I would ever have. I still resented the way he arm-twisted me into going to Germany.

Chapter Ten

On the day before I left, I expected a quiet night alone with Ryan. I brought home some wine and began to make chicken Marsala while he was off riding with the guys. As I was cutting the mushrooms, the phone rang. It was Ryan.

"Hey, babe, what's up?"

"I need you to come to the track."

"The dirt bike track?"

He snorted. "Ummm, is there any other?"

"But, I'm making dinner."

"Put it away in the fridge and get over here, babe."

"Shees, what's the rush?"

"I forgot my effing helmet, and the sunlight's disappearing. I need you to bring it and quickly."

"Fine. Fine. I'm on my way." I hurriedly wrapped everything and put it in the fridge before rushing out the door with Ryan's helmet.

It'll be nice to see the guys one last time before I go, I thought as I started the car.

On the twenty-minute ride over, I thought about how I'd met Ryan for the first time three years ago. It had been two years in the making. We'd met online and had chatted, texted, and called each other sporadically over that time. It was funny to think how close Fontana was and yet how impossible our schedules had made it for us to meet that first time. I secretly had feared that he wasn't that interested in meeting me, so he made excuses. Finally, I made that first nervous trip to California to meet him. Today, it seemed impossible to believe that we had come from such a place. We were a flurry of dates and activities initially. And after only two weeks, we spent a weekend 'away' at a hotel on the strip.

And that was the first time he'd gotten me onto his bike. I was petrified! It was barely dawn, and we were headed up to Mount Charleston for the day. Neon casino lights highlighted the Vegas skyline as he weaved through traffic. My heart was pounding against my rib cage in sheer terror! I remember wondering how I had ever let this man convince me that this would be okay and why he was being such a daredevil. He leaned the bike to the left and right as necessary, gliding effortlessly through traffic. I squeezed my eyes shut tightly and gripped his waist, burying my head in his back, and breathing in the smell of the helmet he'd lent me, wishing his cologne was a tiny bit stronger. I loved the way he smelled and his reassuring demeanor. Even that early on in the relationship, he'd put me at ease. I had tried to relax, letting go of his waist and allowing my hands to fall loosely into his lap and the bulge I had enjoyed just hours before. Driving in the car now, three years later, my belly dropped, remembering how he had learned me so easily, romancing me, pleasing me. I fell for him fast and hard. Even at two weeks, I knew I was falling. Back then, I had tried to rationalize that it had been two years of courtship, so falling for him so quickly was only natural. But even now that seemed silly, since I'd never laid eyes on him.

The more we rode that day, the more self-assured I became. The more I trusted him, the more we moved together and as one with the bike. By the time the city faded into the distance, I was smiling at the sensations the experience was bringing. The motorcycle vibrating between my legs created a hum that made my crotch quiver. The wind buffeted my body with a rhythmic calming beat that felt like the reverse of singing into a fan. And Ryan was solidly in front of me, warming me from the apex of my legs to the crest of my collarbone, blocking me from the worst of the wind, controlling the bike and our destination, guiding our movements without saying a word.

When he finally pulled off the highway and turned toward the mountains, I was comfortable enough to fall asleep on him. I had rested comfortably against his back and was able to focus on the amazing way my body felt. My hands were comfortably resting on his jeans. I could feel his warmth through the denim material, and I wanted him again right then. He had interrupted my thoughts by turning off onto a gravel road which exaggerated the bike's natural vibrations. I reflexively tightened my grip on him, squeezing my thighs together and holding onto his jeans at the inseams. I had felt so comfortable with Ryan, so at ease, and so turned on. That was a constant from the start—sexual energy surging us through the day.

As he had finally stopped the bike, I stayed put, straightening my legs into a long stretch and gripping his jeans a little more tightly. I leaned forward as I put my feet down and slid my hands down his thighs and then back up to his zipper, slowly sliding over the growing bulge in his pants and continuing on to his hips and up his back. I wanted him to know that this was torture for me, and that I was prepared to share it with him.

We flirted and hiked for most of the morning, eventually finding a secluded area with a floor of leaves and grasses. We had originally sat down to 'take a break,' but as has now become the norm, we ended up making love right there. Even as I drove to the track today, I could still smell the leaves around us and see the way he looked at me, hungry and tender all at once. It was a look I'd never seen on anyone else, and it always melted me. Ryan could still have me whenever he wanted, wherever. My stomach clenched at the thought of how soon that possibility would be gone.

***

I was crying and breathing heavily as I pulled into the parking lot at the track. I didn't know whether I wanted to make love to him or cry all over him, but I definitely wasn't thinking about this helmet or the guys. I grudgingly lugged the helmet out toward the track. It was nice to approach slowly and look at Ryan standing there at the fence line with Chris, his bike leaning against the fence not too far down. He had taken my spot for the night, talking to Chris and keeping him company while the others rode. Maybe it was better that he forgot his helmet. The riders zoomed past, some jumping as they got in front of 'show center,' while others just flipped their middle finger. I sniffed up the last of my tears, wiped under my eyes, hoping to erase any signs of the raccoon that crying might have brought, and straightened my hair as I got closer to the men.

"Hey, you two. What's up?" Both heads spun around on swivels.

"Hey, babe." Ryan stepped to me, sweeping me up in one arm and kissing me.

"Hi, love. I got a little something special for ya." I waved his helmet around. "And hey to you, too, Chris." Chris waved meekly.

"Yeah," Ryan toed the ground, "about that...."

"Mmm...what's up?" I dragged the words out in suspicion.

"I kinda have my old one here. You brought that one for you."

"Oh, Lord, what's going on?" Just then the bikes came into view from around the track, and instead of continuing around, they stopped one by one near the fence line. They were all here, even Pat, whose wife wasn't always game for him coming out to ride with the guys. "Hey guys! How's it going?" There was a jumble of 'heys' and 'how ya doings' and 'what's ups' from the crowd. I laughed. "Right back at ya."

"You guys ready?" Nods came back in reply as Chris breached the fence and headed onto the track. He handed his crutches to Mark and got onto Johnnie's bike.

I looked at Ryan. "We'll meet you guys there," he said, and the guys headed off, with Johnnie driving much more slowly than the others.

"What's going on, hun?" I tried to feign irritation, but I was excited to see what Ryan had planned.

"Come one, babe." He took my hand and led me to his bike. Kissing me quickly, he said, "Oops, I almost forgot." And he scurried back to a rock near where he'd been standing and grabbed his old helmet. I stood there, tapping my foot on the ground. "Oh, knock it off. You're the worst actress I know. Get that helmet on and let's get moving."

This bike wasn't near the comfortable ride that his old street bike had been, but considering where my thoughts had just taken me, this ride was poignant and bittersweet in its own way. The hum of the motor between my legs, Ryan warm and self-assured sitting in front of me, and me leaning into his back, I almost felt like I was back on the road to Mount Charleston. I gripped the inside of his thighs and acted scared like I had on the very first day. And when his leg muscles tightened and he turned his head, I rubbed his chest to reassure him that I was fine. He drove slowly over the dirt ridges and hills. This wasn't my first time on the track, but it was a rare occasion. I don't think I had been out here in over a year. He throttled heavily to get up a hill, and I grabbed his chest, smiling. I loved the excuse to hold him.

As we reached the top of the third or fourth hill, the guys came into view, standing around a blanket laid out on the crest of a ridge. I laid my head on Ryan's back and held him close. I wanted to thank him for whatever was about to happen. I knew he had put a lot of effort into planning something for me, and I was thrilled. As we rolled to a stop, I instinctively put my feet down and let my weight rest on the left leg as Ryan leaned the bike in that direction. I took a deep breath and took off my helmet.

Not only were the guys all there, but they had brought Jackie along and Talia as well. I burst into smiles and tears, and hugs. As I made my way to each person to thank them, I felt more joy than I thought possible. I got back to Ryan and was crying my eyes out while my cheeks burned from smiling so much.

"I love you, Ryan Riverton." He smiled and held me until my tears subsided.

"How about we eat?" The guys had a cooler of hot dogs, burgers, and condiments, as well as some beer and soda.

"And chips with bean dip as a side dish," Chris commented. "They were my idea."

"Oh, were they now?" I smiled at him and ruffled his hair.

As I ate my char-burned burger, sloppy with ketchup and relish, I couldn't help but chuckle. My belly was so full of joy-butterflies that it was quivering, making the inappropriate chuckles come.

"What's so funny, babe?"

"Love. Love is funny." turned to face him. "I'm so in love with you and with this moment. I was home, making chicken Marsala for us, and y'know what? This burger tastes better than any Marsala I've ever made."

"Hey, hey, hey, now. Don't eat too much. We can save room for that Marsala. I won't be getting it again for quite some time, and I'd definitely like one last taste."

I leaned in closer to him and whispered directly into his ear, "Why do your words always bring me back to the vision of you making love to me?"

He brought a hand up between us, holding my head with his fingers, his thumb just in front of my left ear as he whispered into my right, "Because that's where I picture myself when I say these things. I want to taste you. That Marsala, too. But for sure, you." My inner thighs reflexively squeezed together, trying to contain the juices flowing into my panties. I gulped and bit his neck, sucking on the tendon that leads straight to his cock. He moaned softly and then pulled away. "Hahaha..." He waved a finger at me, smiling. "Shame on you." I looked down at his jeans, but he was faster, already trying to adjust with the heel of his hand. He shook his head and threw me a sideways glance before heading off to talk to Johnnie.

Mark was nearby so I stepped over. "This is amazing. Thanks so much for helping Ryan put this together."

He kept chewing his burger. Finally, he said, "I didn't really. Just showed up today with a six pack."

"Well, then, thanks for coming, especially without a date," I surveyed the crowd, "that's a surprise."

"I don't bring girls to the track."

I nodded, trying to buy time to think of a new conversation thread to grab. The awkwardness that hung in the air reminded me of a much earlier time in our relationship. I thought we'd long since gotten past these moments. "I leave tomorrow."

"So I heard. Germany, right?"

"Yeah."

"What about Ryan? Kinda thought you guys were wedding bound."

My stomach dropped at the words. There was a part of me that felt guilty for refusing to marry Ryan. And now, here I was, going to Germany alone. "We'll keep in touch. There's always instant messaging and video calls, right?"

He gave me a sideways glance, "I guess." He winced. "If that's what floats your boat."

"It doesn't 'float my boat,' Mark. Ryan 'floats my boat.' But if I have to go to Germany, then I'll make do with video calls and such. What's your issue?" Mark felt far too accusatory and aggressive, and it really was getting under my skin.

Mark jammed a fist into his pocket and eyed me. "You ever think about being with somebody else?"

"What?!"

"I'm just saying. You're at the track a lot. Anybody else here catch your eye?"

I scoffed, fuming mad, "No! What the hell, Mark?"

"Do you love him?"

"You *know* I love him!"

Mark's body relaxed and he shrugged and kicked at a rock near his feet. Looking into my eyes, he said, "If you were my girl, I would never let you leave. If you were my girl, I'd do whatever I had to so that we'd never be apart like that." He looked at me with uncharacteristic warmth and tenderness. Suddenly, I felt vulnerable. I didn't know whether to hug him or back away from this conversation entirely. Ryan's words from the night before rung in my ears. I was suddenly acutely aware of myself. "I'm just saying, a year apart is forever. You never know what can happen in a year."

Tears filled my eyes as Mark was expressing my deepest fears. If Mark could see that Ryan and I would likely end over this, then surely it wasn't all in my head. Even the guy who seldom pursues relationships could see it. I shook my head and admonished myself, *No. Don't do this right now. Of all the times to start thinking this way, you're leaving tomorrow. Get a grip on yourself!* "Y'know, Mark, you're wrong." I swigged my soda, trying to hear and believe my own words. "It'll be fine. I know it will." I downed the rest of my soda. "Now, if you'll excuse me, I need a refill."

I made my way to the cooler.

"Hey, girl." Talia's voice was exactly what I needed at this moment.

"Oh, my God, Talia! I thought you left last night!" I hugged her tightly with my one free arm.

"That was part of the surprise, silly. Do you think these guys could pull this off with me to drill sergeant their asses?"

"God, I love you. I am going to miss you so much!"

"I'm not gonna give you the chance. Somebody's gotta come show you the ropes of social life in Germany. And who better than someone who's been there?" Before we'd met, Talia had lived for a couple years in Germany, a life experience she gloated about regularly.

"I can't wait! I'm gonna hold you to that."

"And so will I," Jackie cut in, "I'm gonna be right there on that plane with her."

"That's gonna be one helluva girls' night out then. Watch out Bavaria, here we come!" And we laughed and made plans for all the things we'd do when they got to Germany.

By the time the sun was setting, I'd made the rounds and talked to each of the guys, intentionally avoiding interacting with Mark again. I settled on the blanket between Ryan's legs and watched the sun setting. Leaning back into him, feeling his breath on my neck, his arms around my body, the heat of his chest against my back, I felt like I could sit here forever frozen in this moment. I held the sides of his legs, toying with the seam of his pants. He kissed my neck and sucked on my ear lobe. "I love you, babe. And I'm gonna miss you so bad when you're gone." I reached behind me, putting my hands at his lower back and drawing him closer. "You're gonna break my back, Jen."

I snorted. "Oops." My cheeks flushed as I scooted out from between his legs and moved behind him, sitting just above him on the ridge over his right shoulder. My left leg bent behind him, I laid my right leg out beside him and put my head on his shoulder. "Is that better?"

He stroked my calf. "Mmmhhmmm." I felt the rumble of his voice against my chest. I was going to miss that.

After the sun set, we cleaned up the place a bit, and then the guys shooed us off, ensuring us that they'd get the girls, the coolers, and Chris back home safely. I gave everyone one more round of hugs, and then Ryan and I headed off for one last lap around the track.

***

The rock in the pit of my stomach grew larger and larger on the way home. I didn't want to go and couldn't imagine what I would feel like next week or next month. Never mind how I would feel by the time Ryan came to see me at Oktoberfest. That seemed like way too far from now, and the empty space between now and then felt like a vacuum of loneliness. My mind flew to the tentative end-date: Christmas. It had crossed my mind a number of times – trying to force myself to relax and at least give us until Christmas. But here, today on the eve of my departure, I thought it might be better to accept the end now, preempt the pain, rather than wait for it to land on me later when I wasn't ready for it.

We weren't home for five minutes before Ryan said something about it. "Stop it," he warned.

"Huh?"

"You heard me. Stop it."

"What do you mean?" I tried to sound innocent and confused, but Ryan was an ace at reading me.

"Brooding. I can see you over there. Wheels running a mile a minute. Lord knows what terrible thing you've foreshadowed, but Jesus, hun. Stop it."

"Ryan, baby… I can't stop it. It makes me sad. I'm so sad to be leaving. And still, I'm afraid."

"Thinking about it won't solve the problem. It might, however, ruin the rest of our night together."

I clasped my hands on top of my head in frustration and took a deep cleansing breath. Exhaling slowly, I told myself that he was right. Besides, I had a long flight to catch in the morning and hours of time trapped in that plane. I would sort this all out. And then I smiled, remembering what he'd said at the track. "Wasn't there something you wanted to taste one more time before I go?"

I have no idea how he crossed the room as fast as he did, but he had me pinned against the wall, hands above my head, kissing me while his free hand reached under my shirt and pushed up my bra, massaging my breast. I wrapped one leg around him and responded just as ravenously to his kiss. His hand slipped from my breast and into my jeans, passing my mound and parting my lips with an investigative finger.

"Mmmm," I moaned as he entered me. It didn't matter that his finger was dry going in. I was already wet enough to coat him thoroughly. And his hand was gone as quickly as it had come. My eyes shot open, only to see him sucking my juices off his finger slowly, pausing to circle his fingertip with his tongue before thrusting it back into his mouth.

"Yep, there was something…" he smiled at me. "But I can't quite put my finger on it." He tapped his finger on my lips, and I could smell the tang of my sex. I tried to snap my teeth at it, but he withdrew and let my hands go. "Now, how about that chicken Marsala?" He slapped my ass for effect.

"After you, sir. I might need your help in the kitchen, and surely I'll need your company." As he stepped away, I fell in behind him and pulled his hips to me, walking in step together as if we were one. And then I stopped us and rubbed the heel of my hand down his swollen zipper, reveling in the fact that he was as turned on as I was. He pushed my hand away.

"Hands off the merchandise, lady. Unless you're buying."

I pushed him forward. "Move along then. On to the kitchen. We've got work to do."

The next two hours were spent making dinner and eating by candlelight. We drank wine and listened to music, talking of when he'd visit in late September and how we'd spend the three months between now and then. I told him to keep an eye out for Chris and see that he's still doing well at the store. He laughed at my mothering tone.

"He's a grown man, y'know."

"I know, hun, I know. But I worry about him."

Ryan just shook his head.

By the time the kitchen was clean, it was time to head to bed. "Tomorrow's gonna be stressful...for both of us," he said. I didn't argue.

This man had been my lover for three years and a friend since two before that. He was all that I had wanted in a man but never found until now. I couldn't imagine leaving him. We lay together tenderly, stroking and massaging each other's bodies to the point of frustration. And then he made love to me. He kissed me tenderly and lovingly, moving on top of me, and pushing my legs apart with his knees. He took his time kissing my breasts and neck, nuzzling my collarbone and my hips. And when he entered me, he looked into my eyes, and we stayed there in exquisite intense pleasure, never breaking eye contact, maybe not even blinking. Tears fell slowly; he kissed them away. He moved on top of me as if we had the rest of our lives, as if this night would never end, as if tomorrow could be stopped if we just didn't stop making love.

I didn't rush him. I didn't want to. I wanted to rest on the edge of oblivion for as long as he could keep me there. Long, slow strokes in and out of my sex, rubbing the underside of my clit as if it were a violin and his cock the bow. Tiny orgasms rocked me over and over again, until I was nearly exhausted. He kept kissing me, telling me he loved me, meeting my stare with strength of conviction, a dare to doubt him. And when at last he began to move faster and in a rhythm my body knew well, I met him thrust for forcible thrust and grunt for groan. I screamed as he tore into me, my legs up on his shoulders, his legs bucking, ramming into my already tender lips and clit. He leaned over, I gripped the headboard with my toes. He fucked me even harder. His arms and neck strained with the force of each thrust. I felt his belly and chest tense on my hamstrings. We reached such a force that I was bouncing off the bed each time he lifted off me. Every muscle in my body ached for release. And when it finally came, it was pure bliss; his cum splattering the walls of my pussy with hot streams of ecstasy. My legs tightened, toes curled, I released the headboard and wrapped my legs around him, holding him inside me to the hilt, filling me, stabilizing me, loving me.

We fell asleep almost immediately.

Chapter Eleven

*A*nd then it was gone.

Life in Munich was like everything I'd imagined and nothing I'd ever experienced.

The company apartment was functional enough. On the day that I walked in, the front door swung open, and it seemed that the entire place opened in front of me and to my left. The kitchen was immediately on my left on the same wall as the apartment door; in fact, if I opened the door too wide, it might've smacked into the side of the kitchen cabinetry. Immediately to my right, as I stepped inside, were two book cases built into the apartment's wall, abutting one another in the corner. There were books already on the shelves, some in English and some in German. *A nice touch,* I thought, immediately feeling like picking one up and settling in. To the left of the book cases and diagonal from the apartment's main door was a balcony. I stepped outside and immediately noticed the trees in the courtyard, lush and green. After living in Las Vegas for so long, this shade of green felt surreal and nearly unnatural. I thought of reading books sitting here on this balcony, allowing the cool Bavarian breezes to waft unfamiliar smells of nature in my direction.

Stepping back inside, the main space of the apartment laid out before me. It was a modest functional space with a sitting area and coffee table on one end nearest the balcony, and a dinette set on the far end nearest the kitchen. The grey carpet was thin and functional. It was so tough and meager that it almost felt like indoor/outdoor carpet. There was an opening in the wall to my right, in the space separating the dining and living rooms. I assumed it was the studio's bathroom, but I was pleasantly surprised to discover a hallway with a bedroom door on each side and the apartment's one bathroom beyond them. Each room was furnished with the basic needs, nothing extravagant, lush, or even homey. I made a mental note to shop for more personal linens and things just as soon as I got the chance, a task I eventually asked a bright young employee to help me with as weeks had gone by, and it seemed I'd never have the time.

The day I moved into the apartment was the last day I remembered having any time for myself. I was busy most days, too busy to fully experience Germany, too busy to even know where in the world I was living. I might've actually been living back in Vegas if it wasn't for the drastic difference in climate and greenery. Watching the seasons change for the first time in over a decade was done through the windows of the store. I checked stock, worked inventory, and opened the Huntington's Sport chain for Europe—their first ever and a flagship store at that. The store was 200,000 square feet of retail floor space and activity areas, about 50,000 square feet larger than our store in Las Vegas. I worked hard to ensure that I stocked the shelves and arranged the store according to my best possible marketing plans. Some areas of the store were decided for me—the indoor golf driving range, the shooting range near the gun displays, and the water feature near the fishing gear. But the rest of the store was mine to design, stock, manage, and maintain.

The differences in culture and activities originally had me flustered, and sales floundered for my ignorance. Europeans required less gear for camping and spent more money on mountain biking and hiking. Setting up sales displays to focus on Volksmarching and minimalist camping was where I finally started to see sales picking up and customer throughput increase. I was exhausted by the time I got home each day.

And the time difference made talking to Ryan more difficult than we had anticipated. Daily video and phone calls faded to weekly, and by August, it was haphazard and random. We touched base in e-mail but it was unfulfilling and became more of a method for empty check-ins and attempts to schedule our next video or phone rendez-vous. Sadly, each of us had cancelled so many times that the other began to get frustrated, more ready to reschedule than to risk disappointment.

I missed him just as much as I had expected, and I resented him for making it sound like it would be a walk in the park. He knew before I ever left that I was afraid of this—these quiet moments, this time to think about our disconnectedness, about losing him forever. And still, he was letting it happen. He said we'd compensate with these calls, he had promised it, and yet he rescheduled or canceled more often than not. It was as if he didn't want or need them.

I needed them. And without them I missed him wretchedly. In the quiet times when there wasn't some obligation pulling at me, when my mind was at rest, I ached for his touch, his kiss, his sex. Just the sound of his voice would have made our separation more bearable.

Sometimes I lay in my bed in the quiet of the night and try to remember what his breathing sounded like. I had old recordings of his voice on my phone from when we had used a walkie-talkie app, and I listened to those over and over again. I even researched a way to save them to my hard drive and rescue them from my phone; time wasted, as I never found a solution. He was trapped on that phone. I found myself clinging to that old worn-out thing, refusing to upgrade, refusing to switch to the company phone as my primary, just because he was there, on that crappy outdated technology. I cuddled with it at night, playing his voice and getting angry when there were hiccups. Sometimes the battery died surreptitiously or the phone unexpectedly reset itself, and when these things happened, I'd fly into fits of anger and want to fling it across the room. I knew better, though; breaking that phone meant losing him. No, I wept instead, and I waited until the phone cooperated, lying awake in the darkness and reaching for those moments when he held me, when he loved me, when his fingers stroked my hip, or when his hand passed over my cheek.

And then the sun would rise, and Huntington's was there. I was driven. I would whip the Huntington's flagship into submission for making me leave him. The staff was afraid of me, but the store was immaculate. Corporate was impressed with the numbers and public impression of the brand name. I had redefined myself in the old way: professional success was my hallmark. I was good at that. *Maybe I wasn't so good at relationships. Maybe Ryan had been a fluke,* I thought, as my old insecurities resurfaced. The distance between us had stretched my emotions to a tight thin hair, ready to snap at the realization of my deepest fears. In the back of my mind, a small voice wagged its finger at me and told me that it had been right all along, that Ryan would abandon me like so many men before him. I tried to ignore the voice. I buried myself in my work, and Huntington's wasn't in any shortage of that. I had to hold on just a bit longer. Soon enough, Oktoberfest would be here, and when I saw Ryan, everything would be clear. My fears would have to wait until then. They'd been standing on the edge, listening hard for any confirmation that they had been right in the first place, but I could keep them at bay, until Oktoberfest at least.

And then he called.

Unexpectedly, on a Wednesday evening, in the third week of August, he called. I nearly swallowed my Adam's apple as I answered the phone with nothing more than a croak.

"Jen?"

I cleared my throat. "Ryan? Is that you?"

"Yeah, babe, it's me."

My breath caught in my throat, and tears instantly fell. It had been a week since I'd gotten more than a banal email checking-in, and his voice struck my ears with such warmth. I missed him suddenly, as if an entire decade had passed, and all of the missing from that decade had been added together and dropped on me in this one instant. "Ummm..." I sniffed, trying to compose clear ideas. "Uhhh...hi...hi, baby. Oh, my God, I've missed you!"

"I've missed you, too. A lot."

My heart pounded in my chest, thumped in my ears, turned my legs to jelly. "I'm... uhh... wow... just... getting home from work and...hey...what time is it there? It must be the middle of the night." I reached for some tissues and tried to covertly blow my nose. Breathing deeply, I slowed the flow of tears and began to regain control.

"Yeah, it's past three in the morning." His voice cracked.

"What is it?! What's wrong, hun?"

"Jen, there've been some things going on here..." He paused so long I began to worry that the call disconnected.

"Ryan?"

He exhaled heavily onto the line. "Babe, I don't want to get into it. I wish you were here, though."

"Oh, hun," I gushed, "I wish that, too." My eyes burned anew. I blinked back the tears and took a deep breath. "Soon enough, hun. Soon enough. Oktoberfest in September. A couple more weeks and—"

"That's why I'm calling," he interrupted. "Jen, babe..."

The silence on the line was ominous. My stomach turned to lead, my throat tightened. "Honey, what is it?" I spoke slowly. *This was it.* I knew it. *The end was happening,* I felt it. He didn't want to say it. "Tell me." I braced myself and willed the contents of my stomach to stay put.

"Jen, I'm not coming. I can't—"

I dropped the phone and stood there, stunned, frozen in disbelief. This really was it! Angry, furious, resenting him, hating him, abhorring the job, loathing

Dullberth, devastated—I was crushed. I couldn't breathe, and yet the sobbing began again, violently this time, choking my throat, aching to be released, but no sound came. My cheeks ran rivers, my nose a bog. I fell to my knees. Fumbling for the phone, I grabbed it and listened. All I could do was listen. My throat would not work for anything but to cough up more tears. The line was quiet. I sniffled, swallowing a noseful of snot and getting a grip on myself. "Ryan?! Ryan?" I was frantic. How could he do this? I had been so vulnerable, so honest, so raw...and still, even knowing how it would hurt me, he had backed away anyway. It was too much for him. I knew it all along. I was stupid to come here. "Ryan!" I screamed into the phone.

Silence.

And for the next two weeks, still more silence.

My life was so full of silence that it was deafening.

I'd called him back that day three times, but twice, the call couldn't go through, and he never picked up on the third time. I called in sick for three days, unable to get up, unwilling to participate in this charade any longer. Each day I would get up and try to get ready for work, but it seemed ridiculous. This job had cost me Ryan. Was it really worth it? How many fishing poles did I need to sell to make *that* okay? Eventually, a pert little German sales girl showed up to ensure that I was okay and see if I needed any medicine or if I needed to go to a hospital. I dismissed her, but the next day, a woman from corporate called, wondering what happened to me. The store. The store. The store. It was always about the profit margin. Fuck. Fuck this whole thing. I can't believe Ryan made me come here. I can't believe Dullberth twisted my arm. I can't believe I let them. I cried incessantly. I spread the tissue paper company's profit margin that week. That's for sure.

The apartment walls were thick with his voice, with the call: 'I'm not coming.' The grey carpet was fitting for the drab melancholy that seeped into my entire being. The rest of the world was muffled. I listened to it as it passed, but only heard it through the foreground of 'I'm not coming.' Why not? Why wasn't he coming? He had fallen out of love in less than three short months. I was sure of it. I had been right all along. I knew this would happen if he didn't come with me. I had said it would happen. And Mark! Damn him for saying it: 'If you were my girl...' But I wasn't his girl. I was Ryan's, and I wanted it to stay that way. If he had asked me to, I'd have quit this job for him. If he had asked me to, I'd have...I'd have...fuck...I'd have done anything to prevent this.

Talia called and e-mailed. I answered, but only because she'd wring my neck if I didn't. She tried to 'talk sense' into me.

"Call him back."

"I did call back. Three times that day! It's been weeks, Talia, and I don't hear *my* phone ringing!" I huffed, still infuriated that my fearful inner voice had been right all along. "And why would I call him now? So he can hurt me again? So he can spell out exactly why he doesn't want to be with me anymore? Fuck that. Fuck him!"

"Jen, seriously?!" She huffed, exhaling heavily onto the line. I could picture her rolling her eyes. "Is it *that* melodramatic?"

I chuckled through my tears. "Yes," I pouted. "Yes, it fucking is. He was the love of my life—"

"And yet he's not worth a phone call?"

"I'm not worth one to him!"

"He called you. You hung up on him."

"I dropped the phone. Maybe he hung up. I mean...I had a meltdown. I...I...."

"Call him, Jen."

"When are you coming? How about you come keep me company since his sorry ass won't?"

"That's how we're gonna handle this? He's a sorry ass, and I'm supposed to be some stand-in?" She huffed again and let it hang in the air.

"Was that a real question?"

Silence.

"Goddamn it, Talia. He fucking broke my heart. I'm not calling him to beg for more heartbreak."

She sighed. "So to be clear, I'm not gonna be your stand-in lover."

I laughed through my tears. I snapped my fingers. "Damn. And I was really counting on that." We both laughed appreciatively. My God I loved her. What an amazing friend she was! Even after a decade, I still felt like we had so much to talk about and learn from one another. We made plans for her visit in November. She'd bring Jackie; they'd stay at my place. We'd all work really hard to drown my sorrows.

***

Contrary to any expectation I had, preparations for Oktoberfest began in late August. The largest of the tents took weeks to build and prepare. They were able to seat thousands at once and that didn't even count the outdoor seating. I could feel Munich beginning to swell with people and activity, even in the early weeks of September. I had arranged to have a vendor's booth out by the Hofbrau-Haus tent, hoping to capture the eye of Americans that would be drawn to the Hofbrau name. Then it was as simple as a few brews, and they'd be talking about our products and our booth with their Oktoberfest co-tourists.

In the weeks that led to the celebration, I was busier than ever and thankfully so, because the sting of Ryan's phone call had not lessened in the least. Each night, I fell into bed exhausted, barely able to think about my phone or drop more than a few tears before passing out and beginning again the next day. The bustle of Oktoberfest was infectious. After the huge tents went up, more and more brew houses arrived and set up tents. Eventually, vendor booths started going in, and services such as telephone booths and taxi stands stood up. Signs, posters, maps, and advertisements were hung all over town, making the place look like it had been ticker taped with images and slogans. And by the end of the second week in September, there was a buzz about town; the hushed anticipation of thousands of voices electrified the air. The place felt poised to burst, and with up to six million attendees expected, it just might do precisely that.

I had expected to take a vacation for the final two weeks of the three-week event; it was supposed to have been Ryan's time. I, of course, had cancelled my vacation, but the swill of his rejection kept me flip-flopping between an apathetic emo and a driven, focused professional. I suspect my staff was confused or intimidated or both. Regardless, our vendor booth was set and stocked. The store was stocked, and the warehouse was packed in preparation; all staff were either scheduled or on standby to cover every day of the event. We were ready, right up until the very first day when it became clear that we weren't.

The store was a madhouse for the entire three weeks. We were awash with tourists. Merchandise was flying off the shelves faster than we could restock. Never before had I had to decide between stocking and customer service, but the loss of either might've meant loss of sales. Too slow at the register, and people lose interest in hopes of returning to the event sooner; no merchandise on the shelves, and people don't find something they'd like to spend their money on. Gross sales were through the roof on things like sports team apparel; carabiners from the Bundesliga, rugby, and other sports; and patches, key rings, and so on. Any merchandise small enough for a suitcase seemed to be what we needed to stock. We stayed late every night, restocking and even moving larger displays aside to allow for more of the 'hot' items to be stocked in preparation for the next day's rush.

I was busy, but I should have been so busy that I couldn't think straight. I wasn't. My body ran itself into the ground from the store to the booth and back again deep into the wee morning hours before starting all over early the next morning. For three weeks, I ran without stopping, and yet I couldn't find enough to keep Ryan from my mind. There wasn't enough running or physical exhaustion to stop the thoughts from flooding in. I found myself wondering if he came anyway whether Germany was the draw and not me. Maybe he was at Oktoberfest, but taking the place in as a tourist, a free man. Maybe he was there with another woman. Maybe he brought the guys along. I scanned the faces of my customers. Surely, he wouldn't be so brazen as to come into my store, but still I couldn't help myself. When I manned the Huntington's booth, I searched the crowds for any signs of him. A few times I thought I smelled his cologne, and I whipped my head in the direction the scent had come from, but he wasn't there.

It was grueling. And each day ended in anger, frustration, and heartbreak. Every day I felt that phone call hanging over me: 'I'm not coming.' Why? How come he couldn't give us a chance? I thought we were magical. I genuinely believed us to be a special kind of couple, something that only comes around once in a lifetime. And I didn't want three years to define the beginning and end of that for me. I wanted my lifetime thing, and now, he had stolen that from me.

Oktoberfest passed but the feeling didn't. It gripped me. He gripped me. Always at the back of my mind was the feelings of doubt and the persistent *what-iffing*. What if I had stayed home? What if I had never let this offer even land on my desk? A simple 'no, thank you' would have kept me safely there with him in our beautiful status quo. What if he had simply agreed to come with me? He would be here right now, and I'd not be trudging through this existence alone. What if Mark was right and Ryan just needed to be man enough to ask me to stay? Why hadn't he asked me? Why didn't he need me enough to beg me to stay for him?

The questions never ended.

The melancholy remained.

The bustle of Oktoberfest had not silenced him, the pain, the memories, nor the questions. In the quiet that followed Oktoberfest, I was nearly deafened by their mental chorus.

And I dreamt of him...often. And it was as tender and loving and sensual as always. He held me, drew me into him, and wrapped his warmth and strength around me. He kissed and nuzzled my neck, gripped my hips and pulled me onto him or pulled himself deeper into me. He covered my breast with his mouth, his tongue flat and smooth, coaxing my nipple out; his hand warming and massaging the other breast. And then I'd wake, grabbing my neck in hopes of catching his head, my crotch throbbing, my breasts cold and unattended, my lips parched and dry. I'd pull the covers around me tightly, trying to bar the dreams from coming back, trying to protect myself from the want of his loving touch. I fucking missed him, and I hated it. The need seemed to be unending and the sorrow a black hole.

Chapter Twelve

*N*ovember finally blustered in with a chill we never see in Las Vegas. And it brought with it my girls. Ahhh, they blew in right on time. Since I hadn't used vacation time during Oktoberfest, I had additional time to spend. The girls extended their trip from the originally planned week so that we had eleven days together. It was glorious and touristy, and absolutely the escape I needed. We traveled Europe by train with backpacks. We dined at fine restaurants, sidewalk cafes, and wineries. We Volksmarched in Bavaria, sunbathed in Nice, and held up the Leaning Tower of Pisa—I've got the photos to prove it. They were supportive, fun, and amazing, exactly the kind of women I needed in my life.

For the most part, we avoided the topic of Ryan, and I was glad for that. I loved being able to focus on this other thing—this time with them. Thoughts of him snuck in on occasion, like when I saw lovers hand in hand on the beaches of Nice or sharing a Cappuccino at a sidewalk café in Venice, but I rejected them as quickly as they rose. He didn't love me anymore, and I had to move on. It had been nearly eight weeks since the phone call, and now it was undeniable. He was gone for good.

"Hey, scoot in. I want to get both of you and the gondola in the background." Talia and I hugged up closer together on the Rialto Bridge overlooking the palaces lining the Grand Canal in Venice. This place was heavenly and unique among all the possible European tourist stops. The narrow walkways and quiet private alleys provided shade and respite from the throngs of tourists in places like Ponte di Rialto and Piazza San Marco. Still, all of it was worth seeing and experiencing. The smell of the water here was thick and laden with a hint of algae and the occasional acrid breeze of a water taxi or motorboat. The architecture reminded me of middle school social studies classes about the Renaissance and everything that Americans fantasize European buildings will look like. The brick and stone construction combined with the romance of majestic church steeples next to quaint sidewalk cafes and the stunning Doge's Palace really can convince you that anything is possible, even a Cinderella or Sleeping Beauty tale.

I squeezed Talia's shoulders. "I love you, girl," I said quietly while we were so close as Jackie snapped the photo. "Thank you for being here with me."

"Oh, please, I'm just here for the Italian food. Hadn't you heard how good it is?" She smiled and poked me. "Just kidding, honey. I love you, too. How are you holding up?"

"I'm fine," I lied.

"Hmmph," she sucked her teeth through pursed lips, "fine, huh?"

"Yeah, I've got you two here." Jackie joined us again, and I pulled her into a side hug. "Right, Jackie? With my girls, who needs a guy?"

"Hey, hey, wait a minute. Hold up now," Jackie cocked her head to the side in disbelief and wagged her finger in the air, "I need a guy. I don't necessarily need a boyfriend, but I need a guy!"

All three of us nodded and chuckled. "Yep...hmm...okay," I said nodding. "Maybe that's why I'm sad. Lack of sex." And then I added more softly, "Ryan was amazing in bed. Whew...." Jackie and Talia exchanged a glance. I fanned myself with my hand, "Whew. I think I should start taking applications because I need a qualified replacement." I forced a smile.

Talia cut her eyes at me and pressed her lips together.

I shrugged and had begun to qualify my statement when Jackie said, "Let's go get some lunch! I'm starving, and this crowd here is worse than a mosh pit anyway." She took each of us by our elbows and guided us off toward Piazza San Marco.

The square itself was a huge open space headed by a beautiful cathedral, Saint Mark's Basilica, at one end and opening to the canal at the other. The buildings on the sides had gorgeous archways under which you could pass to find shade from the sun, and also perhaps dodge into a café for a somewhat expensive bite to eat. Pigeons settled in the open areas of the square and begged from around that café tables. It was a beautiful sight but also packed with even more tourists. We decided we'd do better to head away from the square, and eventually, we found a café a few blocks from the piazza. And just in time, too; I was hungrier than I expected to be.

We'd barely placed our order when Jackie took a deep breath and said, "Jen, listen..." She paused, looking serious and concerned. I felt as if bad news was coming, and she had saved it until this specific moment for some reason. "I need to tell you something. And I want you to hear me out before you shut me down."

"Oh, man, Jackie." I closed my eyes in a long exasperated blink. "Please don't start in on Ryan. I get that enough from Talia."

"Just listen," she placed her hand on mine and shook it with purpose, "and don't interrupt." I clenched my jaw and squinted over at Talia, warning her of the tongue lashing that was to come if she'd put Jackie up to this. "I've been riding lately. And, ever your going-away barbecue, I've been occasionally riding at Apex. Strange thing is I never see Ryan or the guys there...." She paused, looking at me as if something was suppose to sink in. "Not since August some time. I sometimes see Johnnie and Paul, but they are never with the others. And sometimes they even come alone." I wrapped my arms around my chest and shrugged. My appetite was fading and my throat tightening. "I used to say hi to them and talk to Ryan, or even hang out with Chris on the sidelines, but I haven't seen Ryan or Chris at all since the end of the summer." I squinched my face together and shrugged again, offering a loud heavy sigh and looking as bored as possible. "I think something happened; something bad enough to make them stop riding." I relaxed my shoulders and raised an eyebrow, sucking my teeth. "Stop it and listen. You know how much they loved riding. They were out there all the time, at least some of them. And now... none of them? Or at best, only one of them? They never rode alone. They were one of the most responsible set of guys, always making sure there were at least two in case someone got hurt, especially after Chris. And now?"

Jackie was trying to bring hope back. Here I was, barely holding onto accepting the fact that Ryan and I were over, and she had the audacity to bring doubt to that. She wanted me to reconsider even though Ryan clearly hadn't. She wanted me to fabricate some mental excuses for him that would make this okay. I couldn't bear to listen to another word. "Are you done!?"

"I mean, yeah. Can't you see that something probably happened?"

"Yeah, maybe they found another place to ride. Did you ever think of that? Maybe they didn't like my friend riding where they ride, checking up on them for me. Maybe that's how they saw it. So now, yep, something happened. Ryan kicked me to the curb, found another girl, and doesn't want you to know. Seems easy enough to sleuth out, don't you think?" My nostrils flared, as this vacation seemed suddenly more like a trap than an escape.

"I don't think that's it, Jen. Everything doesn't revolve around you." Jackie spat. "Even if Ryan did have somebody else, do you really think hiding it from you is enough to move to another track to ride?"

I looked at Talia. She gave me the 'I told you so' face and nodded back in Jackie's direction.

Suddenly, I wanted away from there, away from them both. I wasn't hungry even a little bit. I wanted my room and my pillows and the somber solitude that my German apartment provided. My eyes scanned the area, searching for escape, thinking of a place to run.

The water! I wanted the water. I desperately needed the ocean, the beach, a tent, a blanket, the sunrise, the gulls, and the swells and crests of waves. Venice would have to do and St. Mark's Square wasn't too far off. "I'll meet you at the water taxi stop near St. Mark's." I threw my napkin on the table and marched off.

The square stood open and welcoming. I saw the pigeons settled in the middle of it, and I ran into them at full speed, chasing them off. Being so aggressive helped dissipate the anger, and seeing them all flutter into the sky made me feel like I was powerful, like I could do anything. I could command a flock of birds to move in a choreographed display towards the sky. It felt like a revelation. A few of their wings lightly caressed my skin in their haste to get skyward, and the feeling was ticklish and magical. My belly bubbled and fizzled like champagne. I ran through them again, but this time, feeling like a four-year-old. I stared at the sky as I ran, watching them all rise up around me. My heart felt full and joyous for those few seconds.

I smiled and laughed at my silly behavior before continuing on toward the canal. I stood and I watched the tiny little peaks of water slap up against its concrete edge. I was mesmerized by the tiny little microcosm that was so much weaker than the ocean but behaved in such a similar way. The gondolas, water taxis, and personal watercraft making their way around the canals was a sight to see in the bright sunlight of midday. The sun danced as little diamonds on the water's surface. I plopped down and inhaled deeply, letting this different sea smell settle into my nose and lungs. Tears bathed my eyes as I longed for the beach; no blanket here, just the hard concrete of this man-made city. It was beautiful and soul moving, but it was not the beach.

Was this to be my new life? If Ryan was the beach, a blanket settled on the sand, cozy, warm, moving, and flowing, then did the Venetian canals represent my new life: water flowing but forged on something more firm and sturdy than the sand? I was uncomfortable here on this canal. I disliked that I could not bury my feet in the sand. I scooted to the edge and tried to dangle my feet in the water, but it was too far down and a little bit dangerous with all the boats coming and going. And algae, thick and slimy, carpeted the steps and edges of the canal. Even if I could stick my feet in, it would be a far cry from the solid grounding comfort that cooling gritty layers of beach sand provide. I stared out across the water and looked at the people on the bridges crisscrossing this glorious place. I loved Venice. I genuinely felt like I was in a special divine location, but it was not the beach. This new life didn't compare to my old one with Ryan. I loved Jackie and Talia, but they were my support system, my friends, not my life mate, not my lover. Could I find another lover like this man who had stolen my heart?

I hated Ryan for putting me in this position. He set the bar so high that anyone I might even consider dating was likely to be dismissed early for one reason or another. Who could possibly hope to match his support and love, his warmth and joking demeanor, his sex played out through each day, one silly fun interchange at a time? I drew my knees to my chest and hugged them, burying my face in the space they created. I cried, letting the tears drop a painted pattern onto my pants. Even as they fell, I watched them and the random way they fell from my lashes. Tears were a companion of sorts. At least recently they had been. I'd become good at crying, and this was a day to let it wash over me and watch the patterns emerge on my pants. I shook my head and smiled at how mindless and numb I had become.

***

"I'll do it," I said that evening back in the hotel as we packed.

Jackie and Talia both gaped and exchanged disbelieving looks.

"No, really, I'll do it. When we get back to Germany, I'll call him."

"Don't do it because I told you to." Talia's voice was stern and almost resentful.

"I'm not."

"Don't blame me either." Jackie was far more sporty in her warning.

"I won't, ya bandwagon jumper-onner." We burst out laughing. "Now, let's get on with this touristy thing. We start fresh tomorrow." I turned to Talia. "Where are we headed, Ms. Tour Guide?"

"Well, I think somebody demanded that we go sip cocoa in the Alps somewhere. So...Switzerland. We'll catch the train here in a few hours, so get your butts moving, ladies!"

"I wonder who had that great idea...hmmm?" I pondered mockingly.

"Bah! Same lady who has all the great ideas," Jackie replied. I puffed out my chest and stood proudly. "Me!" She finished her thought and I stood there looking foolish and acting forlorn which brought a fresh round of hearty laughter.

The rest of the trip went amazingly well. I could not have asked for better travel mates or companions. We three were definitely well suited for one another, but I suppose that's the way of it with three strong independent women.

And then we were home again in Munich. The hustle and bustle of being tourists wound down within hours of arriving back at my apartment. And suddenly, the weight of my promise felt heavier than it had that day in Venice. I tried to think back to those moments sitting beside the canal, feeling the raw sense of Ryan's presence and how silly it would be to throw that away without at least one last phone call. I had gone from watching my tears fall to staring out over the sunset, remembering how many of those Ryan and I had watched at the beach, out camping, at the track, and that very special last sunrise before I had come to Germany. Surely, I could dial his number one last time. It couldn't be that difficult. And maybe he did have a good reason for not coming. Maybe he had reasons for not calling me or messaging me in any medium. I should at least give him a chance to explain. And yet the prospect of dialing his number seemed daunting now.

We relaxed that first night back, and nobody brought it up. Instead, we ate a meager dinner of Muesli, with milk and some fresh fruit; we were all too exhausted for anything else. The next afternoon, I announced that I would follow through with my promise, a proclamation that landed my Adam's apple firmly in the middle of my windpipe. And even now, as I dialed his number, I found breathing difficult. The girls had hugged me and wished me luck before leaving me here to the task at hand, promising to be there just in the living room to hear the good news when it was all over.

And now, I looked at my old crappy cell phone where he lived, and digit by digit, I pressed the numbers into my business cell. Each digit I pressed felt like it was impossible to pound into the phone. And then, finally, I had entered the entire string.

Butterflies swarmed my stomach, and I squeezed and released my toes on the carpet over and over again to expend the nervous energy. My legs bounced up and down. I inhaled deeply and exhaled as slowly as I could manage. Three rings...*I wonder what his voice will sound like. Will it still affect me viscerally like it always used to?* Four, five...*maybe he was screening his calls.* Six, seven...*maybe he was with his new girlfriend, and now was a bad time.* Eight...*no voicemail?* Nine...*this was a dumb idea.* Ten...*now I just seem desperate.* Eleven...*I should hang up.* Twelve...my thumb put me out of my misery. I threw myself onto my pillow and cried. That was it then. It was done. I couldn't leave a voicemail because the call never went there. Maybe he changed his number. Maybe he screened my call. Maybe he wasn't actually available right now, but that seemed the least likely of all the choices after everything that transpired in the past few months.

I bleated into my pillow, and the door creaked open. Talia and Jackie sat on the edge of the bed. Someone's hands were on my back, Talia's voice asking what happened. I told them. They shrugged it off.

"Try again tomorrow."

"Or maybe an e-mail."

"Didn't you guys used to IM?"

I bolted up to a seated position. "It's not that fucking simple! Do you know how hard it was to dial that number?" My voice cracked. "Do you know how long I let it ring? Do you know how stupid I look now? How bad this hurts? No! You don't know. I should've never come to Germany! I should've never let him go. I have no one to blame but myself. I should leave him alone. He's moved on. I know it. I..." I melted into tears again and fell back onto the bed.

"You don't know that he's moved on."

"The truth is you don't know anything yet."

"Give it time. Talk to him at least once more. Find a way."

"Why do you two care so fucking much if Ryan gets another chance?" I shouted at the ceiling and to neither of them in particular.

Talia spoke first. "Look, hun, I've never seen you happier than when you were with him, and I think you should try to get that back. I want you to be happy. And in all the time I've known you, he was the one who brought it out of you. You're beautiful and amazing and powerful and yes...independent as all get out, but you're even more beautiful when you are happy and never more so than when you were with him. You deserve that. You deserve what you had with him, so why not get that back? Or at least find out why you don't have it anymore? Don't you think you deserve it? Or at least deserve an explanation?"

I sniffled but didn't answer at first. We looked at each other for a long time. She loved me and wanted what was best for me. I knew that. And I did want an explanation, and yes, I thought I deserved it. I shrugged. "Yeah, I guess," I said meekly, taking the tissue she offered me and blowing my nose in a most unladylike fashion.

And then Jackie said, "It's way simpler for me. I agree with everything Talia said, but really, I have never seen two people happier than when I saw you two together. He loves you. Not *loved*, *loves*. I know he does and he always will. The truth is I'm jealous of what you guys had. I want that. And if you two can work it out, then I get to stay hopeful that maybe one day, I'll find it, too. I want you to have that because if you have it," her voice cracked uncharacteristically, "then I still have hope."

I hugged her and held her for a long time.

Chapter Thirteen

*T*he hugging and sobbing continued off and on while we packed them up and rode to the airport the next morning.

"You better call me as soon as you get word from him," Talia warned.

"I'm gonna call you anyway, no matter what." I rolled my eyes and bobbled my head.

"And me!" Jackie piped in.

"Girl, you know I'm going to have plenty of work stuff to complain about, and I need to bend your ear so you can tell me how much worse it is at your office!"

"Ugh. Don't remind me! I only have one more day off when I get back to town, and then I'm back to the grind!"

We said our farewells as they headed back toward the gates and through customs. I cried all the way home. Being alone doesn't have to mean you're lonely, but today, I was desolately both.

I fixed a cup of hot chamomile tea when I got home and sat down at my computer, trying to fashion some kind of message to send Ryan. I wanted to seem loving and kind and open and casual. I wanted him to know that I missed him without making him feel trapped. I wanted to do anything, so long as it didn't make me seem like something he needed to shake loose of. How could I convey all that I felt in this message without sounding like a Debbie Downer? I was distraught over him and alone. My world felt barren and colorless, but I couldn't say that. He might think that I was too weak of a woman for him; he might think that I wasn't the woman he used to know.

Maybe I would just say, "Hi, babe. Missing you. And wondering how you're doing, :)" Surely, that was light and airy enough, and then maybe he would answer me and tell me what was going on with him. Maybe he would reply with something as simple as a "Hello, babe." I think I'd be happy with anything that continued the conversation. But if I was so light and airy, would he think I hadn't missed him? Would he think I had just blown off the fact that he didn't come, shrugged it off like I didn't care? Because that wasn't at all what had happened, and I wanted him to know I cared. I sighed heavily and sipped my tea. An hour later, I swigged the last icy swallow of the cup and stared at the computer screen: blank.

I slammed the laptop lid shut, put my cup in the sink, and went to bed. I pulled my old phone out of the nightstand drawer and held it delicately, as if he himself lived inside it. I pressed and held the power button. Slowly, it came to life. "Where are you, Ryan?" I whispered into the chill night air. The phone powered up, but just when I found his voice clips, it shut down, restarting. I rolled onto my back and stared at the ceiling, tears slowly making their way to the pillow through my hair. I remembered that time at the beach, the day of Chris's accident.

I can feel the way you love me...here. I placed my hand over my heart. *And here.* I squeezed my breast, and then I squeezed my eyes tightly shut, wringing the tears from them as I smiled and traced down my hip to the rise of my mound. I smiled through my tears. *And here!* I squeezed my pubic bone and wiped my tears with my other hand.

"I love you, Ryan Riverton," I said into the dark nothingness.

I took the battery out of that shitty old phone and put it back in the nightstand. Maybe another day.

Maybe another day.

***

I dreamt of Ryan that night. He came to me here in my apartment in Germany. He snuck in somehow, and I woke up to find him lying next to me, propped up on one elbow. I looked at him as if I'd been expecting him.

"I needed you." His voice rumbled against my chest.

I reached up and stroked his cheek. "I need you, too, baby. Even now."

"Why did you leave me? Why didn't you call back? Why did you hang up?"

"You abandoned me. You weren't coming. We made these plans months before, and you abandoned me. I...I lost it. I was..." I looked into his eyes; these excuses weren't working. "I'm sorry, baby. I am so sorry. Please forgive me."

He wrapped his fingers behind my head, his thumb in front of my ear, and he pulled me to him. He kissed me tenderly. Any doubts I had about his love faded away, rinsed as easily as soap from a dish. I took his face in my hands and pulled him further into the kiss, pushing my tongue past the amazingly warm plump lips that were upon mine and into his mouth, seeking his tongue, seeking to play, wanting to ignite his lust, our fire. He did not disappoint. His tongue teased mine, drawing me in, poking and prodding. My nipples tensed inside my T-shirt, and suddenly, his hand was there, warm, massaging, softening one of them, and then twisting it again into a peak. My belly trembled and my hips seized. My cunt was on fire, and I needed him to touch me. I grabbed his wrist and wrenched his hand from my breast, pushing it down to my pussy. I placed it there and wrapped my fingers over his, pushing them between my legs and over the growing damp spot on my panties. "Please, make love to me?"

His mouth was at my neck, sucking hungrily, biting almost angrily. I deserved it—and it felt good—like sweet ecstasy. His anger played out on my body. I moaned and stretched my neck. He bit harder. That would leave a mark. I didn't care. His fingers had moved my panties aside and were pushing inside me. Over and over again, he delved deeper into my hot wet cunt. It had been so long since a man had touched me that I was tight, almost too tight for his fingers. His cock was going to hurt. I couldn't wait. I fumbled at his belt, scrambling to get it apart and get to what waited behind it. I wanted to taste him, to ride him, to just feel his cock in my grip one more time. He yanked my panties down. I lifted my legs so he could remove them, but he didn't. His hand was back at my pussy, rubbing from my clit to my ass and back, lubricating everything. And then he massaged my tight rosebud before sliding the tip of his finger into my ass.

"Ooooh…" I moaned and gasped but did not stop him.

I finally had his pants open and pulled his cock free. It was so fucking amazing. I had missed it so much. I ran my finger over the tip, sliding across his pre-cum and glazing the head of his cock with it. He pushed me onto my back. I drew my finger to my mouth; he tasted exquisite, as always. He stood and undressed in lightning speed before leaning over me, kissing me, straddling my hips. And he tugged on my T-shirt hem. "Get this off," he demanded. I sat up and took it off, and as I pulled it over my head, he grabbed my wrists and held them in the air above my head. He kissed each palm and then worked his way down my right wrist and forearm, releasing the arm as he turned his attention to my left arm. He kissed and nibbled all the way down the arm past the tricep and toward the side of my body. The lower he got, the more he leaned into me. I lay back on the bed, offering him the left side of my torso. He bit and sucked. He was far less gentle now. He demanded my body; he was taking it. Still straddling me, he moved downward so he could continue his siege. His balls dragged along my thighs, his cock hovering above them but dripping profusely.

When he reached my hip, he lifted and turned me onto my belly, yanking me forcefully by the hips up to my knees. He pushed his way between my legs, using his knees to spread my legs farther apart. I tried to wiggle to a more comfortable position, but he slapped my ass and gripped my hips even more tightly, pulling me back to the position he wanted me in. Applying heavy pressure at the small of my back and sliding to its middle, he pushed my upper torso onto the bed. I extended my arms out in front of me, bracing against the wall at the head of the bed.

He teased me first, rubbing his cockhead along my slit, sliding just the tip into my hole and then withdrawing. He slid his cock from my clit to my asshole and back again, slapping it on my ass at the top of each stroke. I began to rock in tiny little movements, reaching beneath me and finding my clit three times its normal size. "Fuck me, Ryan. Please give it to me."

He aligned his cock and teased me over and over again so that I thought he would never fuck me at all. And then he slammed into me with full force, and, holding onto my hips, he plowed into me harder and harder, his thighs banging against the tops of my hamstrings, his balls slapping at my clit, his cock stretching and filling my pussy like never before. It hurt at first. He was huge, I was tight, and I wanted to cry out. But I wanted him so badly, and I deserved to be fucked like this. I wanted it; I wanted his animal sex. He grunted as he banged into me, his grip on my hips so tight that I was sure there were bruises. My fingers moved faster and faster across my clit, my head laid sideways on the bed, and my other hand squeezing my breasts and teasing my nipples. The harder he fucked, the closer I was to the edge. I moaned and cried out. His cock felt better and better with each angry slam. He moved his hands to the round of my ass and slid a thumb into my tight little hole. I screamed and exploded all at once. Cum poured from my pussy, coating his cock and balls and sliding up to my clit like a blanket of warmth.

Before I could stop trembling, he pulled out of my pussy and rubbed his cock on my ass. He slid it up and down my ass crack, getting me really lubricated. I knew what was next. We'd only done this a few times and never in this position. He was always so gentle and slow. This position didn't lend itself to that. I leaned to one side, offering that maybe a change of position would be good. He said nothing. Instead, he grabbed my hips and righted me back to the position I had been in. I bit my lip as he slowly pressed the head of his dick into my ass. As the tip slowly stretched my tiny little hole, it felt smooth and slick, but the flare of his head stretched me so far that it made me yelp. He didn't stop. Slowly but without pausing at all, he gave me every inch of his cock. And when he was buried to the hilt, he pulled my hips back toward him even further. He must've been nearly seated on his haunches.

And then it began. Small strokes at first, in and out, sawing my ass, stretching it, moving me as he wished. I winced and occasionally cried out but never stopped him. I took deep breaths and felt his cock filling me, felt the ferocity of his grip on my hips, now aching from being his handhold for so long. And relentlessly, he pounded my ass, pressing his hand on the top of my hips and anchoring me to the bed. I reached for the distant wall. Somehow, it had gotten farther away now, and I couldn't brace myself. I put my hands near my head and grabbed the sheets and held on, trying to hold my ground. The longer he fucked me, the better this felt—his cock now sliding in and out of my tight little ass. I felt every single ridge of the ribbing on the sides of his cock. Each movement was electrifying. "Yes, baby, fuck me. Please. I've missed you so much." I reached under me and fondled his balls, taking breaks to rub my newly swelling clit and finger fuck my pussy.

"Take it." He grunted and thrust so hard that I was nearly knocked off balance. His body was bucking and thrusting into me, both of us were sweating; the smell of sex filled the room. And at last, he seized and groaned. "Yesss, oh fuck, yesss." He pumped his cum into my ass in what seemed like a never ending stream. Shot after shot of his hot cum filled my tight little hole. He collapsed on top of me, and I let my knees slide back, lying flat on my belly now. Slowly, he softened, and my ass squeezed him out, his cum following in slow dribbles after it. He fell asleep just like that, and I was in heaven.

Chapter Fourteen

*T*he alarm was a rude awakening the next morning.

The realization that I was still alone was even worse. My hand was coated with my own cum, and my panties hung sadly off one ankle under the sheets.

"How sad are you?" I said to the mirror. I smiled. "Good dream, though. Really good dream." Still smiling, I tried to remember as much of it as I could. Shaking my head, I snorted a small air giggle. "Even in dreams, you're a good fuck. Damn, Ryan. Will I ever be loose of you? Invading my mental spaces—that's an evil little trick."

I brushed my teeth and moved through the day. Ryan keeping me company in the undercurrent. I tried again that evening to write to him, and every day for a week. Eventually, I gave up and decided that he was safer here in my mental spaces.

***

Christmas in Germany rode in on a Grimm brothers' fairy tale—fluffy snow blanketed the city, lights were strung on light poles and they lavishly adorned every evergreen within miles of town, and music drifted onto the street from shops that smelled of gingerbread and Stollen. Also, there were Christmas markets set up everywhere.

The day of the first snowfall, I sat in the warmth of my living room, sipping cocoa, and watching it coat the trees in the courtyard. The bumble-bee-sized flakes fell erratically, skittering through the air on blustery wind wings. I sat and watched, mesmerized from sunset to nightfall, when the moonlight gave the flakes an angelic glow. It was silent and peaceful, and it had a surprisingly dramatic effect on my demeanor. That night, I slept better than I had since leaving Las Vegas.

The next morning, I rose to find the children's boots lined up in the hallway by the front door of our apartment building. Ahhh, early December meant the arrival of Saint Nicholas, and he'd been generous this year—the boots overflowed with colorful candy and sweets. The sight made me nearly giddy with childlike awe and wonderment. I arrived at work in a better mood than I had in many weeks. Work had reached an even pace. We turned a decent profit, and I was able to work more on management and training than I had been able to in the beginning. The staff was capable, knowledgeable, and friendly. We'd finally found a comfortable rapport, and I was less directive and tense.

On this day, business was nearly nonexistent. Between the Feast of Saint Nicholas and the weather, few customers were likely to come to the store. Ilsa, my assistant manager, made cocoa, and we gathered the staff together near the tents for an indoor camping session. A cardboard campfire set the stage for storytelling, and we took advantage of it, each of us sharing family holiday traditions and memories. I had come to know the staff on a more personal level after Talia and Jackie left, and I enjoyed being with them. Ilsa had done well with the hiring process as I had been busy purchasing stock and setting up the store in those first few weeks.

Our indoor camping session eventually degraded to joking and laughing and telling tales of things that happened on the sales floor. I learned that my staff had originally seen me as a rigid unforgiving tyrant, particularly in August and September. And in an effort to blow off steam, they had perfected performing impressions of me for one another. Each of them took turns giving an impression of a particularly heinous berating. Each were factual, though the impressions felt like caricatures of the truth. I laughed jovially with them as I remembered each event and the stress and frustration that I'd felt. When it was Ilsa's turn, she declined to do her impression, saying she didn't have one. I stood instead and gave an impression of her: prim, proper, well dressed, and perfectly manicured— ever the professional with poise and dignity. She almost felt too polished for a place like Huntington's. I was sure that she could have made millions selling fine jewelry or mansions. In my best Ilsa impression, I attempted to sell the staff a rather brutal hunting knife, exaggerating Ilsa's flair and poise as if the knife were made of diamonds and glass. We laughed together as the afternoon hours wore on.

I released them early and closed the store myself. No matter what the personal price, I was competent here, and it made me feel good to finally feel a part of a team, watching the store become what I'd envisioned it to be, and knowing that corporate would recognize the excellence here. I wandered the aisles, assessing our store as objectively as I could. I felt the warmth of pride and satisfaction, knowing that this truly was my store, that I birthed it and brought it to this stage. We were ready for Christmas and the rush in spring that was sure to come. There was only one customer that afternoon, and he was really just been seeking respite from the bitter cold. I made him a cocoa and gifted him a Huntington's scarf. I'd chalk that up to advertising later.

As I made my way out to my car that evening, I thought of Ryan. I wished he could have seen what I'd done here, that he could be as proud of me as I was of myself. I wished I could have succeeded in both places: my career and my love life. But if I had to choose one, professional success was the sure bet. It never abandoned me, it was predictable, and I could guarantee that I'd achieve the outcome I wanted. Romance was none of those things.

In my apartment that night, I read a book. For the first time since August, I was able to concentrate long enough to enjoy it. I told myself that this was day one in a string of what I hoped would be many.

***

Spring rushed in, and before I knew it, we were approaching Easter. Sales again swelled as people readied themselves for the temperate weather. The staff and I had found harmony and teamwork; they preempted my concerns, addressing them before I found the need to correct. The Huntington name had been established with this flagship store.

As the weeks and months passed, I found peace with my new life circumstances. The ache of missing Ryan faded with time, and I found myself dating sporadically. Men felt dangerous and emotionally unsafe. I found excuses to dismiss them all. None had as much potential as Ryan, and I wasn't willing to risk any of me for anything less than what Ryan and I had had. And so, dates came and went, nobody lasting more than a week or two, with most not making it past the first date. *Maybe it's just Germany*, I thought. *I'll be back to good ol' American boys soon enough*.

I had come to find joy and camaraderie here at the store, and it was there that I spent most of my time, not hiding as I had done in autumn, but seeking the soulful satisfaction that work brought me. I was genuinely able to relax and watch the store find its own German identity while I gradually trained Ilsa to run purchasing, human resources, and the books. I found that the less I directed the front of store, the more esprit and confidence rose within the ranks, which helped with customer service and sales. In truth, though, this was an undeniably wonderful group of people, and I'd miss them when I left.

There would be another store opening up in Northern Germany, but I turned down the position there, asking for a transfer back to the southwest region of the US. I missed home and needed closure on the Ryan saga. I wanted to face my old life and find peace and acceptance. Ryan had had a role in my life and I'd found happiness with him; I wanted to be able to look back on that time with warm nostalgia and not feel the tightening grip of failure that those thoughts presently brought. I hoped that getting home would help me in that regard. I had found a makeshift peace in the past six months by gradually closing and locking the door that led to romance. I focused on all the other facets in my life and just never addressed what was behind that door. I knew that someday I would have to change, and a trip back to a familiar place might help.

The satellite human resource office here in Germany called back to the states. Dullberth was to assign the new guy for the store in Northern Germany. It turns out that Rasmussen couldn't wait to get back to Europe, and I was delighted to learn that in just one year, Chris would replace him as the general manager of the flagship store in Vegas. I beamed like a proud momma. *Damn, I love it when I'm right*! "You go, Chris!" I whispered to him on the wings of the universe. "I'm proud of you."

And so, June came and I turned the store over to Ilsa. She was practically running the place already anyway. The month was filled with packing and last minute shopping for gifts for friends and family and for me—things I bought specifically to remind me of my time here. By the end of the month, I was ready to leave Ilsa, the store, and Germany all behind.

The flight back to Las Vegas was nerve-wracking. I would be on two weeks of paid time off while I said hello to the kids and checked on the house. I knew I would stop in to see Chris but dreaded the possibility of seeing Ryan. I had come so far in the process of healing, and I was petrified at the idea of falling back into that dark place. Maybe I would stop by the old house we used to live in just to take a look and say good-bye, and maybe I'd stop at the track. I needed to be able to put that life to rest so that I could move on and find someone else.

***

As I walked down the jetway, I could barely breathe for the heat. It was miserably hot. How had I ever lived here before? I couldn't wait to strip down to a bathing suit and beach wrap! The airport was comfortably air conditioned, and the sound of the slot machines made me smile. No matter how far I ever went, Las Vegas could always make me smile. I felt like this was my city, like I knew her and she knew me. The slots were only a reminder of her seedier side, the part I never took part in, but that so many of the typical residents and surely tourists delighted in. My steps felt lighter as I approached the monorail back to baggage claim. I breathed deeply and exhaled, grabbing a handhold as the monorail pulled off.

Baggage claim was bustling. There were huge display screens flashing images and trailers of shows here in town, descriptions of Cirque du Soleil, magic shows, variety acts. Random people stood holding placards with names written on them, clearly intended to bring the special guests to their accommodations where they would be invited to lose tens of thousands or more. It felt like a circus even here in baggage claim at the airport. My cheeks began to hurt from smiling.

I approached my baggage carousel, scanning the crowd for either of my children. I couldn't see anyone, except those who had been on my flight with me. Still smiling, as the bags started dumping out onto the conveyor, I finally heard Kelsea's voice over the cacophony.

"Hey, Mom!" Turning, I saw that both she and Zion were here. And they were joined by Kelsea's husband, Blaine, and my first grandbaby.

I ran to them, feeling as excited as a schoolgirl. My heart leapt to my throat, and, suddenly, they all seemed like sparkling, beautiful, perfect people that I'd feared I'd not ever see again in my life.

Tears of joy ran down my cheeks as I finally reached them. "Oh, my God, I don't know who to hug first!" I giggled nervously as I took Kelsea's face between my hands and kissed her cheeks, just as I had done since she was a child. And then I threw my arms around Zion's waist and held him tightly. "So, what are we up to now? Six foot five?" His arms easily spilled onto my back and held me.

"Six six." His deep bass voice rumbled through his chest and against my eardrums.

I looked up at him, smiling and shaking my head. "When will it stop?" He shrugged. I reached up and cupped his cheek. "I missed you, buddy." His eyes were glassy, and he squeezed my shoulders more tightly, resting his chin briefly on top of my head.

I turned to Blaine next and gave him a hug. "Thanks for taking care of my baby and for giving me this amazing young one." I took the baby from his arms, cooing and cuddling him. "You two have done amazingly well. He's absolutely gorgeous." The baby chimed in, seemingly agreeing. "So, tell me everything. I want to know how the pregnancy went and how these first couple of months have treated you. E-mails and those pictures were barely enough to keep me informed! And Blaine, how is your practice doing? Clientele still growing? And Zion, a show on the strip?! I want to know all about it. You have risen like the star you always were, baby. Who says it takes ages to find success in stand-up?"

I had a thousand questions. I had buried myself so deeply in Huntington's that I seldom called home, and when I did, it was typically to check on things quickly before running back to work. Now, standing here in front of my loved ones, I felt reconnected. I realized that I had become disconnected even from my own children. Warm tears fell as we caught up, chatting as the baggage arrived.

And it didn't stop over the next series of days. I reacquainted myself with my family and with my house and the pool. Readjusting to the weather would have been impossible without the oasis in the backyard. I couldn't get enough of my family, and they were happy to see me again, too. We all stayed at the house. This time I stayed in Kelsea's old bedroom, now converted into the guest room. She and Blaine had, of course, taken up residence in the master, and Zion stayed in his room when he wasn't rooming downtown. It felt like we had returned to our old footing in just the first few days. I felt loved, welcomed, and cherished. I knew I was home.

I knew I needed to follow up with some other business, so after a few days of sunning myself, swimming, reading, and other completely indulgent relaxing activities, I set about handling those things.

Huntington's. Chris. I arrived at the store on a Thursday morning and wandered through it as any customer would. He had done well. The place was immaculate, and the end caps and feature displays were spot-on. I wondered if he'd still be on crutches when I saw him, if he'd even recognize me after a year, if he'd talk to me even though Ryan and I were no longer together. I took deep breaths and thought about the days that we sat watching the guys ride, chatting about life, women, and riding. Such a good kid.

He wasn't easily found. A manager not often on the sales floor is a rarity. I headed toward the warehouse, but that turned up nothing, too, except a few warehouse workers pissed that a stranger had just strolled right in.

"Well, actually I am looking for Mr. Jacobs. Do you know where he is?"

"Managers don't answer to warehouse staff, ma'am. But I know we'll have to answer to him if he finds you back here. I'm gonna need you to go."

"Well, if you see him, will you let him know that Jen came by."

"If I think of it, ma'am. Sure will." He rolled his eyes at my apparent audacity.

I spent another hour in the store testing out the camping chairs for comfort, sitting in front of a tent and pretending I was at the beach, and checking out the newest in crossbows and hunting knives. The American displays were so different than what we'd done in Germany—more aggressive and garish. *Yep,* I mused to myself, *I'm back in the good ol' USA.*

Chris neither showed that day nor in the two other times I checked back. It was strange, but I thought that maybe I just wasn't meant to meet up with him. I considered calling Dullberth to see what he knew of Chris—taking the opportunity to gloat—but it wasn't worth it to hear that man's snippety attitude again.

I drove by the house, the one Ryan and I had shared. There was a car there I didn't recognize. I wept as I relived some of my favorite memories. I dared not stay more than five or ten minutes; I can't imagine what the neighbors would think as they saw me lurking along their street in my car, crying on apparent 'stakeout.' I said good-bye to that life as I drove away, and I felt a weight lift as I did. Somehow, seeing someone else's car at the house made me comfortable in the assumption that Ryan had moved on. That single image was enough to make it okay that I do, too.

That still left one more decision: Ryan's parents.

I struggled with whether or not I should stop to see them. I loved them dearly, and surely, his mother deserved some of my time. But I feared seeing Ryan or being asked tough questions I could not answer. I began to dial their number on multiple occasions, and once even let it go to voicemail, but what could I possibly say to them? What business did I even have contacting them now that Ryan had cast me aside? His mother was amazing. Being here in Vegas again and thinking of how life used to be was really difficult. There were so many reminders and so few of them that didn't come with the stab of grief or bittersweet nostalgia over what I no longer had. She was part of that feeling. I still remember her voice in my ear when I last saw her. *"He loves you,"* she had said. *"Remember that when it is difficult when you're apart."* And she had called me her unofficial daughter-in-law.

It was definitely time to leave. I needed to be away from all the melancholic sentimentality that surrounded Las Vegas. After enjoying the Fourth of July fireworks out at Red Rock with the kids, I packed up the car. I was happy to leave for San Diego before the full heat of August lit Vegas on fire; the sweltering heat of the city was already wearing me down. The San Diego corporate offices had just been opened to handle the international expansions. We had new stores planned in England, France, and Italy within the next five years, and

I was to coordinate the rollout, find and organize the initial flagship stores, and help select the managerial staff for each new location. I expected to travel quite a bit, so I purchased a small beachside condo. When I was stateside, I wanted to be comfortable, and the beach was certainly that for me.

Chapter Fifteen

I drove away from Las Vegas and left that old life behind. As I reached the outskirts of the city, I caught a glimpse of the San Diego offices of Ryan's package delivery company; I didn't even flinch. A new life awaited me here, and it began at the beach. I checked in on my condo first, ensuring that closing was still on schedule for three days from now. And then I went to the beach. I did have a hotel room, but I only went there when the chilly California night air chased me from my respite on the sand in front of the ocean. The sound of the waves was cleansing and soothing. They would become the backdrop to my personal peace.

I spent those three days on the beach under an oversized umbrella. I suppose that as I walked out onto the beach, people thought I might be lost carrying an umbrella nearly the size of the ones that go in the center of yard furniture dining tables. I'd bought it especially for the beach, though. It was colored like a traditional beach ball: red, yellow, blue, interleaved with white. It made me happy to sit under it and let the sun work its way around me while capturing and amplifying the ocean in its concave top. I arrived at the beach mid-morning each day and spread my blanket, and then set up my umbrella, arranging it for the best sun blockage. I was able to set the umbrella on the ground so that it was partially a sand blocker as well. It created a little cavern of tranquility for me to spend the day. I read books and wrote. I sat for hours and simply listened to the ocean. I'd snack on trail mix or a sandwich I'd brought, and then I'd nap—the best most decadently battery-recharging naps I could possibly envision.

And maybe I'd wade in the wet sand, just letting the waves lap at my feet and ankles, taking in the sun and the breeze, and watching others walking or playing along the beach as well. If people were too numerous, I'd make a note to try a different beach the next time so that the ocean and I and the gulls could have some private time. Usually, though, it was a perfect mix of people, sun, sand, breeze, gulls, and waves. And by the time I was seeking solitude, people were leaving for dinner. I'd leave, too, but come back after I had eaten or maybe come straight back with dinner in hand. Then I would leave the umbrella in the car and simply walk along the beach with my windbreaker on, enjoying the sound of the ocean surging in my direction, only to lightly caress my feet.

Sunsets were breathtaking. I'd learned to appreciate them the same way that I used to love the beach sunrises with Ryan. The hues of red and orange changed the entire beach ambiance; they indicated that the day was ending, that the sun was slowly sinking away. It was as if the colors clung to the sky, holding on for as long as possible and finally fading to twilight's blues and purples before the sun eventually lost the fight to the night. The gulls sought silent refuge and left me alone with the waves and the sand, now quickly chilling to something far less inviting. At last I would give up, too cold to stay another minute and too tired.

Even after I closed on my condo, I kept up the ritual when time and scheduling allowed. The beach was my best new companion. Sure, there was work and, yes, dates too, but the beach had become my muse.

Work was a willing and insistent companion and would take all my time if I let it. The offices in San Diego were barely even rented when I arrived, so there was furniture to order and janitorial staff to hire, office supplies to purchase and signage and logos to hang. If this were to be our international corporate office, I would make sure that clients would not be disappointed when they come through these doors.

When it came to spending time with people, I found that the good ol' American boys whom I thought would be able to win my heart were as disappointing as the dates I'd had in Germany. Small talk was too small and empty. Intelligent conversation fizzled to talk of work and other trite topics. Awkward silences were common, and I was quick to refuse a second date. Maybe I needed time to just be by myself. Maybe I was destined to be single.

***

For the first few weeks, I lived in my condo with nothing more than an air mattress and my suitcases. It didn't matter; I was happy there. From my parking lot, I could smell and hear the beach. And one flight of steps later, I was stepping into my flat. As the door opened, the entire place really lay out in front of me.

From the front door, I could see directly through the living spaces and right out the balcony to the ocean. It was the selling point of this place for me. I sat on that balcony most nights and let the ocean sing my lullaby before reluctantly traipsing off to my air mattress to sleep just enough so that my work would not suffer the next day. My first purchase for the new place was actually a set of balcony chairs and a small table to set between them.

While I was in Germany, I'd given Kelsea a short list of "mandatory amenities" to be aware of as she looked at all the listings I emailed her; one of them was a balcony with an ocean view. She had done exceptionally well in that department. And even though I purchased the place for the beach location and loved the balcony the most, the rest of the condo was truly well-appointed as well. I felt lucky to have found such a place. The kitchen, tucked in to the left by the front door, had mahogany cabinets, granite countertops, and a stainless steel sink and appliances. The sink was in a kitchen island that doubled as a breakfast bar, allowing the kitchen to be open to the remainder of the condo. And the living/dining area was carpeted in Berber and capped with crown molding. The bedroom sat off to the side through a door cut in the wall between where the dining room and living room would roughly be split. There was, of course, a guest bath and laundry, and it even had a built-in desk nook near the front.

I shopped over the next series of weeks and bought a living room set, a dinette, and a master bedroom suite. Each set of furniture was modest and within my budget, just something to furnish the condo.

In all, I had found my solace, my paradise at the beach.

***

When the boxes arrived from Germany a few weeks after I moved in, I was excited to give the condo a homier feel. The walls were bare and the place felt Spartan. I was ready to add signatures from my travels and make the space a reflection of myself.

I opened the 'functional' boxes first: books and bathroom items, the things that I already had space set aside for. I put things away and flattened boxes as I went. I was surprised at the effect unpacking had on my mood. I was nostalgic about the time I had spent in Germany. Europe was an unforgettable place, and one that I looked forward to visiting over and over again. It was nice to revisit some of the things I had bought while I lived and touristed in that fairy tale playland. Each piece that I unpacked found a space in my new existence. They got a new start just as I was getting one. As I pulled even these basic items out of the boxes, I felt a tug at my heart pulling me back to my flat in Germany and to the memories I had made there.

By the time the bathroom and bookshelves were stocked, I felt a sense of warmth and peace. Going to Germany was the right decision. It was a wonderful experience professionally and personally. And the part of it that Ryan owned was simply a part of life. Maybe he and I were never meant to be. Maybe we would have eventually broken up anyway. Well, maybe not.

I giggled a little at my own self-talk and dragged another box off the stack, tearing the top open. It was from my bedroom. My heart stopped and, for a second, time stood still. My hands were suspended, gripping the edges of the box lid. And my eyes were glued to the few items at the top of the box: bedding, clothing, and my bedside lamp. Why was I instantly so close to tears? I shook my head, and then my body moved like a dog climbing out of the tub after a bath. *Bah! Stop it, Jen,* I chastised. *It's just stuff.*

I pulled the bedding out and looked at it. Just seeing it filled me with melancholy. I felt a deep core sadness, a desire to climb in bed, curl up, and cry. These sheets and comforter represented hours upon hours and days and days of crying, weeping, and mourning. The pillowcase was speckled from an accidental overbleaching once, and I swore that the pattern looked very much like the tear stains from my pants that day in Venice. No, the sheets needed to go. I needed something more beachy and bright anyway. These colors were too heavy and drab. I tossed them into an empty box.

My clothes came next. I stacked them into piles: *now*, for clothes I could wear any day; *winter*, for clothes I might wear again but not until it gets much colder; and probably *never*, for heavy parkas and clothes that I was no longer interested in. This last pile would go to the Goodwill early this coming week. I took the rest of the clothes and put them away in my new dresser or back into a box deep in the closet.

I was down to the final few items in this box, the ones that dripped with bittersweet nostalgia. First was my journal at the bottom of the box, sitting alone, surrounded by writing utensils of varying types and styles.

The pens and pencils lay there, aligned like a mass grave of the massacre hidden in the journal's pages. I picked up the book, tear-stained and maltreated from countless nights of furious scribbling and crying, lamentations and rants, all bearing my pain in grueling detail. I held it in my hands, feeling the worn leather cover and binding. I thumbed through it, listening to the crackle of the tear-drenched and then dried pages. If I thumbed through fast enough, it sounded like applause coming from a distance. I didn't care to read it; holding it was enough. The weight of it couldn't have been more than a couple of pounds, and yet it felt so heavy that holding it made my shoulders sag and my breathing more labored. I got to my knees and grabbed all the pens and pencils in one determined fist. Moving quickly and with purpose, I took the book and the utensils that scribed it and banished them to the closet with those winter clothes.

Returning to the box, I felt lighter somehow. I grabbed the box intending to tear it down when I felt the weight of something else shift inside. I peered inside, half afraid to see what was left: the phone. There at the bottom of that box was the old, useless, tattered, unreliable phone.

I picked it up and held it to my mouth, thinking of Ryan. It felt smooth against my lips, the glass gliding effortlessly over my bottom lip, the metal less smooth, snagging on my upper lip where the power jack was. I stared into space, looking at nothing in particular, and reliving my five years with Ryan. It was true, we hadn't met until after two years, but I counted those two years—they laid a foundation for what was to come. I chuckled to myself at how I used to so vehemently deny that those two years were worth anything. *Amusing,* I thought, *how vastly different a little change in perspective can change the way you see something.*

As the phone slid over my lips, I remembered how good his lips had felt on mine—always warm and meaty. They told the story of his emotion, his drive, and his desire, and they always got me to comply, dragging me to depths of rapture that I'd not known before him nor since. Tears finally ran over my eyelash levies, and I pulled the phone away from my face, resting my head on my fisted hand. His hand used to be there, resting at my cheek, drawing me in, bringing me closer to him.

I headed to the kitchen to get a glass of water, slurping it down without really thinking about anything in particular, except how suddenly thirsty I was.

Setting the glass down on the counter, I looked at the phone again and stroked the glass face. How many times had I argued with this phone to stay on long enough to bring me his voice? Now, I rubbed my finger more slowly and tenderly over its surface, stroking it longingly, lovingly. I pressed the phone between my hands, like I was praying. I smiled. Turning my hands until they were parallel to the floor, I pressed on the top of the phone's glassy surface. *"I can tell how much you love me, I can feel it here...in your heart..."* Tears streamed down my cheeks, and I thought about charging the phone up one last time, listening to him once more...for old time's sake, hearing him tell me he loved me. I looked at it again, smiled, and kissed its glass face. Maybe another day.

I put the phone in a drawer in the kitchen, rubbing the drawer face as I closed the phone inside.

Maybe another day.

Chapter Sixteen

Summer turned to winter, and I was off to Naples. I

spent the next six months getting Italy ready and making quick trips to London to see about the England groundbreaking scheduled for next summer. Time flew by, and my jet lag kept me sleepy or slightly tired often. I didn't mind, it just prepared me for relaxing catnaps on the balcony, listening to the ocean heave in my direction, only to give up at the shore. I was happy. Alone but not lonely. Talia came to see me and so did Jackie. We never spoke of Ryan, though he was always in the back of my mind. I couldn't bring myself to tell them that I had never messaged him. And neither of them ever asked.

In the spring of the following year, I sat on the beach in Los Angeles. I never camped anymore; it's no fun without someone to share it with. Instead, even though the beach outside my condo was amazing, I still made day trips to beaches I liked all along the coast from San

Diego to the north side of LA. On this day, I had chosen Seal Beach in Los Angeles because it was quiet and somewhat secluded, which meant I could visit with the ocean and the gulls without getting smacked in the head by a Frisbee or having sand kicked up in my eyes by a wayward football catcher or kite flyer.

I set up my blanket just after sunrise, upset that I'd forgotten my umbrella, but not dissuaded at all. I settled in to watch, feel, write, sleep, read, and accept what the universe was offering, even if it was the chattering company of the gulls demanding food I didn't bring. I sat there feeling the ocean, smelling the salty air, smiling at and, yes, visiting with the gulls. I wrote a few inspired passages and a poem about my feelings as I sat feeling as tiny as a grain of sand compared to the size and magnitude of the ocean. The day passed as slowly as I could hope for. As the sun was high in the sky, I draped my spare T-shirt over my eyes and tried to nap a bit, the ocean singing my lullaby. Despite my sunscreen, I could feel my arms burning before the afternoon had fully blossomed, and I knew I needed to go. Besides, my lips were parched and tasted of salt, and my skin was tight and tingly, the first signs that I needed aloe immediately. I shook out my blanket, rolled it up, and bid the gulls adieu.

When I got back to the parking lot, I saw someone leaning against my car. "Damn kids," I muttered to myself. I expected they would move as I made it clear that I was heading for precisely that vehicle, so I pressed my key and the lights blinked. I knew this also meant that the doors had clicked unlocked, but the kid didn't move. I adjusted my sunglasses and shielded my eyes, squinting to get a better look.

He saw me and stood up, coming away from the car and heading in my direction. I stopped and stared, grimacing against the sun. And still he walked toward me. My breath caught in my throat. I knew the gait, I knew the frame, I knew that style of dress. I dropped my bag and keys and stood stock still, staring, tears streaming. My stomach turned to lead, my temples tingled and nervous perspiration dotted my forehead. The closer he got, the more I wanted to run. My stomach churned and roiled. My throat seized. I chewed on my lips, I rung my hands together and then tangled my fingers. I could not bend over and pick up the bag and keys. I could not run.

I stood.

He walked.

I cried.

He walked faster.

I flinched as he got to me.

He kissed me.

Without a word, he kissed me full on the mouth.

I couldn't kiss him back through the tears. I couldn't reach for him, couldn't hold him. He broke away from the kiss.

I stared at him, lips trembling, and eyes bleeding tears. "Ryan...?" I choked, my throat had my voice box in a vice grip.

He rubbed my back. "Baby, what is it? Please, talk to me. Tell me you're okay." He waited. I stared. "Say something!" The tears stopped flowing; all I could do was stare. His words came to me through water, my ears hearing mostly the rush of my own blood through them. He picked up my bag and keys and led me by the elbow to my car. He fumbled through my bag, found my water bottle, and twisted off the cap. "Drink something, Jen. For God's sake, drink something."

I took the water bottle with a trembling hand and brought it to my lips. Once the water reached my mouth, I gulped and gulped it down, swallowing mouthful after mouthful. When I had emptied the bottle, I finally looked at him again. "What are you doing here? And why are you just...here. Right here in the parking lot?" And regaining my senses a bit, I said, "And who said you could kiss me? And..." I started crying anew. My stomach continued to seize and clench. I turned away from him and promptly threw up half the water I had just downed. He reached into my bag to find something, but I snatched it from him. "I can take care of myself!" I sounded like a three-year-old in tantrums, but goddamn him for coming back after being gone so long. What was I supposed to do now? I was over him already. I had worked so hard to get past this, and here he was, staring me in the face. I wiped my mouth with my spare T-shirt and fumbled in the bag for some gum to get the taste of stomach acid out of my mouth.

"My father died." I looked up from my search, raising an eyebrow. "When I called you, he was ill..." Ryan's voice was serious. Was he offering an explanation after all this time? Why didn't he tell me that before? Things would have been so different if he would have just told me. "He was really bad...in the hospital. There was no way I could come to Germany knowing he might die."

"You didn't tell me," I suddenly felt terrible for not visiting his parents when I was home in Vegas last summer.

"Jesus, Jen. I barely told you I wasn't coming, and you hung up on me. You didn't give me a chance to tell you."

"I dropped the phone..." I said angrily, feeling the heat of all my tied back emotions trying to spring forward. I was angry and resentful, but now I also felt guilty.

"What?"

I scanned his face, looking for some sense of where this was going. "I didn't hang up. I dropped the phone."

"Why didn't you call me back?"

All the blood drained from my face. My mouth gaped open. "I..." Jackie and Talia had both told me to call him back, and a thousand times I had wanted to but...I didn't want to appear weak. I didn't want him to see me as needy. And how could I mention those three measly attempts on that fateful morning? Suddenly it seemed like I had been the one who gave up on us. "I..." He folded his arms across his chest and began to tap his toe. I squinted at him. *Had he actually raised his voice? Did his tone sound as accusatory as I was hearing it, or were my emotions playing tricks on me?* "I tried..." I looked at my hands, "a few times. But you didn't answer." *Twice counted as a few, didn't it?* "And...why didn't you call me back?"

"I had to deal with my dying father and, at that moment, didn't have the emotional energy to deal with a pissed off girlfriend. I knew you would call back when you calmed down." I looked at my feet. "Seems you never calmed down."

I fumbled with the straps of my beach bag, lips trembling again. "It was bad for me," I began. Then I shook my head, realizing how small and insignificant my pain suddenly seemed. "When did he pass?" I looked at my hands, unable to face him.

"November thirteenth."

"Oh, Ryan, I'm so sorry." I threw my arms around him and hugged him. His arms reflexively wrapped around me and drew me even closer to him. We stayed there for a long time, speechless, but exchanging something far bigger than words. His hands stroked my back and tugged at my tangled, wind-blown hair. I stripped his hat off and kissed cheek and temple and rested my cheek against the side of his head, smelling him, experiencing him. I didn't want to let him go, but he pulled back.

"San Diego? What do they have you doing there?"

I raised an eyebrow. Perhaps next we'd talk about the weather. "Same stuff. Expanding the brand name across Europe. Spent most of the winter in Italy for the Naples opening."

"That's amazing. I'm proud of you. I knew you were gonna sail right through this Germany thing and onto bigger and better things."

I pursed my lips and muttered, "Sail right through. Yep, a real cake walk that was." Ryan squinted at me. I shrugged. "Your father...I don't understand. How did it happen, and why didn't you tell me?"

"I don't want to talk about that right now. We have time for all of that later."

Later? I thought. *What the hell does that mean? Five minutes ago, seeing Ryan again fell into 'never' and now he was already talking about 'later.'* I couldn't wrap my head around what was happening. "Well, what do you want to talk about? I mean, how did you end up here in this parking lot standing by my car? How about we start with that?"

"We're camping a mile and half from here," he said. "I told the guys I needed to go for a walk this morning. Sunrise at the beach is hard for me these days," he cut his eyes in my direction, "nobody to go find sitting on the blanket visiting the gulls without me."

"Ryan, I—"

"So I walked. I walked this direction and would have kept going, but the rock pier sort of forced me to the parking lot. I was on my way through when I saw your car."

"What a coincidence," I said with more malice in my voice than I intended.

He paused and eyed me, an angry edge bringing the tension even higher. "Anyway, I should be getting back."

"What?! You wait for hours by my car just to kiss me and shake up my world? Are you serious? What am I? A snow globe? Not cool, Ryan." He turned to step away. "That's it then?" I asked. "Wait in the parking lot, see me finally, kiss me, and then leave? What was your point to all this?"

"I needed to see you. At least one last time for old time's sake. I needed to actually see you. It was worth waiting by your car for a little while. And that's it."

"And the kiss? What the hell?" I was flustered at the prospect that I might let Ryan slip right through my fingers once again. Stalling was going to have to work until I thought of something.

"Stop it, Jen. Stop trying to tear this moment apart. Dissect it later. It is what it is, nothing else. I just kissed you. I saw what I needed to see."

He saw what he needed to, but I didn't even try. I wasn't ready for it. He surprised me. I didn't even participate fully. I wanted a do over. "And what was that?"

"Jen, it's been great to see you...one last time. Congratulations on the promotion." He turned and began walking away.

"I missed you, Ryan," I called after him, but his pace remained steady. He didn't even acknowledge that I spoke. "I said I missed you!" I called louder, taking a step in his direction. Still no reaction. He was getting away, and I had no idea how to change that. This was a moment to try to begin again, to at least find closure if not a new beginning, and he was walking away from it.

I ran. I left my bags on the ground by the car, and I ran to him. Just as my feet hit the sand, I caught up to him. Grabbing his arm, I tugged, making him face me. "I said I missed you, goddamn it. I missed you and I loved you and I love you still. And please...can we talk about it? I had no idea about your father, and I was..." I tapered off for lack of anything that felt like it sized up to his father's death. My lower lip trembled. He stood there, staring at me, his face not giving me any clue what he was thinking. I cupped his jaw with both my hands, "Can I get a do over on that kiss?"

And without waiting for an answer, I kissed him. It was tender at first, loving and tenuous, fearing rejection. But when he gave me a slight teasing response, barely participating, I was alive again with the memories of how we used to be, how we teased and played, always pushing the other to be more forceful in their pursuit. I pulled him to me and pushed my tongue through our barely parted lips. My heart smiled as our tongues danced together, and his hands found their way to their usual roosts at the small of my back and the under cup of my ass. The kiss must've lasted minutes because when we finally broke, I was winded.

"Is that a better answer to whatever you needed to see?"

He looked down, trying to hide a smile. "For someone who has issues with abandonment, you didn't mind abandoning me, Jen. You left me to deal with one of the hardest events of my life completely alone. I don't know if I can get around that."

"I'm sorry, Ryan. I'm sorry. I really just felt like you had decided not to come, that you had found someone else, that everything I always feared was going to happen was actually coming true. And when you didn't call back, it felt like confirmation."

He exhaled as if the weight of the world was upon him. He scratched his head, and then shook it as if clearing cobwebs. "No, Jen. No. It's not that fucking simple. I don't know what I thought was going to happen when I saw your car. I don't know what I was thinking. But now, seeing you, talking to you and thinking about us, I have no idea how I thought this would play out or why I thought this would be a good idea." He turned and took a step. I watched him moving away from me. Again, I was losing him, and it stabbed at my heart worse than the first time.

"Can you walk away so easily, Ryan? When you know I love you, when you know you still love me, how can you turn your back on this?"

He spun around. "You had no problems doing it. You didn't hesitate to cut and run. Not so much as an e-mail?! Just...just... gone!"

"Not 'just gone'! It wasn't near as simple as you make it sound! I cried my eyes out, Ryan. I was devastated. I couldn't get you out of my mind. But I wouldn't beg you to be with me. I had left you to go to Germany, and I felt like you would abandon me for it. I told you that before I left and then...in August, I believed that you were proving me right. It all made sense. I wasn't going to email you just to grovel and beg! Either you wanted to be with me or you didn't and it seemed pretty clear to me that you didn't. How could I have known about your father? How could I have guessed that there was something else?"

"Because I told you Germany would not break us. Because I told you I loved you. Because I showed you in every way that I could, that we were a forever thing. You were the one who wouldn't marry me, the one who's so afraid of commitment, the one who has had me on a string for more than six years now. If anyone was going to leave, it was definitely you. Off in Europe with business executives and retail moguls and people who think like you do and talk like you do and are interested in the things you care about. I believed we could make it, and I meant everything I said to you before you left. No. You can't lay this at my feet."

I looked at the sand, listened to the sound of the gulls, hugged myself, and felt my paper-dry pink skin bristle at the contact. "No one's blaming you." I began softly, feeling the weight of the decisions I'd made, hearing Jackie and Talia chastising me. "I'm just..." I stepped into his space, lowering my voice even more. "I'm just saying don't walk away. Today. Just don't make this the last time I ever see you."

He looked away somewhere down the beach. "I need time. Time to think. Time to breathe. Time to figure out what I was thinking when I decided to stand by your car today. My number hasn't changed. You could have called it all this time. Maybe you should consider using it sometime." He stepped back and turned to go. I reached for him as tears of guilt silently chased each other down my cheeks, screaming, *"Your fault"* to one another as they fell. He pulled away from my grasp. "Don't. Just stop. I need time. How hard is that to understand? I'm going back to camp. You should go wherever you were headed when you came to the parking lot." He walked away, and I stood watching him for long minutes until he was nearly the size of an ant.

Finally, I turned back to the parking lot. My skin was reaching a shade of pink that foreshadowed a painful week of scarlet, starting before sunset this evening. Gathering up my bags and my pride, I got in the car and headed off to the drug store to find that aloe.

Chapter Seventeen

*I*n the weeks that followed, I called and texted

Ryan sporadically. Sometimes he'd answer. Sometimes days would go by without a word. I felt like we were starting all over again: small talk, benign topics, and general checkups on each other's well-being. Bah, it was all so painful. I spent time talking to Talia about expectation management and whether it was worth the time and effort it might take to repair things with him.

"Honey, I don't know. He doesn't feel very receptive, but......." She took a deep breath and then whispered in a tentative tone, "Can you blame him?"

We fell silent, and I listened to myself breathe while I struggled with the guilt that I felt. "I've thought and thought about it, Talia. We're *both* to blame,—both of us. I mean, he could've called me, too, y'know."

"Yep, he sure could've. And I'm not saying he's blameless. I'm just saying—I mean—well, hun, his dad died."

"Not my fault at all."

"Nope, it isn't. But he was dealing with that and all of the things surrounding that. So, maybe he couldn't come up with the strength to also call you when he believed you didn't care anymore."

"But I thought *he* didn't care!"

"Oh, I know, hun. I witnessed that little belief system at work when I was there with you. I'm aware of what you thought."

"Is this an 'I told you so'? Seriously?! Are you really gloating right now?"

"No. The time for gloating hasn't come yet. I'm just saying be patient with him. It may take awhile before you get the warm reception you're hoping for. And if you can't be patient, then accept that this really is over."

"But I don't want it to be over. God, you know the guys I've tried dating. They're terrible—stodgy, aloof, pompous, narcissistic, broken, low self-esteemed—guys with full sets of past-life luggage. I've tried them all. Jesus, the guy from last week?! The business dinner turned awkward proposition?! Where do these guys come from? And why do they find and pursue me? I just want Ryan, Talia. I want it to be like it was."

"Even if it takes time to get it back?"

"Yes."

"Even if he needs your reassurance and commitment?"

"Yes."

"Then what are you calling me for? Call him."

"I love you, hun."

"I love you, too."

***

I continued to give Ryan space and reassurance, but I knew that nothing would ever be different if I didn't change something. So I dialed his number on a late June afternoon.

He answered after only two rings. "Hello."

"Come stay with me for a weekend."

"What?"

"Come to San Diego and stay with me for a weekend."

"I'm busy with work and stuff. I don't think I can."

"It doesn't have to be this weekend. How about next? I am not going on a trip to Europe again for more than a month. I have regular office hours, and I know that the Las Vegas summer is coming into bloom, and you could use a break. So, next weekend? Or the weekend after that?"

Silence stretched the tension so thin that when he finally spoke, I jumped. "I might be able to come down next weekend, but I'm not sure I like the idea of staying at your place."

"Why not?"

"I just don't."

"It's an open invitation. We don't have to decide that right now." He grunted agreement. "You can bring your bike if you want. There are cool tracks around here to ride...or so I've been told. Glamis isn't too far east of here. It would be really cool to see you ride again." Again a grunt. "Okay. We can plan that as the week progresses. How was work today?"

And conversation fell into the typical meaningless drivel of checking in and making small talk. By the time I hung up, I felt tentatively hopeful at what was to come.

***

Over the next week, we spoke more frequently than we had been, and I loved it. His voice had not changed. It still had its impact on me. I wanted to hear it in my ear again as we lay naked on the bed in the aftermath of our sex. I wanted to hear it at the back of my ear as I cooked in the kitchen and from across the condo as we made plans for the day. I just wanted him near me, and each day that passed made that more of a possibility.

The weather forecast for the weekend was absolutely amazing. I couldn't have asked for a better setting for this time together. He arrived on Saturday morning, refusing to come down Friday night because he didn't want to stay in a hotel and was as yet undecided about staying at my place. This day felt like a trial run at something, and that made the excitement, and nervousness, tangible.

We met for coffee at a nearby restaurant. I offered to show him around town or to do any one of a number of other things, like going to the beach, going to a motorcycle track, going to a movie, and so on. He was quieter than he had been on the phone, but I didn't let that bother me.

"I'd love to show you my place. It's right on the beach, and we could swim or hang out or...."

"Okay. Let's go see your place for starters." He smiled across the table at me. "I've missed the beach. I love Vegas, but I miss the beach."

As I drove, I was silently taking inventory. Was my place clean? Had I made the bed? Would he like my condo even though it was small? Would he be spending the night? As I pulled into my assigned parking space, the butterfly colony in my stomach threatened to fly right out of my mouth. I took deep breaths and

Sunrise Fires

swallowed hard. "I need some water," I said as he grabbed his bags from the back of his truck. I noticed he hadn't brought his bike and wondered why.

Opening the door to my condo felt as if I was looking at it again for the first time. The waves crashed on the beach, white caps glistening in the bright sunlight. It was gorgeous today. The kitchen was clean and still looked as rich and luxurious as it had on day one. I grabbed a glass and poured myself some water. Taking a sip, I offered the glass to him. "Want some? It's filtered..."

He didn't answer. He was walking slowly from the front door toward the balcony, mesmerized by the view. When I took his bags from him, he finally acknowledged me. "Wow. Now that's a view. I love this place if only for that."

I smiled proudly. "I love it here. It's worth the money for beachside. You want some water?" He took the glass from me and took a big swig, handing it back half empty.

"Do you sit on the balcony?"

"All the time."

He opened the sliding glass door and let himself out, taking up roost in the chair I normally sat in. I set the water on the side table and sat down, musing to myself that I was sitting in the chair that I mentally think of as the one for guests. We sat there quietly, watching the beach, the gulls, the people, and the waves for quite some time. And when he finally stopped staring at those things long enough to look at me, I spoke. "So, umm, there is more to this place than the balcony. And it turns out that I'm giving tours today. Do you want to see the rest of it?"

"Sure," he said with the natural smile that I remembered so fondly. "Sure, hun, show me the rest of the joint."

The tour was short. A one-bedroom place doesn't offer much in the way of side trips. Then we spent the afternoon on the beach. We changed into swimsuits and walked right out of the complex onto the sandy dunes. We probably walked at least three miles in one direction before deciding that we were getting hungry enough to turn back around. On the way back, my hand found its way into his, and he didn't reject it. It was amazing to be in this space at this moment in time, holding his hand and walking along the wet sand at the water's edge.

"Jen," he stopped and faced me, "I can't promise you anything. I really have no idea why I'm here, except that a part of me feels powerfully compelled to be."

"Baby, stop. I am just happy that you are here. I'm not asking for promises. I know this thing got broken when I went to Germany. And I can accept that we have things to talk about and work through, but I can't go on dating people who are probably nice enough guys who just seem terrible because they aren't you. You are my yardstick by which all other men are measured, and so far, I can't even find a guy who can get past the first foot. I can't keep doing that without knowing for sure that this cannot be salvaged. What we had was magical, a thing of fairy tales, my own fantasy relationship brought to life. And maybe we never get that back. Or maybe we can't get all of it, but I'm not willing to let it rest without knowing."

"Where'd you come from?"

"What?"

"Where do women like you come from?" We both smiled at the memory. "Cuz I know a few guys who need a woman like you, and it'd be great to tell them where to go to—"

"Nowhere. They can't go anywhere to find another woman like me. There are none," I playfully punched his arm, "but you knew that already."

We walked on, back to my place, joking and laughing for the first time since I could remember, probably since before Germany. As we got back to my place, I hopped in the shower while Ryan headed for the balcony again. Ten minutes later, I emerged, feeling refreshed and sand-free. "I have some wine if you want," I called out toward the living room.

Ryan didn't initially answer. Figuring he didn't hear me, I began to rummage through my dresser for some clothes to wear. "Did you think I could hear you over the ocean out there?" He was standing at my bedroom door.

"Ohhh, you startled me," I said, standing up and pulling my towel more tightly around my body, suddenly feeling shy. "I said I have some wine if you want some. Or there's beer in the fridge, too."

"Wine sounds amazing. Sweet white, I'm guessing...?"

I smiled. "Yea. It's in the fridge, bottom shelf."

He turned, and a few seconds later, I heard the refrigerator open. I put lotion on my body and hurriedly threw on some panties and a sundress.

His voice echoed back to my room, "Where's the corkscrew?"

"In the drawer next to the stove!" I called back.

I expected to find him on the balcony with two glasses of wine, but when I came out of my bedroom, he was standing in the kitchen, looking at something I couldn't see.

"What's up, hun?" I asked, rounding the corner into the kitchen. And then I froze. He was holding my old cell phone, examining it like an artifact. My heart leapt to my throat, and I immediately felt my cheeks burn. I cleared my throat. "Well, now, that doesn't look much like a cork screw." I chuckled and smirked, trying to seem casual. "It's on the other side of the stove, in this drawer." I reached for the drawer but saw that the wine was already open, cork on the counter beside the bottle.

"Is this your old phone?"

"Hmmm?" *Where was this conversation going to go? And what was my fastest road to a new topic?* "Yeah." I shrugged, "Yeah, I just, umm, I never got rid of it." I reached for the phone. He stood more fully upright and held it tightly.

"Why not?"

I felt my eyes sting. *Could he read the importance of that phone? Could he tell that it had been my own personal lifeline, my security blanket?* It was impossible. I took a deep calming breath. "I dunno, just never got around to it." Feigning nonchalance was becoming more difficult.

"There was nothing else in that drawer."

He was pressing for something that I didn't want to give. I felt foolish for what had happened in Germany, for how I had behaved. I felt weak for clinging to this silly phone as if it represented us. And I didn't want him to know any of it. "Yeah, it's ..." It's what? What could I say here? How could I explain why that drawer was a shrine to the phone I could not let go?

"I talked to Jackie."

"What?"

"I talked to Jackie, Jen, before I ever saw you back in April. She told me about San Diego, about your promotion." I raised an eyebrow. "You never asked how I knew. When I congratulated you, you never even wondered how I found out." I shrugged, still preoccupied by the phone he was holding. He pointed at me with the phone. "She also told me about Germany."

I clenched my jaw, vowing to call Jackie just as soon as I was away from Ryan. I was livid at the prospect of what she might've said. "What about Germany? I mean, she and Talia came and visited..." That was it. Surely, Jackie had mentioned the trip and our touristy escapades and given him a general update. I lightened my tone. "We took a whirlwind tour of a lot of Europe. It was—"

"Not what I meant." I froze, my Adam's apple suddenly too large for my throat. "She mentioned that you had a phone, that you kept it in your nightstand. And that it had come to mean something, maybe too much. Something about it tying to me? I didn't believe her. It's so unlike you. You're such a strong woman. So independent..." he trailed off and held the phone out for me.

I took it with a trembling hand, tears not yet flowing. I was willing them to stay back, willing them not to embarrass me further. "I don't know what to say," I choked.

"Didn't you wonder why I waited by your car at the beach in LA? Why I walked right up and kissed you? None of that was a surprise to you?" His eyes met mine, but I was wrestling my lower lip and chin trying to stop the quivering; there was no way I could form comprehensible audible words so I shrugged lamely. "I had to know. Part of me absolutely thought Jackie was just slinging guilt and being a protective friend, trying to make me out into some bad guy I wasn't. I couldn't picture you being crushed and devastated and sad like that. I wanted to hope that it was true but I really wasn't sure. So when I saw your car on the beach, I just figured it was perfect – no pressure, no build up, no planning – just wait and then see the truth for myself on your face when you saw me unexpectedly. I was sure that I could tell how you felt if I kissed you." He rolled his eyes and laughed quietly. "That first kiss told me that the entire thing was a big mistake. I felt like a schmuck for even daring to hope."

"Stop it," I finally said. "It wasn't a mistake. I was just dumbfounded. I felt sick; I think I was in shock. I never thought I'd see you again – I was sure you had moved on, found a wife, probably settled down by now. To see you walking toward me..." my nose tingled and tears swelled my eyelids, "I lost it. My head was swimming when you kissed me; I don't even think I was on earth at that moment."

"Why? Why does it seem like it was so traumatic for you? Or shocking in such an overwhelming way? I really don't get it, Jen." He put a hand on my shoulder and squeezed. "Tell me your side. Tell me what happened in Germany."

I lost the battle with my tears. "I can't. It seems so trivial now, compared with you losing your father. We've never even talked about that. And even though it felt intense when I was there, it now seems like I was being immature."

"I want to know, and I'm ready to listen." He put his arm around me. "I *need* to know, Jen."

I leaned into him, resting my forehead on his shoulder, letting my tears flow and drop to the floor between us. I thought of Venice and smiled. I thought of the bleach stains on my long since discarded pillow cases. I thought of the gallons of tears I had shed over this man in the past couple of years. They represented a love that he deserved to know about. Maybe after six years, it was about time that I opened up to him. I inhaled deeply, and blew it out slowly.

"Your voice," I began, my own voice cracking. "It has always been amazingly grounding for me." I lifted my head off his shoulder. "I've loved it and complimented you on it a thousand times." He looked into my eyes, confused. "Well," I smiled and winced, holding up the phone, "your voice lives in this phone. We used to talk on that walkie-talkie app, and we had entire conversations that I could relive when I missed you." I paused, remembering powering up the phone and feeling the electric anticipation. "Well...as long as I could get the phone to cooperate." I laughed, thinking of the thousand times I nearly chucked that phone across the room for being infuriatingly uncooperative. "Which mostly it didn't do."

"Oh, my God," he breathed, "that stupid app I told you to download when we were still doing the online thing?"

I nodded, feeling sheepish. "It keeps a pretty good history of conversations. I don't know how far back it can go, but I listened to our last few conversations hundreds of times while I was in Germany. I mean...we used the app right up to the very end, so ...you really loved me by then. And..." I looked at the phone, remembering the way his voice reassured me, the way I allowed it to comfort me even through the terrible audio of that silly shitty phone. "Ryan, when I listened to those conversations, I could tell that you loved me. I had no doubt about it. I could hear it in your voice. I believed you when you said it, and I needed to hold onto that." I looked up from the phone into his bewildered face and sniffled. "Or maybe I just wanted to believe it," I admitted.

His eyes narrowed, and he shrugged as he asked, "Why didn't you call me back that day?"

I cringed at the memory and looked away from him. "I..." Why didn't I call him back? Why did I so readily believe that he had found someone else? I had no answer that I would ever be able to defend. "I don't know," I finally whispered. "I really don't know. I tried three times right away; the first two didn't go through and the third just rang and rang. After that," I shrugged feeling suddenly oafish, "I gave up." Looking back on it now, that day carried some measure of confusion and maybe a hint of shame for me. Grasping for anything that might reassure him, I continued, "And in November, before the girls left, I tried again. I was really hopeful that day..." I looked at the phone still in my hands, reliving the disappointment one ring at a time. "You never answered then either. Didn't you get my missed calls?"

"No. It didn't go to voicemail?"

"No. That actually made it worse too. Not being able to leave a message and not knowing if I would get up the courage to dial your number again after such disappointment."

Ryan's questions kept coming, and my answers, even the lame ones, also flowed, though some took time and contemplation. We talked for hours about what had been the end of us, about what he went through as his father lay in that hospital bed, about my mental state during Oktoberfest, and then when the girls visited. I told him everything, even about the week trying to draft an e-mail that I finally gave up on. It felt good to get it out, good to finally release my weak inner child to him, to finally have enough to lose...that trusting him was the only option I had left.

Chapter Eighteen

*B*y the time the moon was shimmering off the ocean, I was exhausted and starving.

"Can we take a break and eat something, please? I'm starving."

Ryan looked outside as if he just realized the time. "Oh, my God, how long have we been talking?" He leaned back and stretched.

I shrugged. "Hours. We moved to the couch a long time ago. It's been long..." I threw myself back into the couch, the back of my hand on my forehead. "Throat parching..." I raked my neck with my nails. "Stomach draining..." I grabbed my stomach. "Hours." I sat up smiling. "Aren't you hungry?" I poked his ribs with my elbow.

Releasing his stretch, he rubbed and then patted his belly. "Hmmm. Yep, I guess I am running on empty. What's open around here? Can we order out Chinese or something?"

"Bah!" I scoffed. "At midnight? I don't even think you can do that in Vegas! Fast food or else we cook something here."

His eyes came alive. "I haven't seen you cook in ages. What do you have here?"

"I'm mostly out of town, so I don't keep much. I think I have some eggs and maybe leftover steak from a business dinner the other day. I can make us some omelets." I offered.

"I'd love that." As I cooked, he poured us some juice and sat on the large counter next to the stove.

"Clearly, you have more faith in my cooking skills than I deserve. I can't cut steak without a countertop, bub."

He acted dejected but moved, choosing instead to sit on the much smaller counter above the drawer where the phone had been enshrined. "This kitchen seems awfully small for you. I remember you loving the kitchen at our place in Vegas."

"Do you still live there?"

"No. I moved in with my mom for a while after my dad passed. And now, I have my own apartment close to work."

"Any girls been to that apartment?"

"Not sure I like this line of questioning..." he cautioned.

"I'm just curious. I mean, I dated a little. So, did you...?"

"Yes, Jen. Yes, I dated. There was no one until a few months after my dad passed. So, no...nobody ever came to our place. At least, nobody you didn't already know. I had the guys over once or twice. But that's about it."

"So, the new place has had company? As in overnight company? Move in company? What kind of company?"

"Jen, I never stopped loving you, but for a while there, I sort of hated you, too. I needed you, and you were so self-absorbed and shortsighted that you couldn't be there for me as I thought my woman should have been. It doesn't matter who's been in my apartment. It doesn't matter who I've dated and whether or not we've kissed or made out or had sex or had sleepovers." He reached for me, grabbing me by the arm and pulling me until I stood between his legs. "What matters is that I'm here now. Let's talk about us, about this, about the future, about our *now*. If you want to visit the past, then let's talk about our past, even the parts that hurt. But the rest of it is sort of irrelevant."

I felt like a reprimanded child, especially since I knew he was right. "I'm gonna burn your omelet," I said lamely, stepping back to the front of the stove and flipping the eggs into a perfect omelet shape.

"You always were an amazing cook."

"Thanks."

And so it began again.

Ryan and Jen.

He stayed the night, though really we never slept, so I'm not sure I'd call it spending the night. We talked about the store in Germany, the plans for Naples, and how the store construction in London was coming. He told me of his promotion to mechanical supervisor over ten others who all fixed aircraft for an airmail package delivery company. He told me about his employees, the challenges he faced with some of them, and how proud he was to have moved into a management role. It was amazing to reconnect.

Finally, I said, "We should probably sleep soon. It's definitely Sunday morning now, and I think your last yawn used all the energy you have left."

He looked outside. "Nope. Not so sleepy that I won't stay up just a little while longer. Go get dressed into something warmer and meet me right back here in less than five minutes."

As I changed into long pants and a T-shirt, I looked at the clock; it was nearly five thirty. I was exhausted. I wondered what he had planned and was intrigued to find out, but I silently prayed that it wouldn't take long.

"Okay. Now what?" I said, reemerging from my room to find him in jeans and a T-shirt as well. He pulled on a sweatshirt. "Is that it? No sweatshirt? I said 'something warmer.' I'm not sure a T-shirt is gonna cut it out on the beach at this hour."

"Well, you didn't say we were going outside, sheesh." I feigned irritation.

After I pulled on my jacket, he walked me out of the complex and onto the beach. As we reached the line where soft dunes give way to harder packed damp sand, he pulled a blanket from his bag and laid it out. "After you, madam." He motioned for me to sit. I obeyed, casting him a querying glance in the grey light of a newly breaking dawn. "I won't go one more damned day near a beach without watching a sunrise with you, Ms. Simmons." He announced it impertinently and with great aplomb, and then he plopped down next to me.

I laughed, smiled, and laughed even more. It was a priceless moment that in six years we'd never shared, despite all my promises to wake him 'tomorrow' or 'next time.' I put an arm around him as the sun cast its first yellowish orange hues across the horizon. "I love you, Ryan Riverton."

By the time the sun was a full disk low on the horizon, it was light enough for us to look into each other's faces. We joked that exhaustion aged us at least a decade. The bags under his eyes were obvious as I am sure mine were, and his skin was dull and pale. We definitely needed some sleep.

As we walked back to my condo, I asked him to stay and at least take a nap before hitting the road. "I'll sleep on the couch if you want, or sleep with one foot on the floor. No matter what, you've got to sleep a bit before you go."

"I'll stay for a few hours, babe. And I would love to lay with you. But," he faced me, brushing my hair off my shoulders, "Jen, I won't have sex with you."

My stomach flipped, and I suddenly felt ashamed. He made the statement so seriously as if he needed to ward me off. I had not been thinking about sex at all, though part of me sort of knew it would happen if he agreed to sleep in the same bed with me. Our energy had always been physically electric. I was confused and felt the sting of rejection. "Ummm, okay...?" I continued walking back to the condo. "Seems a strange announcement to make. I wasn't implying sex at all."

"Good then." He smiled. "Not having it shouldn't be a problem."

"But, why? Why'd you say it? Why do you feel that way?"

He opened my condo door and let me go in first. Closing the door behind him, he leaned against it. "Because I can't see straight when we're sexually involved. Because you drive me crazy, and you know it. Because I don't want that again until I am sure that I want all of this again." He pointed back and forth between us.

"'All of this?' What's that supposed to mean?"

"It means I love you, but we've both got scars, or, at least, wounds that need to heal. Tonight was an amazing start to that. Better than I expected to be honest. But that doesn't bring me back to the man I was before Germany. It doesn't make me want to beg to be your husband like I used to. It makes me cautiously optimistic about the potential that we can work this out." He took my hand and led me to the bedroom. "Look, I love you. I just don't want sex to make us run away with this thing. I can't wait to have sex with you one day again. And parts of me want that more than others. You aren't the only one complaining about the new boundary." He stroked my cheek. "I have no doubt that any problem we are going to have won't originate in the bedroom. I don't want sex to be the fix to problems that do arise. I want it to be an addition to something that is already put back together."

"I want that, too." I looked him over once, allowing my eyes to linger at his waistband and just below. "But you have no idea how I've missed it," I said in an impish voice.

"Fuck, baby. Me, too." He pulled me onto the bed, and we crawled towards the pillows together. "You think I don't miss that? Your sex was amazing, your body is ridiculous, and your enthusiasm and playfulness get me hard just to think about it." He lay on his back and motioned for me to nestle in. "I can still remember parts of you so clearly that my hands can almost feel them again...on their own."

I lay on my side, head on his chest, one leg on top of him, and the other straight down beside his. He stroked my back and the side of my body, tracing a line from my lower ribs down to my waistline and up to the rise of my hips. I wanted to protest that making our bodies wait was asinine and high school-ish, but the sound of his heartbeat in my ear, trace of his hand at my side, and the feel of the warmth of him beside me all conspired with exhaustion to silence me.

I woke up alone; a note beside me on the bed. He had to get back to Vegas. He didn't want to wake me. Call him when I get up. He loves me—still. That last sentence carried me through the next week.

Chapter Nineteen

*O*ver the next series of weeks, Ryan and I once again found footing. We started off dating 'with no expectations,' and moved rather quickly back to being exclusive. I was hopeful that we might still find what we had lost.

I also made time to meet Jackie for lunch and discussed with her how Ryan knew so much about my time in Germany. As we ordered our deli sandwiches, I pressed her for an explanation. She said she'd seen him at the grocery store and spilled the beans about everything. Right there in the frozen section, all of my heartache and pain was dragged out. I mused at how fitting it was that it happened in the frozen section. It turns out that Ryan had been just as confused and angry as I had been. He'd not told her that his father died, only that he'd had some things to deal with and couldn't come to Germany.

"Jen, he was furious! You should have seen when I called his name. He spun around as if the Grim Reaper was calling after him, and he wasn't prepared to go without a fight. I tried to ask how he was and stuff, but he was giving me short choppy one word answers through gritted teeth. It kind of pissed me off, so I got a little mad and asked if he was dating again and if he was happy. But of course, I didn't give a shit if he was happy at all – I was just so angry that he was being such a prick! Before he could answer, I told him that you weren't happy—not for a long time—and then I told him how much you had loved him, how he broke your heart, and how miserable you were and stuff. Mostly, I was trying to make him feel bad for being such a douche and leaving you like that. And when he said he just had 'stuff to deal with,' please! I was totally done with him and the conversation. Stuff?! Really? That's the best he could do?"

"Why didn't you tell me?"

"Are you serious? You've been such a basket case about him, constantly picking this thing apart and never really getting closure. Fuck, every time his name gets mentioned your eyes roll to the back of your head and you start huffing and sighing like you've run a marathon. No thank you. And to be honest," her toned softened and she glanced at the floor before continuing, "I didn't want to open the wound that finally seemed to be healing. You had finally moved on and bringing up the 'frozen foods' incident might have slowed that down. I mean really..." the spark in her eyes returned. "What would have been the point? He didn't tell me anything except maybe that he didn't have any better excuse than you did for the breakup."

"His dad died, Jackie," I said, feeling surprisingly defensive on his behalf.

"Damn! Really?! Well, he could've said as much! And..." She paused and looked around. "I wish there was a crowd of people here to hear me say this: *I was right!* I told you in Venice that something happened! I told you!"

I rolled my eyes and shook my head. "Yes, Jackie, you did. Eat it up. Say whatever you want. You were right, and I was wrong. I was too insecure to see it, and it cost me—a *lot*."

"Have you told Talia yet?"

"Yes."

"And did she say that she told you so, too?"

"No, I think she is reserving that moment for later...maybe when we see each other face to face." I laughed genuinely.

Jackie laughed, too.

"I deserve it, I suppose. At least, from you two." I smiled at her.

"It doesn't matter now. I can't wait to see what happens next with you two. So, how's it been going so far?"

Conversation faded into friendly catching up. I told Jackie about recent developments with Ryan, and with Naples and London. She told me about her recent scuba trip to New Zealand and her most recent love interest. By the time I headed back to San Diego that evening, I was smiling from ear to ear. It had been great to learn that Jackie had not betrayed my trust and I was delighted to have been able to spend the entire afternoon catching up.

***

As the summer dragged on, Ryan and I continued to reconnect. I planned a trip to see him in Vegas on one of my last few weekends before my trip to London. "If I arrive on Friday afternoon, do you think Chris will be in? I've not seen him since before Germany."

"Dunno. He's a nut about that place, but he also keeps his vacation hours down to a minimum. Thinks he's some kind of big shot now. I don't think you realize the monster you created." Ryan chuckled

"Hah. Big shot? Well, hey, he is the general manager of a Huntington's and faster than anyone else has ever made it to that post. So, I think I can forgive a little big shot—itis." Truth was, I had been wondering about Ryan's motorcycle and about all the guys for a while now. I'd not seen them at all since my return from Germany, and Ryan never mentioned them anymore. I'd even considered going to see him at the store or calling him from my offices in San Diego under a premise of corporate business, but I decided against it.

"I dunno. If you see him, tell me how that goes."

"Do you not see him anymore, hun?"

"Been a while, I guess."

"I'm surprised at that."

"Life. Schedules. Shit gets in the way. He used to invite me out to bars and clubs and VIP-this and reserved-section-that, and girls...all the time with the girls. We're just different people now, I guess."

"Wow, honey. We've not really talked about them— none of them."

"What's to talk about? Listen, I've gotta run. Mom's calling on the other line. Probably firming up dinner plans. Still going Saturday night, right?"

"I can't wait to see her."

I hung up the phone, excited about my upcoming weekend in Vegas and hopeful about seeing Chris, the 'Huntington's Big Shot.'

Four days later, while walking through the front doors of the store, I was pleasantly greeted by a young lady arranging a display. "Hello, ma'am. Welcome to Huntington's. Anything I can help you find?"

"In fact, there is something. Your general manager, please. Mr. Jacobs. Is he around?"

"I believe he might be. Is there anything that maybe customer service can help you with?"

"No. I definitely need him." Realizing that she was looking a little nervous at an apparent customer seeking the general manager, I took mercy on her. "We're longtimo friends. I've been out of town for a while, and I'd love to see how he is doing."

She immediately relaxed. "Right this way, ma'am. His office is just back here."

She guided me to Rasmussen's old office and knocked timidly at the door. "Mr. Jacobs...there's someone here to see you."

I heard rustling, and finally, the door came open. We stood awkwardly for brief seconds while he took time to register who I was. "Oh, my God! Jen Simmons. *The* Jennifer Simmons? Can it be that the prodigal daughter has returned? Jillian, do you know who this woman is?" The girl looked left and right, and then shrugged sadly. "This is Jennifer Simmons, the fastest rising retail clerk. Went from clerk to general manager in eighteen months, I think, and off to regional and then corporate within four years. Isn't that right?"

"Something like that, Chris. Now stop. The girl is intimidated enough." Turning to the girl, I whispered, "I'm just Jen today, the lady who came to see Mr.

Jacobs. And I thank you for the escort. I think there is a display that needs you more than we do."

She smiled graciously, looking relieved as she turned and fled.

"Now, as for you, Chris Jacobs, I was the fastest rising store clerk until you came along. General store manager within a year is unheard of!" I hugged him. "Congratulations, hun. Are you gonna let me in or what?"

He flung the door wide open and swept an arm out in front of him. "After you, m'dear."

The office appeared far more comfortable and lived in, now that Chris was occupying it. Rasmussen had been tidy, professional, and nearly industrial in his designs. Chris had sports team pennants hanging on the walls, photos from sporting trips he'd been on, a small putting green set up in one corner, and a comfortable leather couch across from his desk. "Wow, I love what you've done to the place. What happened to all the Huntington's stuff that is supposed to be in a store manager's office?"

He made his way around to his side of his large mahogany desk, his pronounced limp tugging at the nostalgic part of me. "Supposed to be? Are you here to inspect me? If I knew that, I might not have let you in." We laughed. He sat down in his leather executive chair while I found a seat on the fluffy leather couch. Looking around, it was quite a contrast between professional office and man cave. But somehow, Chris was pulling it off.

"No, Chris, I'm telling you, I'm not here as corporate. And besides, I love this office set up—just wondering about it. I don't think anyone else has ever done more than hang different pictures, or, in the case of Rasmussen, take down all the pictures completely."

He rolled his eyes. "Yeah, Rasmussen. What a character he was...." We chuckled.

"Good at his job all the same. And you should be grateful for it because his success helped turbo boost your own."

"Sure, I guess so. He was pretty stiff and stodgy if you ask me. Corn cob up his butt. Besides, I heard they were looking to find me a store to manage anyway, even if Rasmussen hadn't been picked up for Germany."

"Is that so? And where'd you hear that from?"

"I know a girl," he began, his face softening as he spoke, "she told me. We were getting serious and ..." his eyebrows raised as his eyes found mine. He straightened in his seat and he cleared his throat, "and that's all you're getting outta me, corporate. I can't reveal my sources." He pointed a sharp index finger in my face.

"Chris, Jesus, it's just Jen. That's it. I have no business here in the southwest region anymore anyway. I'm international development now."

"So I'd heard." He looked at me seemingly for the first time, almost sizing me up. "How's Naples coming?"

"It's gorgeous. I can't wait for the grand opening. Should be October or latest of early November, so people have time to shop for the holidays."

"Will you be there for it?"

"Most likely."

"Taking any up-and-coming pups with you?"

"Such as...?"

"Such as an old friend and someone who has potential to join you in the corporate ranks one day?"

I smiled warmly at the thought of having brought him into the Huntington's family and possibly mentoring him into corporate. "I don't know, hun. And I won't make you any promises." I smirked at him appreciatively; "you definitely have an eye toward your future, eh?"

"Of course. How else will I catch up to you?"

I chuckled humbly, redirecting conversation, "Chris, seriously, how have you been?"

He shrugged. "I'm fine. Never better."

"Ever gotten back on that bike of yours?"

"Nope, sold it. Shortly after...I mean, just you know, after..." He hesitated awkwardly. "Shortly after you left for Germany."

I squinted at him. "After I left for Germany? Be serious, Chris."

"Oh, I'm serious." He leaned back in his chair and swiveled back and forth looking at the ceiling. "Ryan can't cook like you, and sitting on the sidelines alone without you or your cooking wasn't worth it." He stopped moving and looked at me, smiling broadly as he finished his sentence.

"Do you guys do anything together anymore? I really have such great memories of times spent with you guys, almost like being with Ryan's second family."

His eyes narrowed and his lips tightened into a thin line slightly turned down at the corners. We looked at each other silently for a few seconds before he broke eye contact and turned away, "Bah. Not family at all." He grabbed a football off the bookcase behind him, throwing and catching it in a perfect spiral lightly tossed toward the ceiling. "Just guys who hung out to ride really, and maybe do other stuff. Lately, can't get anybody together, even for a drink at a club...even when I get us the VIP section and a bottle."

"Maybe beers at someone's house would be more comfortable?"

"Enh. Maybe." Toss, catch, toss, catch. "Doesn't much matter anymore. No one's really around much."

"Where'd everyone go?"

"I dunno. Busy, I guess." Toss. Catch. "Pat's gone. Divorced, and it was messy. Had to move to Minnesota cuz she went back to stay with family, and he was chasing his kids. He'd never see them otherwise. Paul's around, I guess, but his new girl's kinda tight with the kitchen passes. Johnnie's around, too." He caught the football and sat up. "And then there's Ryan...." He raised an eyebrow and pursed his lips. "He's around...but never goes out anymore either." The tension in the room was tangible but I couldn't tell it it was anger or hurt that thickened the air between us.

"It is sad to think of not going out there and watching you guys ride."

"You two back together?" He asked with an air of nonchalance.

"We're talking and seeing where things go. I'm going to spend time with him this weekend. Maybe I can arrange something - we can all get together for a ride at the track. We can meet at Apex—"

"Told ya," he interrupted, "don't have my bike anymore." He leaned back again and resumed his personal game of catch.

"Then come sit with me on the sidelines."

"Better to try to get them together at Randsburg in Cali. No one's gonna go to Apex."

"Why not? You guys used to love that place. I've got some great memories from being out there. Remember my going away?"

"Not everybody has good memories out there..." Chris trailed off, and I suddenly felt insensitive for bringing up the place where he'd hurt himself. "Anyway, let me know what the guys say. See how many of them are willing. Let me know if something comes together."

"I will, Chris. I will. And if I do, are you in?"

"Let's just start with you doing it first."

I left shortly thereafter, feeling like something was definitely off. This version of Chris bore some of the old Chris characteristics, but he had changed quite a bit in the year I was gone. I wasn't sure that Ryan was right about him becoming a bit of a pompous ass; I felt something else darkening his usual childlike enthusiasm. *No doubt I wasn't the reason he stopped going to the track, but what was?* I hoped to get the boys together again this weekend and sort out whatever happened to them.

Chapter Twenty

$\mathscr{I}$ met with Ryan at his apartment that afternoon, and we barbecued some burgers for lunch, slpped beer, and were playful. After dinner, we settled in on the couch and started a movie on DVD. Being there beside him was wonderful and warm and felt like old times. It reminded me of how things used to be, and it brought my questions back about the guys, why I'd not seen Ryan's bike, and so on. "When's the last time you rode your bike or got together with the guys?" I began as the movie slowed to a boring part.

"I don't," he answered plainly. "Sold the bike after..." he trailed off.

"What, hun? After what?"

"After the group sort of stopped riding." His voice was firm and tense.

"Hmmm," I paused the movie and sat up, "that's it? Just that simple? I doubt that very much. What happened, babe?"

He sat up and reached for the remote. "Nothing. Nothing happened." His tone was nearly angry. "Let's just watch the movie."

I held the remote above my head, smiling and trying to return to our playful mood from earlier. "Nope. You'd never give up riding like that. I could cry over you selling your bike. Tell me, hun."

He sat with his elbows on his knees, arms hanging out limply in front of him. He stared at the floor. "Mark," he said, as if the single word would be enough. I waited but he did not continue.

I set the remote on the table and turned to face him. "Mark what, hun?"

He looked up at me, tears beginning to pool in his eyes. I reached toward him, but he pushed my hand away. "Don't."

"Honey, what happened?" I ignored his rejection and pulled him into me, holding him tightly. "What the hell has you so worked up?"

We sat there endlessly, the silence filling the room to bursting. His tears began to make a small circle on my shirt, warming and then cooling my chest just below the collarbone. And still I waited. My mind went back to Jackie's announcement in Italy about the boys not riding anymore. She said she had seen some of them but never in a big group anymore. *Was Mark among them? Had she said she'd seen Mark? And come to think of it, I don't remember Chris giving me an update on Mark either. What happened? And was it what Jackie had said? This thing that happened broke the group up, and now, they never rode together anymore?* I wanted to know. The minutes dragged on endlessly and I began to feel the ominous weight of Ryan's silence; it was clear he was devastated by something

Mark had done and the ticking of the clock in my head got louder and louder by the second.

When he finally began again, his voice startled me. "He's dead."

His words smacked me across the face. "Oh!" I gasped. I never would have guessed that. I could not have ever envisioned that he was gone. I searched for words that might soothe and comfort Ryan; how could I possibly soften the pain? "Honey, I'm so sorry to hear that. I know you loved him like a brother. I know it must've been hard." I rubbed his back not knowing what else to say, feeling stunned by the news that Mark had died so young and at a time when Ryan had so much else going on.

Again, the silence dragged on. It was excruciating sitting here, waiting for him to decide what to tell me and then find the strength to say it. I knew there was more to it. Mark's sudden death was likely devastating for him at the time especially with his father's illness also weighing on him. I wanted to know how it happened and how Ryan had dealt with it; I guessed it was probably a car accident since it was so sudden, but it seemed strange that he would still be so emotional about it after so much time had passed. And there was no way Mark's death would stop Ryan from riding. That alone wasn't enough.

"Will you tell me how it happened?"

"At the track," he began, "he went there alone. We never go alone!" he blurted.

"Okay. Apex? Where you always used to ride?"

He nodded. Things were now coming into perspective – no wonder Chris had been so sure that no one would ride at Apex this weekend. "The ridge that Chris got hurt on."

"What about it, babe?"

He sniffled. "He went around from the top and drove off at full speed."

I clapped my hand over my mouth. There is no such daredevil move as that; it was an impossible jump. The ridges were too close there, and he was sure to wreck. "But honey, that's...there's no way he could...it would be..."

"Suicide." He finished my statement.

All the blood drained from my face; I felt like lurching into dry heaves in rage, sadness, and frustration at my helplessness. Instead I belted out question after question in rapid-fire succession, each one louder and more shrill than the last, "What was he thinking? Where the hell was his head at? How could he possibly have thought that was going to work out? And why go alone?" My head swam with the grief that I knew Ryan felt and with confusion over his friend's decision. My thoughts skimmed through my own library of memories of Mark searching for signs of the daredevil spirit an act like that portrayed; it didn't make sense. Mark was not impulsive or adventurous at all; he didn't have that kind of personality. Confused, I held Ryan as he sobbed quietly into my chest. "I'm so sorry that happened, so sorry that he was so irresponsible, so sorry that he's gone." I began to rock with him softly, trying to picture the rest of the crew and how baffled they would have been at discovering what had happened.

"He intended it. It really was suicide."

Ryan's words had an immediate, violent, visceral response. "Oh!" I gasped as my arms reflexively drew into my chest and I doubled over. My stomach suddenly turned inside out on its way up my throat, my mouth watered in an attempt to dilute the acid already making its way up from my stomach. I couldn't breathe. I couldn't speak. I couldn't even think. My ears buzzed so loudly that I couldn't make out what Ryan was saying; something about a note, his own terms, not being found in time. I lurched, dry heaving, my eyes bulging until they felt like they'd pop out, my ears burning from the force of the heave. Ryan's hand was on my back, rubbing, soothing. I allowed my arms to fall to my ankles and rested my chest on my thighs, folded in half, giving up, sobbing.

Finally, I regained enough composure to speak softly, almost afraid of the answers, "But why? Why? What was so wrong with his life? He had you guys and his family," I sat up again, anger replacing shock, "and he could have any girl in town. Shit, I think I met half of them through his one-date process." I spit the words out, "Ryan, why? What the fuck was so wrong with his life?"

He took a deep breath. "That's just it, Jen. He couldn't find someone." He placed a hand on my forearm. "He dated and dated and dated and never found 'the one.' His note…" He winced and trailed off.

My eyes searched his face, imploring. He briefly met them and looked away again, biting his lip. He shook his head. "It's enough, Jen. Enough to know that he was unhappy. Let that be enough."

"That's what the note said? Tell me, honey. I don't understand how you stopped riding, how this event took away your happiness in it, how it convinced you to sell your bike. I loved watching you ride, seeing you so happy and free." I squeezed his hand and we sat for a long time, breathing, holding each other, weeping.

At last he took a deep breath and began again. "It was one week after they diagnosed my father stage three and inoperable. You had been gone for about two months. They found him at the track, dead for at least two days. And his note," he choked again, "his note," his eyes met mine. He swallowed hard and took a deep breath. "He basically said that if you and I couldn't make it, then nobody would ever be able to love him...that there was no hope, and he was tired of the loneliness and sick of pretending and a bunch of other stuff that didn't make sense."

I couldn't breathe. He blamed us for his suicide? How could he blame us? He had been so bitter at the going away barbecue. *Wait, could I have prevented this? Oh, my God! Ryan probably felt so responsible.* Tears poured down my cheeks as my eyes met Ryan's again. "Baby, I..." What could I say? How could I even begin to make him feel better? "I'm so sorry that that happened... it wasn't our fault... it couldn't possibly have been. There's no way... he...." The words came in spurts, and I wasn't even sure they were the right ones. *How could I begin to soothe a wound that was so old, especially when I wasn't there to help support him through the first time? How could I say anything that might help him to find solace? And why? Why would Mark write such things? He had to know that it would kill Ryan to know it, to read it. And how fucking selfish and unfair of him.* Anger began to roil inside me. Tears dried up as my jaw tightened into a teeth grinding clench. Suicide alone was selfish enough, but to also blame us was preposterous. I had been selfish, too: selfish with Ryan, short-sighted, focused on my own desires, goals, and fears. And here he was, drying his tears and blowing his nose, spent. "He's fucking selfish," I proclaimed. "Selfish and shitty and weak. It was a terrible thing to do, baby. It's not our fault. It's not your fault. We aren't responsible. There's no way. We can't be! It isn't right!"

Hysteria was taking over and I was nearly screaming. Ryan stopped me. "Shh shh shh shh," softly, he placed his fingers over my lips. "Stop it."

"But, honey," my lower lip trembled, threatening to pour new tears down my cheeks, "he...." I took a deep breath and began again. "I...I wasn't there for you. I didn't know. And then, your father..." My head bowed as I looked at my hands. I focused on my lap as I tried to make sense of all that Ryan had been through. "I was selfish, too." I breathed, hardly a whisper.

"What?"

"I was selfish," I looked up and into his eyes, "I wanted things to go my way. I feared they wouldn't. I saw only my fears coming to life and didn't trust you, trust us, enough to hold on...to ask questions, to let myself be more vulnerable, to be there for you, to..." I began to cry again, "to do anything that a girlfriend...that a friend would have done. I'm so sorry, Ryan."

"I hated you for it." His statement stung. "I hated you despite how much I still loved you. Not for the suicide, you didn't know. How could you? Just for disconnecting...you just bailed." His jaw was set and his face stoic. "For months I didn't ride. The track reminded me of him and the stupid idyllic picture he had of me and you. It seemed such a farce. We seemed so fake, like somehow I didn't know anything about us at all. Like our relationship had all been bullshit. Like I had been some companion for the present. I felt so out of sight and out of mind, and I hated you for it."

I sat there, letting his feelings wash over me. I had been so alone, felt so abandoned, been so sure that he had abandoned me. That he didn't want me, that I had been cast aside. Hearing the other side of it changed my perspective on everything. I remembered the phone call and how devastated I'd been, the grey feeling of my apartment and the feel of my pillow, damp and musty, for the next three days from my endless tears. And my anger and resentment were misplaced all this time. My confusion over having been jilted completely was incomprehensible all of the sudden. The phone, e-mails, a letter, or carrier pigeon might have begun to mend this so long ago. But instead, I had gone this other way and screwed it all up.

"The guys..." he eventually continued, "we tried to set times to ride, but eventually, we all dropped out and just stopped showing. My dad's illness made it worse. Johnnie helped me move back into my mom's, and then I don't think I saw him for four or five months. You asked about the guys the other day. The truth is I really don't know about them anymore. Chris is the only sap who can't let go of the fact that it's over. He tries to get us together, and we all avoid or make excuses. He's such a pompous ass now, anyway. I dunno, Jen. Everything just was different. My bike was the least of my concerns. Riding didn't bring me the escape and comfort that it used to. It brought memories of what had happened since that summer. The track. The curve where we had your barbecue. The spot where Chris got hurt. Imagining finding Mark. Picturing you on the sidelines, watching, laughing, and joking and then when we were done riding, all of us hanging out to eat. None of the good shit existed anymore, and in all the places where it had, all I could find was ...pain, death, morbid shit." He took a deep breath. "So I focused on my mom, helping her get on her feet again after Dad passed. And

I worked my ass off and took on all the overtime they'd give me. I figured, fuck it. Take care of the shit I know and," he shrugged, "I sold it the following spring, maybe around May."

"Do you miss it?"

He shrugged again. "Maybe sometimes. Or maybe I just feel nostalgic about it. Like you feel about high school prom once it's over. I don't try to figure shit out the way you do. It just is."

I leaned into his chest and wrapped my arms around him. "I don't know how to make it better or how to take back anything that has happened. But I do know that I love and appreciate you, and I want to try again." Though he placed his hands on my back and held me, he was silent and unmoving. I sat upright again. "Do you?"

"I want to have what we used to have. And I know that's bullshit. So, really I just wait and watch to see what happens, each day, each time I see you. See how I feel. See how we are together. See what this becomes." There was a dull heavy ache in my throat and swallowing wasn't helping clear it. "I love you, Jen. Probably always will. But we've got some heavy shit to deal with. Mark is just one thing. And really, he is my cross to bear."

"Not alone," I rasped. I cleared my throat and started over. "Not alone. You don't have to deal with it alone. Not anymore. And we can work through..." *Through what?* I thought. *Through a year and a half of pain and resentment? Through anger and hate?* "Our stuff," I ended lamely.

The evening wound down in a somber mood. There was an awkward distance between us, and dinner seemed an afterthought, simply out of necessity and habit more than need or desire. We slept in the same bed, though it felt like I was back in Germany again.

When we woke, I kissed him, and we held each other, but each of us was staring off into some other place we'd rather be. For me, that place was one where we were comfortable again, where joy, sensuality, and love coalesced into a beautiful happy life together. I went back to the summer before my departure to Europe, and, lying beside him again here and now, imagined that we felt today as we had back then.

"I should get back to San Diego," I said later over my coffee cup. We'd barely said three words to one another since last night, and it seemed that it would not get any better before dinner tonight at his mother's house. I didn't want to face her like this. And really, what would be the point?

"And dinner? What do you want me to tell my mother?"

"I'll tell her. It's the least I can do."

Dialing her number a moment later as I sat on the balcony, my stomach felt tense. I feared her rejection and anger.

"Hello?" My heart jumped. I was actually surprised that she answered.

"Ummm, hi, Mrs. Riverton. It's Jen."

"Mmmhmm. Hi."

"I'm calling because I wanted to reschedule our dinner from this evening. I need to get back to San Diego earlier than I anticipated."

"I see." She wasn't making this any easier.

"I am so sorry for this." Silence hung in the air. "Maybe we can meet for a cup of coffee or something before I head out this morning." I surprised myself with this invitation and suddenly became nervous.

"Why? Why would we meet for a cup of coffee, Jen?"

What was I thinking? Of course, she won't meet me. I felt like she sat in judgment of me, expecting me to prove something to her, needing me to say the right thing. And I had no clue what that was. I didn't have the energy to try for anything other than the truth. "Mrs. Riverton, I would love to see you personally, privately, to talk, to apologize, to lay eyes on you after so long, and to hopefully begin again." Silence. "I understand if you don't have the time. Or," I paused, recognizing the heavier reality, "or the desire. But I wanted to try, to at least make an effort. And I was hoping that you would be willing..."

"What time did you plan on leaving town this morning?"

"Probably ten or eleven."

"There is a French patisserie on the south side of town, on your way down the interstate."

"I know of it, though I've never been there."

"I'll meet you there at eleven."

"Thank you, Mrs. Riverton. I look forward to seeing you again."

"I'm not sure I feel the same."

As I hung up the phone, I wasn't sure if I dreaded seeing her again, or if I was elated at the possibility of seeing her and beginning to make peace. Whether Ryan and I ever worked out or not, his mother was an amazing woman, and I respected and appreciated her immensely. On a personal level, I needed to feel like I had done all I could to show her that and to make up for not having been there for her and her family as her husband had passed. We were close, probably closer than many true mothers and daughters-in-law, and then suddenly we were nothing. There had to be a reckoning. It hadn't originally been my intent when I called her, but it seemed like today, reckoning would begin.

I packed my weekend bag and gathered my toiletries as Ryan showered and got dressed. "Get everything settled with my mother?" he asked as he pulled his shirt over his head.

"Likely not, and I apologize in advance for anything negative that comes to you this evening over dinner on my account." I didn't bother telling him about our coffee date; I didn't want to risk his intervention or judgment. I zipped my bag and stepped over to him. "Ryan, I love you and your family. And I loved you when I was in Germany, too." He looked past me out the window. "I missed you then...." I stroked his unshaved cheek, "and I miss you now." He didn't look at me. I kissed him just beside his lips, unable to meet his face square-on, and unwilling to force the issue.

As I pulled away, his face turned, eyes closed, and his hand snaked up the front of my body, his fingers hooked around my neck, his thumb taking its place at the front of my ear. He guided me into a tender kiss, gently pressing his lips into mine, moving them together and drawing me into him. I felt like I was falling into an abyss—one of love and of feeling wanted. His free hand moved to my hip and he kissed me again, dragging his lips away from mine and onto my cheek. He laid a trail of kisses from my lips to my neck, allowing his hand to fall away from my ear and trace the full round rise of my breast before sliding it under my arm and drawing me into a hug. He held me for a long time, his breath warm my neck where his kisses had just been. "I love you, too," he whispered into my ear. Intermittently, he kissed or nuzzled my neck. I matched his slow tender affection, breathing him in, loving the feel of his pulse against my lips as I kissed his neck. Finally, he broke the magic. Pulling away from the hug, he said, "You should go. San Diego awaits."

I cleared my throat and looked at my watch. I had fifteen minutes to be at coffee with his mother, so I didn't argue despite the fact that tearing away from this moment actually caused me a sense of anguish and fear that I'd not get it again. "Okay. You're right. I should." I gathered my purse and my bag and headed toward the door. He walked me out, and we kissed one last time before I drove away. I cried a bit on the way to the patisserie, though I really had no idea why. Fear about facing his mother? Sadness about the time with Ryan? Nostalgia? Happiness about the beautiful tender moment we just shared? Thoughts of where that might've led made me smile. Even in that nonsexual, awkward moment, my body had responded to him. My panties were damp from the way his lips pressed mine, the way his tongue and mouth teased my neck, and the way his hands felt around me. They brought back memories, physical ones, the kind when the body was all on its own and separate from the mind, and those memories flooded back every time he touched me like that. I took a deep breath and reminded myself to be optimistic and positive. He loved me still. I smiled as I pulled into the parking space and locked the car.

***

I sat at the front of the bakeshop for ten minutes, waiting on Ryan's mother, thinking, wondering if she was going to show up. I reveled in the smell of fresh baked bread and pastries of all kinds. The front of the place was a bakeshop with a display case where you could buy pastries of all types. They were beautiful and colorful—jelly and fruit-filled confections, alongside coffee cakes and cinnamon rolls. I watched customers come in and buy pastries. Others came to the counter on their way out after dining, intending to take a box of fresh pastries home with them, and still others came in pairs with loved ones, asking for a table in the back. It was a wonderful place and one that calmed me; a perfect choice on his mother's part. It represented Caroline Riverton perfectly, warm and calming in an unspoken indescribable way.

The minutes ticked away, and I had just decided that I'd give her another five minutes before leaving when she opened the door into the foyer. I stood up and smiled. She nodded and continued walking toward me. I held my arms out to hug her. She offered me a lean, accepting my hug but not reciprocating it. The hostess led us to a table, handed us menus, and stepped away.

I took a deep breath, urging myself to sit upright and be strong. "Mrs. Riverton, I am so glad you decided to come."

"I'll only be having a coffee. I don't have much time." Her tone was noncommittal—not angry, not warm, just plainly stated. I had no idea what to expect.

"Me, too. Just coffee." I set my menu at the edge of the table, unfolded my cloth napkin, and placed it on my lap. Smoothing it onto my thighs felt good and reassuring as I considered how to begin. She sat across from me in the booth, her slate blue eyes somehow seemed more dull than when I had last seen her and her hair more grey, too. She must've been nearing sixty though when I left for Germany, I don't remember ever actually thinking about it. Now, she looked like a senior citizen, frail and weary, skin more wrinkled and shoulders sagging. Still, she sat there proudly, indomitably across from me; the strength that I had always admired about her seemed to radiate from her still.

"I am so sorry to hear about," I paused searching for the appropriate reference. 'Jim' was likely too familiar and 'your husband' likely too impersonal. "Mr. Riverton." I finally said. She tore her eyes away from the window and looked at me. "I am also sorry that I wasn't there for you. That I didn't know. That Ryan and I weren't talking then."

"As I recall, it was you who weren't talking..." She pursued her lips and raised an eyebrow.

All my muscles tensed, reflexively defensive. I swallowed and breathed through the desire to defend myself and point out that Ryan never called me back or contacted me in any way. Instead I nodded. The waitress came back with coffee and asked if we'd like to order. It was a relief to know that she'd not be back anytime soon.

"I regret that Ryan and I weren't talking. I regret my side of that. And I take responsibility for it. You were important to me. You are important to me still. I admired you and loved you and missed you. When I came home from Germany, I wanted to come see you but..." I tapered off, somehow feeling like my thought process back then might come into question. She tilted her head slightly forward, urging me on. "But I thought that it might be weird or awkward. What if Ryan was there when I came by? Or what if it was no longer okay? What if I was being stupid to even consider it? I second guessed myself and I chickened out. I had no idea that if I had come by, I would not find you living happily here with Jim right by your side as it has always been."

"You hurt Ryan." Her tone was sharp. "He was devastated by so much in his life at that time, and you literally couldn't finish one difficult conversation with him before you quit the relationship." I opened my mouth to say something, anything, to stop her, but she raised a hand. "No. Let me finish. I don't want to hear your reasons or excuses. Your side may matter someday but not now." I closed my mouth and looked at my silverware. My coffee begged for creamer, and maybe sugar, too. The spoon wanted to be held, the cup needed to be raised to my lips. My legs wanted to move, to get up, and run. My jaw begged to be unclenched and set free to defend myself against her accusations. My stomach churned. And I just sat, listening, understanding that this was the reckoning that I had expected.

"I thought I knew you before you left. And certainly, I knew how much my son loved and needed you. I told you that and asked you to hold onto his love and remember it. Do you remember that conversation?"

My eyes stung with tears at the shame of having disappointed her. I remembered the moments she held me and spoke to me so lovingly, the wink she gave me as we left her house that day. When she had said, 'He loves you like I've never seen him. Remember that when you're missing him in Germany,' and she had called me her unofficial daughter-in-law, it made me feel like she was my own mother who had warned me of something and even told me how to avoid it. And then, after I had disappointed her, she was now asking me why I hadn't listened to her. I was six years old again, sitting here in front of this woman whom I respected so much. "I remember."

"And yet you couldn't be there for him. You couldn't hold onto his love for even three months." She shook her head and took a sip of her coffee. "I know he is seeing you again. And I cannot stop him. But I am not as open to the prospect." I silently cried as she spoke. "I loved you, as I would any daughter-in-law, sometimes even as the daughter I never had." She paused and shook her head. "I loved and trusted you with my son. I blessed the relationship and encouraged him. He found such joy in you, and I wanted him to have that." She paused and pointed a finger at me from across the table. "And you abandoned that. You left him standing alone at a time when your love should have been his leaning post." She took a deep breath and continued through gritted teeth, "In the time since you have been gone, I have guided my family through some of the most...grief...the worst..." her eyes were bloodshot and I thought they glistened with tears, but none fell, "the worst events of our lives." She finished her thought, barely audible. Looking into her mug, she sipped and swallowed slowly as if the coffee were mud.

She sniffed and began again more firmly, "We are different now. All of us. Even you, dear. Ryan is not the same man you knew before Germany. Find a new relationship with a new man, even if the new man is Ryan, but do not try to rebuild what was lost. It is gone, and so is that man." I finally stirred cream and sugar into my coffee and gulped a huge swig of it, sucking up my tears and sitting more upright again. Was she accepting that Ryan and I were dating again, giving her blessing, giving me advice? Or was I still being chastised? I couldn't tell. I just listened and nodded intermittently.

"The man you left behind when you went to Germany is dead. Think of it that way, and do not try to force my son back into that old mold. I wanted to see you over for dinner tonight because I wanted to see you interact with him. You leaving today; it reeks of cowardice. This will not be easy, and I'd rather my son start new with someone else." Maybe she wasn't accepting us after all. Maybe this coffee idea was a pretty bad one. I still had a long drive ahead of me, and this was a terrible way to start it.

We sat in silence for a long while. It was likely only four or five minutes, but it felt like twenty. I wondered if it was my turn to speak, if she was waiting on me. I had so much to say, though at the moment, sentences weren't readily coming to my head. I cleared my throat, feeling as if it was now or never. "I love him," I began not knowing what I'd say next. "I love him as much as I ever did. I was wrong and selfish in my insecurities and fears. It hurt him and you and...." I was so relieved that these were the words that were flowing and not the angry defensive ones that also sat just behind these sentiments. "And I am so sorry." I reached across the table and grasped both of her hands. "I loved you as much as any daughter-in-law could love a mother-in-law, even more. I loved you as a friend and advisor. I loved you as Ryan's mother.

"He was the love of my life. I knew that then, but feared that I was not his. I know what you said. I heard you, and, in that moment, it felt so reassuring and real. I am sorry that that feeling faded or was washed away in the sea of my insecurity. I cannot help that now." I did not know where these words were coming from, but she hadn't stopped me yet, so I kept going. "What I can do is love him still and always. I can build with him a relationship that we fashion together. I don't expect or even require your blessing," she squinted at me, her lips a thin line, "but I would like it. And what's more, I would like to rebuild a relationship with you." I stopped. The words stopped stringing themselves together in my head, and I was blank, afraid of her reaction and hoping that I had not said too much.

She squeezed my hands, looked me in the eyes, and nodded. "I will wait and see how this goes. I will not discourage him anymore than I already have, but I am not hopeful about your future. I respect this." She motioned to the table. "It took guts to invite me out alone. Without Ryan here to shut me up, I had no idea what I'd say to you. I respect that, and it reminds me of why I liked you." I beamed and squeezed the one hand that remained in mine.

"It does not mean that I like where you and Ryan are going. Trying to recapture the past is impossible. And trying to overcome such pain is something I cannot fathom. I am willing to watch and wait. You leave a lot more now with this new job, I understand. Is that correct?"

"Yes, I do, but—"

"And you expect that these trips will be different for you emotionally?"

"Yes, they are. They are already. I—"

"And are they different for him?" My mouth sat agape. "Or is each one another little Germany relived?"

"I...I hadn't thought of it that way...."

She asked more questions and made points on how difficult the road back into Ryan's life would be. She said that he may accept my role for a time, but she didn't know if he'd ever trust me in a lifetime way again. She asked if I could find peace in that kind of love—a partial love—a love that was not going to ever reach the heights of our previous relationship. She pressed me for my intentions and for my level of commitment to our success. We spoke in a respectful but wary way. By the time noon came, I was exhausted. I couldn't believe that it had only been an hour.

Her phone vibrated and chimed. "I have an appointment, so I have to go." I nodded and smiled weakly, looking for some sign that this had gone well. She didn't oblige me. "Thank you for the coffee and the conversation." I moved to get up and hug her, but she held her hand out and waved me off. "Don't get up. I'm in a rush, nearly late already."

"Thank you for meeting me, Mrs. Riverton. I really appreciate the time and opportunity."

"Yes, yes. It's fine." She sniffed dismissively. "Appreciate my son." She looked at me sternly. "Appreciate his time and the opportunity he is giving you now. Appreciate that, and we will have begun something."

And with that she left me sitting there alone in the patisserie. The smell of the pastries no longer brought the comfort that it had an hour ago. At this moment, I wanted out of there and back to the smell of the ocean and my condo.

Chapter Twenty-One

The drive home was awash with memories and feelings, all revisited through the new shades of perspective that Mrs. Riverton had added and the new revelation of Mark's suicide and Ryan's abandonment of riding. I reconsidered him and me and what we might become. My new job had me on the road a lot, and his had him comfortably living there in Las Vegas. Would we ever live with or near each other again? And what about this dirt biking thing? I wanted so desperately to see him in that specific happy place again, to watch him ride and to feel the joy rolling off of him; but was that selfish of me too? Was Mrs. Riverton right? Was Ryan really a whole new man? One who no longer desired riding, who no longer found joy in it? Was I wrong to want it for him again, to want him to find that joyous place on the track again?

I passed up the Zzyzx exit and smiled, remembering how he and I had talked about meeting there back when we were online chatting before we ever met. It was the precise midway point between our homes at that time, and, even though there wasn't a town or solid rest stop there, we thought that meeting there might still be memorable and special to just the two of us. I had pictured camping in the nearby state park and maybe hiking through the trails. Maybe Ryan could even bring his dirt bike. I smiled at the memory of having been so full of anticipation about meeting him after so long.

I drove on and continued to reevaluate all that had happened, smiling, laughing, or crying as the memories washed over me. I loved Ryan and couldn't imagine life without him playing a role...even if it was not as my romantic interest. I relived some of our most intimate passionate moments, like the way his hands felt on my body, how his lips and tongue so adeptly stoked my bodily responses, bringing us further into passion and sexuality. His lips on my neck this morning had felt exactly as they always had—loving, tender, and warm while also being insistent and sensual. My pelvis responded to him, seizing and melting, dampening my panties and hardening my nipples. I could feel him touching me still. Always. Just a passing thought in that direction and he was again in my presence, my body responding, reacting, igniting, ablaze with desire for him.

By the time San Diego came into view, I was exhausted emotionally and physically. I fell onto bed as soon as I walked in the door, not even bothering to change my clothes.

***

Ryan and I met two weeks later on my last weekend before the trip at the National Park off Zzyzx. It was a nostalgic weekend of reconnecting and making new memories. When I had suggested it to Ryan, he was instantly on board. We camped among the trees and hiked through the days. On the second night, as Ryan built the fire, I pulled a couple of beers from the cooler we'd brought.

"Do you think we can make it?" I asked, handing him one of the bottles.

He looked at me over his shoulder. "The fire?" He smiled. "Oh, I got this. I did fine last night. I just need a minute." He winked and turned back toward the fire pit.

I smacked him on his ass and plopped down on a nearby log that we'd dragged over to make a bench. "You know what I meant."

"And I don't have the answers. I know that we'll make it through this weekend." The kindling caught fire, and he blew on it, encouraging it to grow. "I know that I'm enjoying you and this time together. Ask me about that stuff. Don't ask me about the future." He stood and joined me on the log as the fire slowly crept its way around the remaining wood in the pit. He kissed me as he sat down. "I love you. I know that. And now..." He paused and took a deep breath. "I think we've about exhausted what I know at this point."

I leaned into him. "Liar."

"Wanna eat?"

"Yeah, I'm starving."

We worked together to roast hot dogs and pull together a camping-fashioned dinner. I liked how much closer we'd become over the past month or so; I wanted it to continue. I was leaving the following week for the UK and had a sickening feeling of déjà vu tickling the deepest recesses of my mind. I worried that somehow this short trip, after such a period of healing and rebuilding, might actually be the end of us. In my head, I knew it wasn't true, but a part of me feared it anyway. I watched him move around the fire and the campsite, his muscles flexing and moving, the fire casting playful shadows across his jawline. I couldn't see his face clearly, but I wanted to; I wished I could see thru this dim light of dusk, past the smoke, and through my own fears and insecurities into the comfort and reassurance that his eyes held. My eyes traveled over him as he moved. God I missed his body. I missed touching, stroking, holding, pulling, dragging, playing, sucking, kissing, nibbling, nuzzling, fucking. I wanted him now, as much as ever. I'd have preferred to have him for dinner instead of the roasted hot dogs and beer. I handed him a bun as he came back over with paper plates.

He took a stick from me and wrapped the browned hot dog in the bun. "Dinner fit for kings," he proclaimed, setting the dog on a plate and handing it to me. I laughed and handed him another bun. "What? It's perfect. Fast, easy, smoky, yummy." I cocked my head and raised an eyebrow. "Okay. Maybe 'yummy' is up for debate. But still."

As we ate, we joked and laughed. I stole opportunities to touch him, and he didn't resist me. Later, as we lay on the blanket in front of the fire, I kissed him, tasting the charbroiled hot dog flavor and reveling in this moment. I propped myself up on one elbow and looked into his eyes. "I love you, Ryan."

He was staring up at the stars, his arm folded behind his head as a pillow and his other hand resting by his side. "I love you, too, Jennifer," he replied absently.

I turned to stare at the stars with him, lying there shoulder to shoulder, both lost in thoughts somewhere up in the heavens. His shoulder rolled a bit and his arm followed; his hand snaking its way on top of mine, and his fingers sliding into the curl of mine. I squeezed them and still we laid there. Out here in the wilderness, away from everyone else, in the sounds of nature and surrounded by the stars that you can never see from the city, we felt whole and completely sated. I needed for nothing else. I wanted only for this time with him to last. The canopy of trees above us held small groups of twittering nestling birds and the occasional hooting owl. The wind rustled through the leaves, and they waved a shrugging naïve shy hello to us lying so far below. The smell of pine, dirt, and decaying leaves rode the wind into our campsite and across my body. The fire was hot on my right side, and his body warm on my left. The night air chilled the tips of my nose and toes despite the fact that I had shoes on. I could hear his breathing and feel his pulse as it beat in his fingers.

I'm not sure when I fell asleep, but, at some point, the howl of a distant coyote and the bitter nip of the desert night woke me with a start. The fire had died to smoldering embers, and Ryan and I were still lying there uncovered, except for the extra layers of clothing we were wearing. I watched him sleeping for a few minutes, his lashes holding his eyes bound shut, seemingly tied to his cheekbones. His lips, plump and relaxed, begged to be kissed awake. His chest rose and fell in the slow rhythm of deep slumber. I smiled seeing him so peaceful. The moon shone bright enough to light the campsite in a grey silhouette. I took advantage of the light to open the tent and arrange our sleeping bags before waking and coaxing him back into the warmth and safety there.

"Mmmm." He drowsily pulled at me after he was inside his sleeping bag. I kissed him, his lips warm and meaty. My heart sped up as his tongue pushed into my mouth and his hand wound around my waist. We kissed slowly, sleepily, tenderly, gradually building in intensity. His hand moved up my body and into my hair. Grabbing a handful, he pulled my head back, released the kiss and bit and kissed the taut muscular line of my neck that he'd exposed.

"Ahhh," I moaned. My skin came alive at his touch—goose bumps rose, a chill ran up my spine, and my pace quickened even further.

"You smell amazing." His voice was guttural, animal, and sleepy. "...always smell so fucking good." He bit my neck and pulled me further into him, giving him better access to the side and back of my neck...and to my ear. "I've missed you, Jen. I want you. I want you so bad."

His voice bounced off my eardrum, each beat was a tiny stroke against my clit. Blood rushed to my cunt, and I struggled to maintain a solid breathing pattern. "Baby," I rasped, "you feel so good."

He suddenly stopped. His eyes flew open and met mine in the inky black that surrounded us. He unzipped his sleeping bag and pushed me aside, smoothing it out. I smiled knowingly and unzipped mine, handing one side to him. We spread it out on top of his and zipped them together. I missed this, the old way we slept together, before Germany, before everything was all screwed up. I took off my jeans and sweatshirt and slid into the sleeping bag bed, zipping up my side. His arm fell out, opening the spot where I always used to sleep. I placed my head on his shoulder and snuggled into his side. His arm draped behind me, his hand loosely at the small of my back, lazily stroking with sleepy fingers.

He lifted my chin and looked at my silhouetted face. I could see nothing more than the outline of his head but was reassured by his breath on my cheek. "This is amazing, Jen. This weekend, this time together. I never stopped loving you."

I melted a little at that moment, drawn into him soulfully and completely, wanting the kind of connectedness that feels complete. I wanted to crawl into his body, wrapping him around me as a jacket and disappearing into him, into us. "Me neither. I never stopped loving you either. And I don't want to. I never want to stop loving you."

His arm tightened behind me and pulled me even closer into him, his other arm drawing around me. He kissed my forehead. His heart pumped in my ear. My own heart thudded in my chest, and together we breathed each other in. I dozed off again to the sound of his body and the feeling of him entangled in me. If only life were always this simple.

***

The canopy came alive a few hours later and dragged the veil of slumber grudgingly from around us. I felt like someone ripped my cocoon off far too soon. I looked at Ryan's chin, his jaw, his scruff. I smiled and scratched it like I'd seen him do so many times. He smiled and grabbed my hand. "Morning." His voice rumbled with the gravel of unused vocal chords. He kissed my palm. I gushed emotionally and physically; I didn't think my panties would ever stop being wet until I was out of his company.

"Hi, love," I stretched, "it seems like somebody wants us up." The cacophony outside seemed as if the birds had descended specifically on our campsite.

He chuckled. "We should get up anyway, I suppose." But instead of moving toward getting out the sleeping bag, he turned toward me, pulling me into him, and grinding his hips into me. "Or else we might not get up at all." His cock was as awake as the birds outside, and I pictured the damp growing circle of pre-cum that was likely marking his underwear.

I kissed him, biting his lower lip. "Do we have to? Would staying in this beautiful bed for a little longer be that bad?" I gave him the softest weakest ingénue eyes that I could muster.

He traced the side of my body, his hand settling on my hip, gripping it. He gave me a playful shake. My breasts jiggled, rubbing against the inside of my thin sheer bra, nipples instantly protruded, reaching toward him, becoming obvious even through the bra and T-shirt. His jaw tightened as the movement caught his eye. He looked from my breasts to my face and back again, swallowing, his nostrils flaring. I traced up my own side over his hand that still held my hip along my ribs, and finally coming to rest on one of my breasts, wrapping my fingers under the weight of it to calm the tingle and using my thumb to soothe the tense nipple. I slid my hand slowly between us across to the other breast to do the same. His lips fell open as his hand came away from my hip and snuck under the bottom of my T-shirt. He moistened his lips with a thick wet tongue and leaned in to kiss me.

His hand crawled up my ribs, indecisive, as his kiss lingered slowly savored on my lips. I felt loved, cradled by his arm behind my back and the warmth of his body in front of me. His lips teased and played but did not push. And when I tried to lean in, insistent, he pulled slightly away. Still his hand crept. My skin tingled, there was a band of electricity wrapped around my arms and across my chest. Every nerve reached for him, begged for his touch, stretched out as if climbing to the surface just to be nearer to him. At last, his fingers reach my bra line, solid wire creating a barrier that meant he had to actively make a decision. I'd have preferred if he could have stumbled onto my breast and rode the passion into our oblivion. His thumb lifted the wire slightly and then traced the soft skin underneath, nearing my armpit and then nearing my sternum. His fingers stroked the line of my bra and along my ribs below it. I broke away from the kiss to let a pleading gasp escape my lips. I turned my face away from him, toward the pillow, and pushed my neck in his direction, arching my back to give him more of me.

"Fuck," he whispered, barely audible. His hand slid behind me and drew me fully up against his chest, his fingers deftly unclasping my bra. His hand raced back to my chest, palm flat, chasing up my ribs to the now loose underwire. And finally, he was there, squeezing, massaging, stroking my breast as his mouth at my neck drew another moan from me. He kissed down my neck to my collarbone, stopping to kiss or bite the places he had so long ignored. I wanted my shirt off. I wanted him now. His hand was not enough. I wanted his mouth on my breast, licking the tender line where the breast transitions to ribs, sucking the rounded swell at the sides and bottom, grazing the nipple. And still his hand massaged. He rolled my nipple between his thumb and forefinger. "Yes," I breathed. My body undulated involuntarily toward him, pressing into him, grinding against him. I was nearly breathless as he raised his wrist enough to move my shirt up and off my breast allowing his kisses to continue their downward trek. I held my breath; he exhaled a hot plume of expectation onto my eraser-tipped breast. I bit my lip, slid my hand into his hair, and pulled him closer. A hardened warm wet tongue flicked my nipple. "Ah!" It came out as sharp as if someone had slapped me. I pressed my lips together, holding my breath, allowing the anticipation to course through me. I whispered, "Please, baby…Fuck, I need you. I need you, Ryan. Stop teasing me." Both hands were on the back of his head, his ears rested on my wrists. "Please do what I know you want to."

He was squared up and level to my chest and clearly distracted by what he saw there. But he looked up into my eyes, holding his breath, and then exhaling slowly, his hand moved ever so slightly before his head did, and for the next few minutes, I was lost in oblivion. His mouth and hands kissed, licked, sucked, and teased my chest, neck, arms, and face. Clothes were a blur as they piled up to the side of us. His skin contacting mine was a new experience, each point of contact celebrated more than the last, bringing me to a state of ecstasy and anticipation that I'd never before known.

He grinded against my thigh, his cock rigid and dripping profusely, lubricating along his grind line and making me wonder if he would cum before we even had sex. Our bodies bucked and banged against each other, moans and heavy breathing intermingled, hands racing to rediscover parts long since visited. As his palm passed over my mound, I froze and parted my legs, tilting my hips in his favor. He gripped my pubic bone, the heel of his hand grounding me to the earth, his fingers poised to send me to the heavens. I was soaking wet, and I knew he could feel it, even now, without delving into my hot pool of sweet juice. I rode his palm, grinding my pubic bone further into his hand. He met me pulse for pulse, pushing harder against me and giving me something stable to grind against. His fingers warmed my engorged lips but waited to enter me. Instead, he let them tap and slap against me as I bucked against him.

"Mmmmm..." I moaned, nearly whining, bucking ever faster against his hand. My moans came faster and louder. I felt desperate for the orgasm that was hidden under his fingers. I was nearly screaming, my fingers scratching into his skin as I gripped and pulled him into me. His middle finger slid easily into my slit and could have disappeared all the way inside me, except that he chose to trace the soft line of my swollen pink lips, sliding and drawing small circles and shapes along the slick surface as he forged upward. He stopped before giving my clit the attention I was screaming for. My voice joined the birds in waking the forest that morning. "Oh. Oh. Ohhhh. Yess, yes..." I held him even closer, parted my legs even wider, tilted my hips even more toward his hand. And again he parted my lips, dipping three fingers all the way into my pussy. Deeply and solidly, he thrust them; over and over he pushed into me. My legs quivered before the orgasm fully struck, and then his thumb joined the rhythm, flicking across my clit each time his fingers were buried in my sopping wet pussy. I couldn't wait any longer. "Yes. Ahhh. Fuck. Mmmmm. Goddddd! Yessss!" I screamed and shook and rocked against his hand as I shattered and disappeared.

The world ceased to exist in that moment. There was nothing but me and this feeling of bliss...and of nothingness. I could not tell how long it lasted nor how loud I was nor if he was enjoying it or not. I couldn't think about any of that. I couldn't think at all. I only cared that he keep doing what he was doing and let me stay here, lost in this abyss.

The crescendo slowly waned, and his hand slowed. Tears wet the corners of my eyes. My mouth was dry and my throat suddenly sore. "Mmmm." My eyes were wide, and that vocalization was all I could muster, though it sounded harsh and gravelly. I tried to wet my mouth and lips with a parchment tongue. My throat seized in a sandy swallowing motion. I coughed and gasped for breath. Closing my mouth again, I wiggled my tongue, willing wetness to alleviate my inability to communicate. "Mmmm." The warmth of bliss settled over me as I began to realize my surroundings again. I sidled into Ryan's chest, seeking the reassurance that his presence and stability gave.

He smiled at me, tracing a thin cold wet line up from my pussy to my belly button before bringing his hand to his mouth. It was open, waiting, but first, he inhaled deeply. "Damn, baby, I have missed the smell of you." He sucked his fingers one at a time, pausing after the first to say, "And the taste of you." He smirked knowingly at me.

Finally, I was on earth again, and realizing what had happened, I returned his smirk with a nod. My mouth watered watching him. Finally, I could swallow comfortably again. I drew his hand from his mouth, kissing him briefly before licking and sucking one of his fingers clean. As I drew his finger into my mouth, he tried to pull back, but I had a firm hold of his hand and didn't release it. Instead my eyes bore into his, and my tongue swirled around the left and right side of his finger before tickling the length of it, paying particular attention to trace the outline of his fingerprint. My free hand reached down and stroked his cock in time with my tongue's motions. He groaned and rolled onto me. His kiss was nearly forceful, hungry, insistent.

As he settled between my legs, I instantly wanted to cum again. I tilted my hips and pushed them toward him, loving the feeling of his rock hard cock squeezed between our bodies. He reached down between us and lifted my leg, putting my knee on his shoulder and leaning against my hamstring. Instantly, his hand was again between us. He slid his hand up my sloppy wet pussy on his way to grabbing his cock. He dragged its tip once roughly through my slit, from the clit to where he wanted it, hovering just outside my warm wet hole. He stayed poised for less than a second, his eyes locking mine, before thrusting into me fully, all the way to the hilt in the first thrust. And from that moment, he was relentless.

He stared into my eyes while he thrust into me over and over again. Each thrust coming more forcefully and faster than the last. His arms and neck flexed and released as he fucked me. God he felt good inside me. He kissed me, nuzzled my neck, and sucked my breasts. "Fuck, Jen. Your pussy is so fucking tight." All I could reply was a slight nod and a smile. My breath was coming in rasps, and my pulse raced as he bit my jugular and thrust into me again. He pulled my other leg up to his shoulder, and he knelt upright, pulling me toward him, his thumb alternated between stroking my clit and joining his cock at the entrance of my pussy, sliding back and forth lubricated by our sex. The veins stood out on his neck as he strained, and his jaw clenched and relaxed.

His nostrils flared. He bit his lip. And still his cock plunged deeper into me. "Yes, Ryan, that feels so fucking good, baby." I put my hands beside my hips and felt his thighs slam into me, strong and unyielding. He slid one leg off his shoulder and held the other up. My entire body turned, and I slid the released leg under him, between his legs. He grabbed my thigh and pulled me onto him harder and harder. He leaned forward, my knee nearly in my face, his cock fully inside me with every thrust. I reached between us and stroked his balls, gently squeezing and releasing, feeling them swell. With my other hand on his shoulder, I pulled him further onto me and into me. Moaning and whining, each thrust took me higher. He held my leg tightly and reached a fever pace. His balls seized in my hand, I gently coaxed them one last time before my hand stole away to my engorged clit. I barely touched it before my body rocked over and over again in wave after wave of ecstasy. His cum spurted again and again all over the inside walls of my pussy; he came so forcibly that I could feel it. Hot streams of cum endlessly poured into me.

We gradually slowed our pace until he collapsed beside me, and we drew the sleeping bags around us again. I don't think we said a word as sleep dragged us back under.

Chapter Twenty-Two

*I*n the days that followed the Zzyzx camping trip, I got ready for my trip to London. It felt different than recent trips had. I was on edge as I packed. Ryan felt distant, our relationship felt like it was in jeopardy, I could not focus on the task at hand. The ghosts of Germany loomed over me as I checked in at the airport. I called Ryan as I sat at the gate, waiting to board.

"Hey, you," he answered cheerfully. "Not going? Can't bear to be away from me, can you?" He laughed.

"Ha!" I replied, wondering how he was taking things so lightly. "I'm at the gate, waiting for boarding."

"Ahhh. What's up?"

"Just thinking of you. And of us."

"And what are you thinking about me and us?"

"About what a great time we had this past weekend."

"Mmmmhhmmmm...."

"And about how much I love you."

"Amazing thoughts to be having," he spoke in a singsong way.

"What are you up to?"

"Just got off work, early in fact, and I'm heading over to my mother's to check up on her. It was a great day at work actually."

I smiled. His joy was infectious. "I am so glad to hear that, love. I didn't really have anything cool or important to say. Just that I love you, and I hope I'll see you very shortly after I return in ten days." It was an obvious baiting comment, fishing for him to alleviate my fears. I felt foolish just as soon as I'd said it.

"It won't be soon enough, that's for sure. Have a safe trip, babe. I'm pulling up at my mom's, so I'm gonna let you go. Knock 'em dead, like you always do."

I snorted through my nose. "Like I always do. Thanks for saying it, hun. Tell your mother I said hi."

"I will." And he was gone. I briefly jumped to the moment in Germany when I held the phone and prayed for him to still be there, on my knees, breathless with shock, the pit of my stomach and endless black hole of fears realized. I felt sick. My heart pounded in my chest, and my eyes burned. How had we come to this place? Why hadn't I listened to Jackie and Talia and my own heart tugging me in his direction? I had been so proud and so fearful at the same time. Too proud to reach for him, for fear that he'd truly abandoned me. I shook my head. *Stop it. Stop doing this shit, Jen. Go to London, handle your responsibilities and handle this trip the way you now wish you had handled Germany.* It doesn't seem such a hard thing to do. I knew that this trip was a measure of closure for me, a miniature reliving of a nightmare, a way of beginning over again.

Ryan occupied an undercurrent of thoughts as I arrived in London and met with the general manager and construction foreman. We ran over how construction was going and what the GM envisioned stocking on the store's shelves—what products would sell best in London and so forth. He was astute and a native Briton, so he had a leg up on cultural understanding that I had lacked in Germany. This store would do well when it opened next year. We were hoping for late spring or early summer for the grand opening, and it seemed that the store was right on track.

While I was there, I had time to consider Ryan and Germany, and the new relationship that we were building. I really thought about what love meant and what it required. Today, it seemed ridiculous to believe that nothing should change in a relationship. I remembered feeling so strongly about ensuring that everything stayed the same, for fear that I'd lose the magic of what we had. And now, it seemed so obvious that things are always changing—it is the very nature of life. And I should simply accept that change is a part of that. I didn't mind the changes that had taken place in my own life over the past couple of years. The professional experience in Germany had been an amazing learning experience and had launched me into this amazing new opportunity to travel and still find success within the Huntington's store that I loved so much. I had moved to San Diego, finally finding a place near the beach where I could truly feel at home when I was home. And my kids were now out of my house and living their own adult lives. Through all of these life changes, I was fine, and I found joy and happiness.

So why hadn't I been able to accept that the same is true in love? I had destroyed my relationship with Ryan because I was so convinced that we could not survive the changes that Germany brought. Looking back now, I realize that we likely could have survived and saved ourselves quite a bit of heartache and pain if I had not been that way. I called Talia in hopes of working it through.

"Hey, hun. How've you been?"

"Oh, Talia, being here in Europe, now that Ryan and I are together again, it gives me the creeps and has me stuck in introspection, self-dissection. And I wonder if you will talk to me about what you saw when you were in Germany that winter."

"Oh, girl." I picture her rolling her eyes as she sighed heavily into the phone. "Why are you revisiting this? Planning on a bath of razor blades and alcohol later this evening, too?"

I laughed at the imagery. "In fact, I've skipped straight to battery acid skin lotion..." I paused. "Okay, maybe that's too far. Disgusting imagery, too. No, hun, I'm fine. I just feel so far away from the woman that I was. I don't really understand what was happening or why I completely cut him off like that."

"Honey, you walked around in a little cloud of insecurity. You were so sure that he was going to leave you that you basically begged for it."

"That's not true. I was afraid of it, sure, but what the hell do you mean, I begged for it?"

"Jen, Jesus, every time the guy breathed the wrong way, you were sure he was going to leave. And you spent time and effort making double and quadruple sure that he knew he was always free to go. You reminded him that he could leave so much that, shit, anybody would actually begin to wonder if you wanted it to happen."

"I just... I guess I just thought that if he knew he was free to go but he still stayed then, I would know for sure that he wanted to be there. And if he felt like he *had* to stay then, I would feel more like I had somehow imprisoned him."

"Why'd it have to be so melodramatic? What if he simply stayed because he loved you? And what if you told him you wanted him to stay and you were glad he did?" She took a deep breath. "Back then, you would never do that. Somehow, that made you feel vulnerable, like admitting that you loved and needed him was somehow giving him the reins on your heart. The truth is if you both love each other, it happens anyway to some extent."

"Wow. That feels pretty profound"

"Look, Jen. I tried to tell you in Germany to just call him, to reach out and show him you needed him and loved him. You spent so much time and effort being sure that he didn't know that you were vulnerable, that you fell into a helpless little hopeless depression. Do you think that isn't vulnerable? Do you think somehow you were strong in allowing yourself to be like that?"

"No. I guess..." I trailed off not knowing what to say.

"Do you think Ryan saw your relationship as real and authentic, and you as a strong woman when you did that?"

"No. He basically said as much. He wondered if the whole thing hadn't been as deep and true as he'd thought when we lived together. He thought I had played him."

"In the end, you didn't look strong or act strong; he got no special messages of strength and independence out of what you did. So instead of not appearing vulnerable or instead of appearing strong and independent to him, you appeared uncaring and callous." I began to cry, sniffling into the phone. "Jen, honey. Stop it. Stop trying to rebuild or relive or analyze the past. Whatever you are doing isn't gonna do anything for the present. Did you learn from it?"

"I hope so," I sobbed.

"Tell me about you and Ryan today. What is the relationship like?"

"I love him as much as ever, if not more. And I feel like he loves me."

"That's the same as always. What else?"

"Mostly, I called you because I remember being so afraid of changes, any changes at all. And right now, I'm feeling at peace. At least, I'm at peace about the changes that have happened in my life in general. I'm trying to see change differently. And truth is I'm wondering why I saw it as such a demon before."

"Mmmmm. I think you were insecure. And maybe you still are, but you've nothing left to lose in terms of Ryan. Maybe you should try to see yourself through his eyes or through my eyes, or Jackie's or any number of people at Huntington's or through the eyes of your kids. Be at peace with our image of you, and maybe you will find that the things that worried you before aren't worth sweating in the long run. Listen, girl, I've gotta run. Roller derby practice starts in half an hour, and I'm not ready at all. I love you. Stop worrying!" She picked up her pace as she wound down the phone call, ending with, "And next time you call, I wanna hear about European adventures. They're far more fun."

"I love you, too, hun, and thanks."

"Ciao! Or Ta-ta or whatever they say in London."

Chapter Twenty-Three

*C*oming home from London felt far better than any return from a trip in the past year. I was excited to drive to Vegas and see Ryan this coming weekend. The weight of Germany had been lifted off my shoulders, and I loved the prospect of the ways that Ryan and I would grow and change as a couple and individuals in the coming months and years. Things felt on course, and I was happier than I could remember ever being.

As the carousel went around for the twentieth time and my bags still didn't appear, I chuckled that Murphy's Law had foiled me again. Someone's bags had to be the last ones off the plane, and I guess they were bound to be mine. I sipped the coffee I'd purchased upstairs near the gate and settled into a chair. My bags weren't going anywhere, and now was the perfect time to breathe and relax.

I took a few cleansing breaths and smiled at my life's circumstances. Who gets to travel to Europe on a regular basis and stay in all the best hotels in the most beautiful cities? And who has children who are independent and standing on their own two feet so early in their adult lives? And friends like Talia and Jackie were priceless; I couldn't imagine going through life without their companionship and counsel. I took another deep breath and smiled as the carousel came around again without my bags. Still time to think about Ryan and his family and friends, and what they'd brought to my life. He was amazing, supportive, and loving in ways that I had only imagined might be possible as I'd dreamt of boyfriends and lovers when I was a child. He was one of the most fulfilling relationships I'd had in my life, and I was grateful for this second chance. I'd grown since the first time around, and I was better for it. My bag finally came into view, and I giggled privately at the timing. Maybe Murphy likes me after all. He knew precisely how much time I'd need to recenter myself and find grace and peacefulness.

I finished my coffee before getting up, letting my bags cycle three or four times in front of me before swallowing the final swig and grabbing them off the belt. My step was light as my bags rolled behind me. I could smell the sea almost immediately upon exiting the building; it didn't matter that there were taxi cabs, cars, and people all around. Whether the smell of the ocean was truly present or not, I could smell it. Maybe it was just anticipation, but I didn't care. There was peace and solace in the thought of it, and I almost glided across the parking lot.

There was someone leaning on my car as I approached. In the dim light of dusk, I could only barely see his silhouette, but I knew exactly who he was. I let go of my bags and ran over to him, throwing my arms around Ryan's neck and smiling from ear to ear.

"What are you doing here?" I breathed into his ear.

"Saying hello to my girlfriend...?" He sounded shocked at my enthusiasm and surprise.

"I mean," I stepped back from the hug, "what about work and such? I mean I wasn't expecting you, and I am super excited that you are here. I totally didn't expect it and—"

His kiss landed mid-sentence and tasted of the cola he'd been drinking—sweet and bubbly. I kissed him back enthusiastically. Gradually, he tapered the kiss to a pace of warmth and love; his tongue dulled enthusiasm's sharp edge and deepened the kiss' emotion, firing the slow burning embers of familiar passion - unhurried, every second worth savoring. His hands moved slowly over my curves, one of them finding my cheekbone and drawing me tenderly into him further. His lips played softly over mine, warm and full, teasing my exuberance into a more serious affection. And then he slowly wound us down and broke away.

"That's more like it," he smiled. I sighed but did not reply. Instead, I leaned into his chest and wrapped my arms loosely around his waist. "How about we get those suit cases before someone decides they've been abandoned?" His hand ran down my back and cupped my ass before giving it a playful smack to get me moving toward the suitcases.

Once they'd been retrieved and placed in the car, I was surprised that he stepped to my passenger side door. "Ummm, where's *your* car?"

"Do you mind if I ride with you?" He paused and gave me a smart ass smirk. "Because I can find other transportation. Y'know this place is crawling with cabs and busses…"

"No, of course not. I was just…" I scanned the parking lot for his truck. "How'd you get here?"

"Get in, love. And let me in, too. I've got plans for you."

As I drove, he gave directions, guiding me to turn left or right as required. And when he wasn't guiding me, we talked of my trip. My hand drifted to his leg, palm flat on his thigh. It was real; he was here, in my car. London definitely wasn't another Germany; it was the antithesis of that. I smiled as we drove on.

As we pulled into the parking lot, I was unsure if I even wanted to leave the car. Being in Ryan's presence privately was enough. The restaurant was an Italian place I'd never tried before. I hadn't planned on a heavy dinner; in fact, might've ended my day with a simple iced coffee on my balcony if he'd not shown up. I looked over at him in the passenger seat, and he was nearly bursting with excitement. I smiled and blushed, completely overwhelmed at the energy coming from him. Seeing him like this made me want everything and anything that was in store for me.

I leaned across the car and kissed him. "Thanks, babe. This is an amazing surprise."

His smile broadened. "The night is still young. Thank me when it's over." His tone was playful, happy, and almost cautionary. I squinted at him, and we both reached for our doors. He was around the car and at my side just as I was standing up, "Madam…" he offered me his arm.

"Oh, my!" I feigned surprise and embarrassment. "I don't mind if I do, sir."

We stepped together to the restaurant entrance. Once inside, the hostess guided us directly to a table where there was a vase of flowers already in place; my breath caught in my throat. When my eyes flew to his face, Ryan was still smiling broadly. He motioned for me to have a seat. As the hostess stepped away, he gave her a nod of gratitude. The flowers were a mixture of carnations and roses, and the smell of them was intoxicating. I reached across the table to hold his hands. "What's this all about?"

"I wanted your homecoming to be special. I've missed you." He nodded toward the flowers. "Read the card." My hand trembled as I reached for the card tucked so neatly among the stems of the flowers, held in place by their stiffness and the weight of the buds above it. I drew it out and immediately caught the faint scent of Ryan's cologne. I drew the card to my face and smelled it, looking at him as I did. "I carried it around most of the day...what?!" I think his cheeks flushed with the slight hues of embarrassment. I smiled, already delighted by the evening. The contents of the card would no doubt make the evening even better, but we could stop right here and still this would be one of the most beautiful memories in my life.

I slowly and carefully tugged the card open, and then withdrew the contents. The card was simple—a flower on the cover and no words at all. The inside too was without factory-imprinted words, only Ryan's handwritten, tightly scratched ones. Already, my eyes burned at how personal he had chosen to be. Already, my heart ached for the time we'd squandered. The thought that I could have been with this man uninterrupted for the past six years overwhelmed me. I felt surrounded in a cloud of fantasy. My lower lip quivered as I read his words:

Jen,

I have missed you while you were gone to London. I love you now even more than ever. And I am ready to start again, wholeheartedly and without reservation. You are the love of my life.

Yours,

Ryan

Tears spilled onto my cheeks as I laid the card on the table. I stared at it and him alternatively for long minutes, trying to regain composure. Finally, I exited the booth and climbed in on his side, wrapping my arms around him and kissing him, his cheek, his neck, his face, his lips. "I love you, Ryan. I adore you. I am grateful for you and for this life we are building. This is the best homecoming ever."

The waitress walked by, and Ryan waved her off. He took my hands into his and looked me in the eyes. "I have no idea how we get to a place where we live together again, but I do know that I love you and that I am willing to work on us even from Las Vegas while you live here. There is no way to recapture what we used to have exactly as it used to be, but I'd love to build something new with you." His mother's words rang in my head. I immediately went back to that patisserie a month ago.

"I couldn't ask for more, love. I can't wait to see where our future takes us."

I didn't move back to my side of the booth. Instead, Ryan and I sat side by side and ordered appetizers and drinks. While we awaited our appetizers, Ryan said, "There's something else......."

"Honey, I don't think I can emotionally handle much more."

"Another surprise..." I shook my head. "Yep. But I'm not sure how you'll feel about this one." I took a deep breath. "You asked earlier how I got to the airport, well ..."

"Yes... go on, Ryan. Stop it with the suspense already!" I punched his arm playfully.

"My mother dropped me off."

My stomach dropped. "Umm, honey..." I paused trying to do the math. Ryan's parents had lived in Vegas happily since their retirement more than four years ago. So if she was here in California, what was she doing here? It seemed like the math should be simple enough, and yet it wasn't making sense. "I don't understand, love."

"We came down here together."

My heart began to pound in my chest. His mother was part of the plan all along. I had not seen her nor talked to her since the patisserie, and even that had been a secret from Ryan. How would she react? What if she didn't approve of us? I had not had a chance to show her how much I loved her son and how much I'd changed since we'd spoken, changed since Germany really.

"And she is coming here to meet us for dinner."

I gulped and suddenly, all sound was muffled by the sound of my heart beating in my ears. I didn't relish the idea of a showdown right here in this restaurant. What if she saw the flowers? What if she didn't think I was good enough for Ryan? I breathed in deeply and slowed my breath, my pulse responded as well. "Ryan, hun, I met with your mother, before London and—"

"I know. She told me."

"It didn't go very well. She made some really good points..." I tapered off as I thought about the implications of seeing his mother right here, right now, right after Ryan has made it clear that he is willing to go all in on our relationship. "Baby, I'm not perfect. And I might not be the woman your mother would choose for you, but I am looking forward to building this life together, and I really hope that she can accept that. Accept us."

I took a deep breath. Ryan had chosen me; his mother didn't need to. Yes, it would be nice, but in the end, what mattered was Ryan's choice...and mine. Seeing his mother would be fine. I would love to see her and reassure her that I love her son and that he is in good hands. "When does she get here?"

"She'll be here any minute. And I am excited for you two to see each other again. You two are the most important women in my life."

"Your mother is an amazing woman, powerful and strong. I've always respected her. She sets the bar high for any woman who might hope to be in your life."

He smiled and kissed both of my hands.

As our appetizers arrived, so did Mrs. Riverton. I immediately stood and hugged her. "Mrs. Riverton, it is so good to see you again."

She nodded. "You, too, Jen. How was London?"

We took our respective seats at the table. "London was beautiful and productive. The weather is bitterly cold, but the city is beautiful always. And the store is coming along fine. I really think they hired the right guy to manage it." Her face was soft and open, more welcoming than I had anticipated. "How have you been?"

She waved me off. "Oh, fine. Fine. Always fine."

Conversation flowed easily, cordially through appetizers and dinner. Mrs. Riverton was such an amazingly regal woman, proud and strong, unwavering in her love and support of Ryan, but solidly a force to be reckoned with aside from him. She spoke of golfing the many courses around Las Vegas and the surrounding area, of planning her next trip with her retiree travel group, of the recent books she'd read, and of taking hikes up in Mount Charleston. I admired her and thought that her inner strength and confidence made her still one of the most attractive and sexy women I knew. I felt at ease by the time I'd ordered a cappuccino for dessert.

"So then," she began with a voice a bit louder and more stern than dinnertime conversation. "How about you two?"

I looked at Ryan; he offered no shield. I swallowed and looked back at her. She dabbed the edges of her mouth with her napkin and looked only at me. It was clear that she intended for me to give her the update and not Ryan. "I love your son, Mrs. Riverton, you know that."

"And I see he loves you, too." Her eyes cut to the flowers in the vase beside her. "Is that enough, do you think?"

I looked at my palms. "It's not enough without patience and effort and introspection...." I fumbled through the words, and no matter how hard I stared at my hands, I couldn't find a script there either. "Listen, Mrs. Riverton, I'm not perfect. But I am learning, and I think that my relationship with Ryan has potential that I have with no one else. Not before him, not when we were separated, not any time in my future. Ryan is who I want to be with. And I think that decisiveness is where you will find that love is upheld and strengthened." I exhaled and smiled at her. I felt good about having stood up for myself and for the knowledge that what I was saying was the truth that she needed to hear.

"I know that you love each other, Jen. And, to be fair, my son's feelings have never wavered. When we met at the coffee shop, I spoke as a mother protecting a son whom you devastated. Today, I sit here as a woman in awe of the way you two love each other." She blinked away tears forming at the corners of her eyes. "You two remind me of my Jim and me early on..." Her voice cracked, and Ryan reached for her hand.

"I am so flattered that you can see glimmers in us of the magic that you and Mr. Riverton shared. I can only hope that Ryan and I can grow into the couple that you two were."

We talked a bit more over coffee about a number of things, including the hotel where they were staying. I offered for them to stay with me, but of course, Mrs. Riverton refused. "Of course, I am sure Ryan will stay. I am a third wheel to that. Besides, I made plans to visit my friend Norma; she lives in a senior's apartment community in Rancho San Diego."

"Oh...? I didn't know you still had friends down here."

"Never lost touch. And now with Jim gone, seems I am in need of the company."

"It is so nice that you have your friends." I said. "Still, would you like to have brunch the day after tomorrow?"

"I would love that," She replied graciously.

I smiled though, truly, it beamed from my soul. My heart felt so full I thought it might burst.

Chapter Twenty-Four

*A*nd so, the weeks turned to months and seasons changed. Ryan and I became stronger and more sure of ourselves and our love over that time, and somehow, the distance seemed like nothing anymore. We spent the holidays in Vegas with his mother, and the spring brought him to San Diego most weekends. I was living in a whirlwind of bliss and joy unimaginable when Ryan and I began this journey.

It was on an early summer morning, as I sat pondering the world and my blessings alone on the beach. The sun was not yet rising, and it was just me and the gulls sitting happily on a blanket, with my toes buried in the cold sand. The seagulls cackled a greeting, and I smiled into the summer dawn air. Ryan still slept in the tent. I'd wake him soon enough. I just needed a few more minutes. For now, I was enjoying keeping company with the gulls.

I pulled my hooded sweatshirt a little tighter around me and gave myself a hug. The brisk air of an ocean side morning was refreshing, inspiring. Inhaling deeply, I let the salted-sea smell fill my nose and lungs.

Good morning, world, I thought, and I smiled at the idea that I could possibly greet the world all at once. But the ocean always made me feel that way, like I was a part of the universal energy, and we were all communing, even a sleepy Ryan back there in the tent. I would wake him before the sunrise, but I had a couple more minutes until then.

"Good morning, beautiful."

I jumped, startled, and settled into another smile.

Ryan.

His love was warming. My soul alight.

"Hey, baby," I said as he settled on the blanket beside me.

"I didn't like waking up alone. This little scene feels like déjà vu." He draped an arm around me and leaned into my shoulder.

"I...swear I was going to wake you." My eyes were on the silhouetted ocean and the swells and crests of the waves. The massive heaving and the tender lapping of the ocean upon the shore were even more powerful and moving here in the grey just before dawn. "Baby, in just another minute or two—"

"I know, Jen. I know." He brushed a tear away from my cheek and replaced it with a kiss.

I lay back on the blanket, smiling. I hadn't even realized that tears were falling. The sky was barely beginning to be visible. Stars were disappearing, but the hues of daylight were not yet here. I looked at Ryan, my eyes meeting his. Smiling, I tugged him toward me, "C'm'ere, ya big lug."

And when he kissed me, the ocean disappeared. There was no sky, no sand beneath my feet, no blanket at my back, only Ryan's insistent lips upon mine.

I kissed him back, playfully at first, in the joy of the morning and the rediscovering of his love. Plump soft and insistent, his lips plied for more. His hand, strong and warm, drew my body into his. I pulled away from the kiss. "I love you."

"I know."

"I don't mean it in some fairy tale bullshit way."

"I know, babe."

I kissed him more passionately and pushed into him, guiding us until he was on his back, and I was half on top of him. My leg slid between his knees, pelvis aligned with his hip. I stretched and tilted my hips, grinding against the side of his thigh. As my tongue played with his, my free hand roamed his chest and hip. I snaked my hand up his shirt and onto the warmth of his belly, fingering the hair that grew there.

His hand stroked my back, reaching past my shoulders and into my hair. He broke from our kiss and guided my neck to his mouth. I moaned as his tongue flicked my sensitive tendon. I reached for the waistband of his jeans. The button seemed impossible to undo with one hand, especially as I was distracted as his tongue and teeth continued to electrify me through adept sucking and nibbling at my neck. He slid a hand under my sweatshirt, tank top, and bra, finding my breast eager for his touch. I gasped and arched my back, pressing my breast into his palm and extending my neck further, heightening my sensitivity. With his zipper finally fully down, my hand easily found its mark. I gripped his cock through his underwear and found him hard and throbbing already; his boxers bore a small but growing damp spot.

He laid back on the blanket, alternating between watching my facial expressions and closing his eyes in pleasure. As I slid my hand under the waistband of his boxers, our eyes met. Smiling mischievously, I explored his underwear, intentionally avoiding his cock. I pressed the heel of my palm into his hip and massaged down the front of his pelvis to his balls, giving each one due attention. He grabbed my wrist, and we locked eyes.

"What?"

"Stop."

I kissed him playfully. "Stop what?" I smiled and my eyes narrowed.

"You are the biggest tease ever."

"We're on a public beach."

"Is that it? That's why you torture me like this?"

"No, of course not, love. It's the excuse that happens to be at hand. That truth is I love the way you fuck me when you can't stand it anymore." It was a challenge, and he knew it.

He wrestled his way on top of me and settled between my legs. He pinned me by my wrists, holding them near my head, and he kissed me forcefully, passionately. I squirmed and writhed, kissing him but struggling to free myself at the same time. He finally broke the kiss. "Marry me, Jennifer Simmons."

"What?"

"I said marry me," he kissed me tenderly, "I want you to be my wife."

We stayed there, looking at each other, holding our collective breaths. So much had happened since the last time he dared ask me way back when I believed marriages change things, when I was sure I didn't want things to change, when I was convinced that if things were perfect, change might bring them falling down like a house of cards.

I bit my lip. In this moment, none of those fears came to mind. In this moment, his request seemed so late, so overdue, and my 'yes' felt right. My 'yes' was bursting in my throat, begging to be screamed out. What Ryan and I had was a forever thing. It was special. I had had two husbands who didn't deserve that title, why not have one who did?

"Yes," I whispered finally. He leaned in closer to me and offered his ear to my mouth. I licked his earlobe, drawing it into my mouth, sucking it briefly before whispering, "Yes, Ryan Riverton, I would love to be your wife."

Heather Labarge is a 24 year veteran of the Air Force, a business owner, and the mother of two. Always interested in writing as a form of creative expression and personal outlet, she has written essays, poetry, erotica and fiction for years.

Sunrise Fires, a heartfelt sensual romance about a woman's early steps away from self-sabotaging thoughts and behaviors, is her debut published work.

Today, Heather lives in Las Vegas, NV and continues to work full time for the Department of Defense while also writing, raising her son and speaking publicly on self-love, self-sabotage and her personal journey to find one while rebuking the other.

Acknowledgements

This journey has been an eye opening, soul freeing experience but the process could not have happened without the love and support of so many.

To each person who allowed me to use their namesake, thank you.

Ryan, you were ever my champion, encouraging and supporting me long before the process began – your kindness is indelibly inked on my creative spirit.

Kelsea and Zion, your patience and love are my heart song; I love you both beyond measure and am humbled to call myself your Mom.

To Talia, I've lately called on the reader in you but I've relied on the strong supportive best friend in you for years. There are no words to express the depth of love, warmth and trust I have for you.

Thanks to Jackie, John, Magie and the others who suffered through the advance copies – you helped me iron out the wrinkles and smooth away the rough edges so that the warm heartfelt moving love story could shine through.

Heather LaBarge

Christene, Greg, Tom, Rama and the community of authors and support staff – you made the 'work' parts of this so much more bearable and kept the train moving forward even when I wanted to jump the tracks and move onto the next thing.

And Charlene, when the finish line approached and I thought I had nothing left to give this marathon, you appeared, supported, reinvigorated, and inspired me such that finishing became a breeze.

And last to Exalted Peacock, LLC for giving me a platform from which to dive.